TROUBLE WITH PRODUCT X

TROUBLE WITH PRODUCT X

by

JOAN AIKEN

LONDON
VICTOR GOLLANCZ LTD
1973

© Joan Aiken 1966

First published 1966
Reissued 1973

ISBN 0 575 01647 7

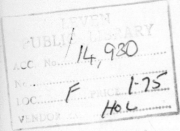

Printed in Great Britain by
The Camelot Press Ltd, London and Southampton

This book is in affectionate remembrance of my time at J. Walter Thompson. No real advertising agency, of course, in the least resembles Salmon & Bucknell; none could, and stay in business.

CHAPTER I

It was finding the up-ended pram that finally tipped me headlong into the midst of the trouble. And even then I didn't guess how bad it really was—that it had already caused one death, and would cause another. Of course the true beginning was long before that, when Gareth Dunskirk stepped ashore from the yacht at Savona, one blue Mediterranean day, first laid eyes on Cara Marcello, and mistakenly conceived her to be the complete and ultimate status symbol that would give him the edge on his friends Tigger and Mait. Maybe it all began even earlier than that when those two spoilt children, Gareth and Cara, kicking and screaming in their respective cradles, both somehow acquired the notion that Providence intended them always to have everything they wanted.

However, what you might call my first official intimation of my future involvement with Product X came on a bleak, nasty Monday just after Christmas, when George Salmon called the whole of his creative staff together to tell us about the new account the agency had won in the teeth, or so he would have us believe, of a dozen hungry competitors.

Salmon and Bucknell isn't a large advertising agency. Salmon is the only living partner; Bucknell died of a surfeit of tranquillisers called Lullabuys, which were later withdrawn from the market; we didn't handle them, I am glad to say. Our agency makes no attempt to enter the lists against such giants as B & H or JWT. On the contrary. The personal touch is what we aim at; "just one happy family," someone is sure to say satirically during any major row or crisis. And somehow, regrettably, it does always seem to come about that our clients become more and more *part* of the family; beginning from business lunches with George, they proceed to rustic weekends at his Maidenhead cottage, and then Mimi takes their wives shopping and I am roped in to escort their children to the zoo, and Tom photographs them, and by this time they are practically living in the office and we know every last detail about their asthma and dry-rot and income-tax problems. Not to mention vice versa. I am not always sure if this is an efficient way to run a business, but it is the way George can't help doing it.

But in general we do all get on pretty well, and the agency certainly has been a haven in time of trouble for me. If not big, it is fairly thriving. At that time we had some good lively accounts, an American firm called Faireweather Foods, and Franz Oesmacher the couturier, and National Peanuts Week, and Midinette Washing Machines, and Funshine Furniture Products, and Bom the Meat'n Milk Drink, not to mention the government of Turkinistan. This last gave us many a headache, as it consisted of nothing but a dozen feudally-minded sheikhs, of whom the less said the better, driving around the desert with their harems and their Cadillacs, but at least it was picturesque and looked well in the Annual Report.

So there we were, sitting round in George Salmon's room, which was the only one where the carpet had pile and the chairs were comfortable, sipping coffee which Jimmy O'Riordan had obligingly fetched from the cafeteria on the ground floor. Our office was in Paris Garden, not a very good prestige area; "south of the river" we tend to say, rather than Southwark, but it's convenient for the Old Vic and Waterloo station. The firm is too small to run its own canteen, but we do have an experimental kitchen where we can thaw out Faireweather Prefab Kebabs and try them for edibility.

I was feeling happy.

I suppose some people feel happy all the time and get used to it, hardly notice it, but I've learnt to hoard the feeling in the way rheumatic sufferers do when the twinges let up. Christmas was safely over, and I had a good new suit on—I'd rushed out and bought it in a splash of extravagance on Christmas Eve to match the jade beads Tom gave me—and old George Salmon had met me in the corridor and told me our Midinette commercials had won a Monaco Award—so I was prepared to love everybody.

I nodded at Susan and Jimmy and slipped into a seat by Mimi. She showed me the colossal tinselly Christmas card she'd had from his Excellency the Emir of Turkinistan.

We were giggling over its message—

> Had I a magic carpet, o my houri
> I'd fly with thee across the wide Missouri;
> We'd consummate our love in astral regions
> 'Mid pomegranates, peaches, and pot-pourri!

"Why the wide Missouri, I wonder," Mimi said.

"He was running out of rhymes, obviously"—when George came in, beaming from ear to ear. Behind him was Tom Toole, our art director. I hadn't seen him since before Christmas. He gave me a serious look and came round to sit by me. My heart did a gentle thump.

George remained standing. As usual his appearance was that of a Man of Distinction—silver hair and a handsome buttonhole—but slightly frayed. His wives never look after him properly and he is always too busy paying out alimony to look after himself.

"Well, friends," he said, "I can see we've all had the usual kind of Christmas, so I won't tax your aching heads and hobnailed livers with anything too difficult to grasp. I just called you in to tell you about our new client, Dunskirk and Son."

We all pricked up our ears. I'd already known there was a new account in the wind, for George had dropped me a heavy hint in the passage just before the meeting, but the name Dunskirk did not ring any definite bell. Pharmaceutical products? Breakfast foods? Lingerie? Or what?

George was going on with his speech. "Dunskirk are a very up-and-coming firm," he said, in that warm, encouraging way he has, which immediately tells you that he is making the very best of some pretty substandard circumstances and which, I am sure, is why his wives are always leaving him, darling though he is.

"They have been established since 1920, when old Dunskirk began in a small way making hand creams and toilet soaps. Since World War II, as you know, they have expanded to cover the whole range of cosmetic products; the ladies will of course be familiar with Gay Gal beauty products."

"Merciful providence," muttered Mimi under her breath. "What *are* we coming to?"

I dared not catch her eye. When I was twelve, and embarked on the secret venture of trying cosmetics for the first time, I remember buying a Gay Gal Flaming Flamingo lipstick and some Coralline powder which probably started my indifferent complexion on its downhill path. In those days, only five years or so after the war, Gay Gal cosmetics weren't nearly so prevalent in the south of England as they are now; old Dunskirk, a Lancashire man, started very successfully by marketing his products to mill girls and factory hands in the midlands and industrial north. Cheapness was Gay Gal's main asset; the things soon became a familiar sight: greasy, lumpy lipsticks in striped black-and-pink

9

containers which looked chipped and sordid even in the display cases, curdled face creams in opulently shaped jars like jelly-moulds. After the first few years one came across them every-where, in chain stores and supermarkets and haberdashers and country post-offices.

Mimi pursed her lips and I could see she was thinking, as I was, that Gay Gal products were no great feather in the agency's cap. However old George was still beaming, like the pussy that's swal-lowed the cream, right in our direction, plainly guessing our thoughts. In spite of his apparent simplicity, old George is really quite a shrewd customer; I've often been tripped up by forgetting that.

"The new Dunskirk line, however," he said, "is of quite a differ-ent order. Dunskirks are introducing a perfume selling to a higher income group which they hope will raise them into the luxury cosmetics class and be the beginning of a line of—ahem—carriage-trade products. Perhaps the ladies would care to sniff."

We nodded at him encouragingly and he pulled out an un-pretentious little brown sample-bottle and handed it to Mimi. With some difficulty she extracted the rubber stopper and sniffed.

"My, my!" she said. "That's quality goods! Can I have a drop to try, George?"

"Better not, just for the moment, Mimi dear. This is the only sample they've let us have at present. It's in very short supply, as I gather it's still to some extent in the experimental stage. I suppose that may not be the final smell, either, so you'll have to hold your horses on descriptions till it's finalised."

"It's not bad the way it is." Mimi passed the bottle to me. I sniffed, and agreed with her. It had a sharp woody tang, very pleasant and astonishingly potent. Most perfumes remind you of one particular fragrance or another, but the curious thing about this one was that it smelt like nothing else one could put a name to—and yet had this terrific authority.

"Very nice indeed. Unusual." I handed the bottle, which was labelled Product X, to Tom, who smiled at me and said, "I'll say it's okay if you endorse it, Martha. I can't tell Chanel No 5 from Lapsang Souchong."

Suddenly, as if a cloud had passed over the sun, I had a moment of queer, bleak misery. I remembered another voice saying, "Buy one if you want, darling; they all smell alike to me. Quite honestly I prefer the way you smell yourself."

Why can't we abolish memory? I drew a deep breath, willing myself: Forget it. Bury it deep, it's gone. Make your mind a blank.

Tom's eyes were still on me; I smiled back at him and said, "It has—I suppose you could call it a woody scent. Nice and sharp. And powerful! I hope they don't go and stick in a lot of amber or jasmine and sweeten it up too much."

Susan and Jimmy were trying it now, and Susan was exclaiming at its strength though she said she liked a nice sweet scent herself; Jimmy was enthusiastic and thought it could easily become one of the really great, classic perfumes. Tom was still watching me; I realised that I'd gone back to my old habit of instinctively hiding my left hand under the large blue copy pad I carried, and impatiently pulled it out.

"Well!" George said, when everyone had commented and chattered sufficiently. "That perfume's our new baby, friends—we're taking over the whole Gay Gal range, of course, but the perfume's a case of starting from scratch, so I'll call a planning session on it when everyone's had a chance to do some creative thinking. Officially it will be in the capable hands of Martha here, as Mimi's rather tied up with Oesmacher and the Emir at the moment" (ribald cries) "but as usual anyone who has a brilliant idea is invited to put it forward."

That was the way Salmon and Bucknell worked. In theory Mimi and I wrote the copy, Jimmy handled the production side of TV commercials, and Tom was the art director, while Susan looked after media and technicalities, but in practice we all mixed in with each other's jobs and the system worked surprisingly well, perhaps because we all got on with one another.

When the meeting was over, Mimi and I went along to the office we shared. Mimi sank back in her chair, stuck her feet on the metal wastepaper bin, pressed her fingers to her eyes, and said, "Lord, Lord, have I the father and mother of all hangovers! What's the matter with you, mon vieux, touch of the miseries?"

Mimi is a good friend. Her full name is Maria Irina Mikhaelovna Dourakin. She doesn't look the way I imagine Russians should—tall and classic, with ballet faces and smooth black hair. Mimi looks like an elegant gnome. She is small and bony and immensely energetic. Her hair is black, to be sure, but it stands up off her high forehead and crackles with electricity. She has an angular face, huge green eyes, a nose that Caesar might have envied, and clothes that *everyone* envies. Some of her outfits come from top fashion houses, but as often as not when one asks, "Mimi, where *did* you get that miraculous jacket?" she'll say vaguely, "Oh, I picked it up at a sort of street market in Northampton that time we were there going over the Funshine factories, remember?" She got on famously with the Emir of Turkinistan, who called her his gazelle and his bird of paradise when he wasn't lavishing less printable endearments on her.

Now she gave me a bilious but shrewd scrutiny and said, "Anyway, Christmas is over, and that's something to be thankful for, as every female knows. You look to me like a girl that needs a drop of vodka in her coffee. Come on, let's get out of here and have ourselves a pick-me-up."

"I don't know what's the matter with me," I said. "When I came in this morning I was fine. Goose walking over my grave, maybe. Somehow I just can't feel very enthusiastic about this Product X."

"Gay Gal's a squalid little firm, say what you like," Mimi agreed, shrugging neatly into a military-looking topcoat that had come from Rome and was modelled, with startling success, on the uniform of the Vatican Swiss Guard. "Still, the stuff smelt all right—remarkably so. I shan't object to some free samples. What'll we call it, let's think of names."

"Carriage Trade," I suggested morosely, pulling on my plain black reefer (with my height and colouring I can't afford to wear startling coats). "Or Just U."

We met Jimmy, looking Irish and distraught, in the lift, and he explained that he was riding up and down because his secretary had flu and so he wasn't able to do any work. He came along with us and we went to the Feathers, which is just round the corner from the office. It is one of those cosy, old-fashioned pubs where you can also get good coffee. We sat by the saloon bar's roaring fire and had a thoroughly pleasant, foolish time thinking up extravagant and outlandish names for our product. Luckily the bar was empty; it was still too early for the lunchtime crowd.

"It ought to have a French name," Jimmy stipulated. "Cannebière? Corniche? Bois de Boulogne?"

"Coup de Grâce."

"Hors de Combat."

"Not bad," I said. "The commercials would be à l'outrance tournaments, tremendous bashings with swords, and the Queen of Beauty fluttering her hankie in the Royal Box."

"Pretty," Mimi agreed. "Why not call it A l'Outrance?"

"No one could pronounce it, acushla."

"You forget," Mimi said. "We're in the higher income brackets now, where they all go to French finishing schools. Still, perhaps you have a point. What other things do they have in combats, gages, crests, coats of arms—"

"Battleaxes."

"Oh, very funny. Can you imagine someone saying, 'A bottle of Battleaxe, please'?"

"A battle of Bottleaxe," Jimmy suggested.

George Salmon came into the pub, where he often had an early sandwich lunch before rushing back to his flat for an hour to try and solve some matrimonial crisis. We waved to him and he came and sat down by us. Mimi said cheerfully,

"We've decided to call our new product Round Table."

"A little political, don't you think?" George said, after one anxious glance to make sure she didn't mean it seriously. "Makes me think of labour and management getting together."

"We want something chivalrous and Arthurian, anyway," Mimi said contentiously. She is always on the point of being irritated with George because he hasn't much sense of humour, but her goodnature always saves her in time.

"How about Guinevere?" from Jimmy.

"No one would know how to pronounce it," George objected.

"We're in the higher income groups now," we all chorused, and George looked anxiously round the bar, which was beginning to fill up.

"Camelot, then."

"Would get muddled up with the musical."

"Tintagel," I suggested, my attention wandering to a counter-card with a turreted castle advertising Round Tower Stout.

"Tintagel? That's not bad," George said judiciously.

"Oh, I didn't mean it seriously."

"No, but I like it. It's interesting and distinguished. That's what we want to aim for. I'm sure this is going to be one of the really great perfumes, like Arpège or Chanel No 5; we want a name to match. That's what we must aim for, something out of the common, don't you see; not just vulgar sex appeal, something more haunting than that."

"More haunting than *sex*?" Jimmy said incredulously, but George was away on his hobbyhorse and not to be drawn. He is a poet manqué, he likes to remind us from time to time; while up at Oxford he published two slim vols called *Expostulations* and *Orgasms*, of which he is now rather ashamed, but it pleases him to think that he could do a lot better now if only he ever had the time.

"Haunting," he repeated firmly. "Nostalgic, evanescent, evocative—that's what a perfume ought to be. Perilous seas in faery lands forlorn, that sort of thing. I want us really to go to town on this thing, see if we can't make advertising history with it."

"Soft sell, George?"

"Soft sell always registers most in the end," George said, "particularly in the cosmetics market." This is another of his pet theories.

Mimi always becomes cynical and mutinous when she sees the creative gleam begin to glow in George's eye. She stood up firmly, assembling her calf handbag and beautiful gloves.

"Bedsocks," she said firmly. "That's what I must buy. Would you believe it, not a single pair of bedsocks did anyone give me this Christmas—and me entering on my thirties. Coming, Martha? Or would you rather stay with the oracles?"

"I'll come," I said quickly. "I need some fresh air."

"You go on thinking along the lines of Tintagel," George admonished me. Then he looked at his watch, drained his double whisky, and, muttering, "My god, my god, Eloise will be wondering where the hell I've got to. She's not at all well just now. Excuse me," he rushed from the pub.

In fact a couple of months went by before we started serious work on Product X. Dunskirk and Son were having production difficulties, apparently; for some reason the second batch of perfume hadn't come out nearly as well as the first. Understandably, they were rather cagey about accounting for this.

Meanwhile George, Mimi, and I had been taken on a conducted tour of the factory. One of the first things young Gareth Dunskirk had done, apparently, as soon as he was old enough to have a say in policy matters, was to insist on moving the firm from Lancashire to London, to get away from the aura of clogs, shawls, and cobblestones. The industrial drift to the south-east was not yet in full swing at that time and they were lucky enough to snap up an excellent bomb-site in south Wimbledon, beside the railway and

14

conveniently placed for the Wimbledon Squash and Badminton Club.

"It'll give us a much better image," Gareth kept telling his father who, obstinately, pined for the factory hooters and black puddings and good-tempered factory hands of Bruddersford.

"Down here they're like a lot of Duchesses," he grumbled. "Give 'em two-hour coffee breaks an' a lavatory apiece, they'd still not be satisfied."

In fact the works were modern and handsome enough. We couldn't help being impressed when we stepped through the insulating double doors into the perfumery department; it was small, but obviously well-equipped. There were glass-topped benches and elaborate smelling booths, screened off from the rest of the room; thermostats controlled the temperature in the laboratory, and a perfume "keyboard" had its shallow shelves stocked with a fantastic range of aromatics and essences. A waft of violet scent drifted about, but it was kept down to a bearable minimum.

"My son designed every bit of this," old Dunskirk told us proudly. He was obviously delighted to have a chance of boasting about Gareth, for whom he had a rather pathetic adoration. Personally I considered Gareth Dunskirk an utter toad; I was glad he hadn't been able to accompany us on the escorted tour. He was away in Italy on a buying trip, apparently.

"What *does* one buy in Italy?" George asked in the bright, hearty tone of someone who is not going to listen to a single word of the answer. He glanced at his watch.

"Eh, well, there's Bergamot Oil, that cooms from near Reggio," old Dunskirk answered in his slow, precise way. I don't know if he was a typical Lancastrian, but he seemed very North country to me. He was a small, round, thickset man, solid, like an underdone doughnut, freckled and balding, with a fuzz of very short sandy-white hairs on the back of his head. His pale-blue eyes were small, twinkling, and shrewd, and he was nearly always smiling, as if he found life a very pleasant, easy, sensible affair. He went on: "And there's Orris root, that cooms from near Florence—"

"Doesn't it sound Shakespearian," murmured Mimi. Tiring of old Dunskirk's careful exposition and George's synthetic interest, she wandered off and gazed at a row of glass tubes like organ pipes leading up through the ceiling, down which thick, globby liquids slowly oozed, having filtered, we were told, through hundreds of grammes of talc.

I looked into a cupboard full of tightly-stoppered brown and green glass jars, and was ravished by the names on the labels: Coriander, anisefennel, juniper, nutmeg—

"Did you know there were nutmeg *addicts*?" Mimi muttered, coming up to peer past me. "I bet Gareth Dunskirk is one."

"Hush!"

—elemi, galbanum, myrrh, opoponax, styrax, camomile, dill, estragon, origanum, pennyroyal, peppermint, rosemary, rue, tansy, verbena, wormwood.

Besides the bottles there were massive twenty-five-kilo earthenware crocks, five-hundredweight drums, great glass carboys in wicker cases, and mysterious chunks of crystalline material.

"Indeed? That's interesting, remarkably interesting," George Salmon was saying. "And tell me now, what actually is there in Product X?"

Old Dunskirk halted suddenly in the middle of a spiel about their cheaper perfume range, and their difficulties with ethyl acetate. He looked rather embarrassed.

If I'd been near enough I'd have kicked George; evidently his had been the one question that shouldn't be asked.

"Eh, well," old Dunskirk said at length, "ye know, a perfume is a very complex product—it's a blend of hoondreds of different substances, some natural, some artificial. In the olden days, they used to blend substances that all had similar scents; nowadays the fashion is more for what ye can call dissonance in perfume. It's not onlike music, really; ye build it up and up, like a bit of orchestration. Soomtimes it can take years to blend a perfume so as to carry out the inventor's idea—it needs some substances in it to make it carry, ye see, and some to give it body, make it last longer; ambergris is one they use for that. Ye reduce it to powder and add alcohol—a solution of that will last for months, but of course on its own it's heavy. It's the proportion of one element to another that's important."

"And in Product X?" persisted tactless old George.

"I think I'd better ask my son Gareth to tell you about that. This perfume's his brainchild, you know. I'll get him to have a talk with you when he comes back from Italy. He'll be home on Thursday with his new wife."

"New wife? Has he got a new wife?" asked Mimi, discreetly changing the subject by taking an interest in clients' affairs.

"Aye, he's joost got wed to an Italian girl."

16

"But, Mr Dunskirk, how exciting and glamorous," I chipped in, seeing George's eye roam once more to his watch (poor George; Eloise was on the point of leaving him). "Have you met her?"

"Nay, not yet. By all he says, she's as beautiful as an angel. I only hope," old Dunskirk added pessimistically, "that she's steadier nor the last. A flighty yoong madam *she* was, and no mistake."

I nodded sympathetically, remembering that Gareth's Number One wife had run off with a bandleader from Blackpool. It had been a boy-and-girl affair; Gareth had married her when both were in their teens and both, I gathered, regretted it almost at once. Luckily that was before we took over the account, so we weren't called upon to condole and commiserate. For his father's sake I too hoped that Gareth had made a better choice this time; old Dunskirk was a nice old boy and deserved a better son. But the chances didn't seem particularly high—I imagined Gareth's taste would run pretty true to form. He had a mania for acquiring possessions—hi fi, cameras, transistors, cars, film projectors, TV— the one feature all his belongings had in common was that they were built for show, not wear, and that they were soon thrown aside.

"Any road, he's fair smitten with this one," old Dunskirk went on. "Saw her first last soomer when he went cruising in Brad Maitland's yacht, went back for anoother look in October—it's my belief he popped the question then, but couldn't get her to say aye or nay—and this time evidently he's fair worn her down wi' persistence. I daresay it's on account of Miss Cara that yoong Gareth has been so keen on buying Bergamot and citrus oils this last halfyear."

"Is her name Cara? How pretty."

"Cara Marcello. Cara Dunskirk it will be by now," her father-inlaw said prosaically. "They got wed in Italy so they would be able to have the honeymoon aboard Brad's yacht."

"Lucky things. Well," I said mendaciously, "we'll look forward to meeting her very much. Now I really thing, Mr Dunskirk, that we have wasted enough of your time—"

"Eh, but you'll stop and have a coop of tea, won't you, Miss Martha and Mr Salmon and the other yoong lady—?" Mr Dunskirk was always a little in awe of Mimi and never slapped her on the bottom and addressed her familiarly as lass, the way he did me.

"Why, that's very kind of you, Mr Dunskirk—"

Obviously his feelings would have been mortally hurt if we'd refused—he really was a nice old boy—so we took the lift up to the Dunskirk family maisonette on the top two floors and were helped by his housekeeper to a vast Lancashire tea, practically a four-course meal, with ham and parkin and fruit salad. George managed to excuse himself and slip away, explaining apologetically that his wife had an appointment with a specialist and wanted him to escort her. Mimi and I admired the view of the railway from the window and ate our way steadily through (at least I shan't need to cook tonight *or* tomorrow, I thought) while our host told us rather touchingly that it had always been his wish to bring happiness into the lives of womenfolk with his cosmetics, in memory of his dear wife.

"Would you believe it, when Moother—that's Mrs Dunskirk that was—when Moother were a yoong girl, her folks were that strict that if she even put a bit o' rice powder on her nose, her Dad would send her straight out to t'pump to wash it off! And no coloured clothes o' Sundays, nothing like that. Why, I remember once when we was courting, she coom down in a white dress on a Sunday afternoon, and her Dad made her go straight back oopstirs and put on her black. So she were main pleased when I first started my little business. 'I like to see a bit of colour on a lass's face,' she used to say. Aye, she'd be fair proud to know how well the business is doing. Happen she does know."

"Is it long since she died?" I asked gently, as Mr Dunskirk had gone off into a sighing reverie.

"Twenty years, lass. Eh, I do wish she could see yoong Gareth now. I'm that proud of this perfume he's invented. I always knew he had it in him to do summat o' the sort. Do you know, Morleys soomhow got wind of it, and made us quite a good offer? But of course we wouldn't sell, or rather, Gareth wouldn't; I'm leaving Product X entirely to him. Making a sooccess of Gareth has been my whole life's ambition, you might say, since Moother died. He was only a toddler then, but a bonny little chap." And old Dunskirk showed us photographs of Gareth, fat and repulsive in a pram, in a velvet collar, in boy scout uniform. At least he had thinned down as he grew up.

"Isn't it a bit risky to let your whole life revolve round another person?" I suggested doubtfully. "Children grow away from you —I know it's trite but it's true."

"Nay, you wait till you've soom of your own, Miss Martha," old Dunskirk said in that exasperating way parents have. "Gareth wouldn't dream of leaving me. He's a canny lad; he knows he can do better by sticking wi' the old man that he would elsewhere."

That rang true; Gareth had inherited his father's shrewdness about money, without the accompanying generosity.

"And when he's had a look round, and found his feet, he'll soon settle down," the proud father went on. "The lad's got a real flair, Miss Martha, I can tell you. He'll fairly wake up the old business when he gets going; be a shot in the arm to the whole cosmetics industry, shouldn't wonder. He'll have new ideas, you see; that's what a college training does for you. That's what I missed, so I was determined Gareth should have it, and when they opened the new Bruddersford University it seemed like the intervention of Providence!" He beamed at us a little wistfully. "Gareth's got intellectual interests and friends now; there's nothing like intellectual interests to stimulate you in your work."

"No indeed," I agreed earnestly, hoping that Tigger and Mait, the only two of Gareth's friends whom I had briefly met, were not typical. Mait, the Brad Maitland who owned the honeymoon yacht, was older than Gareth, perhaps twenty-six or twenty-seven, a smooth, dark, fleshy man, with one of those fruity voices like a hothouse tomato, all culture and no taste; I didn't like his lips, either, they were too red and full. He seemed to have plenty of money and no visible means of support; like the bumblebee he flouted the laws of thermodynamics. In theory he acted as overseas sales representative for Dunskirk and several other firms, which gave him a convenient pretext for flitting off to the continent at frequent intervals; in practice I felt sure that he made his cash by less legitimate means. He talked a lot, knowledgeably, about the export business, but one felt this was just a front; his real passions seemed to be fast cars and rather infantile bawdy stories, so far as I could judge from personal experience.

Tigger Shand had been a college friend of Gareth's, also studying chemistry. He may have been a brilliant chemist; I wouldn't know; but in other respects he seemed stuck fast in adolescence. He was thin and unimpressive, with a hatchet-face and mud-coloured eyes, but he dressed dazzlingly; Gareth revered him as a wit, on rather insubstantial grounds, and he talked with a peculiarly artificial pop-American accent. One could imagine him at school, throwing waterbombs at the girls, producing stinks and explosions in the lab; I felt sorry for Gareth's new wife, faced with this classic pair of husband's cronies. Among the three, Mait seemed the leader and I trusted him the least; I had heard him making jokes, tiny, knowing subversive digs at old Dunskirk behind his back, and Gareth laughing at them sycophantically. I was sure it had been Mait who taught Gareth to despise the solid, unpretentious little firm that had provided his bread and butter and been old Dunskirk's pride for so many years.

Thinking of all this I said, "Honestly, Mr Dunskirk, a college education is *nothing* in comparison with experience and know-how like yours. And enthusiasm."

"Well, and hasn't Gareth got enthusiasm!" He beamed triumphantly. "Look at that grand new lab he's fitted up, and now Product X has come out of it! I tell you, Miss Martha, this is nobbut the start of big doings!'

"Martha, we really *must* go," Mimi put in here. "I'm due to see some Funshine rushes at the Wandsworth Astoria—supposing I shall ever be able to make it there with all this tea inside me. Goodbye, Mr Dunskirk, and thank you for entertaining us so spendidly."

He opened a door on to the fire escape and showed us how we could go straight down without having to return through the works; I was rather relieved, as I didn't think I could stomach the sight of great pans of emulsifying face-cream after such a heavy meal.

"I'll ring you in about a week, Mr Dunskirk," I said, "and make a date for you to come and go through what we've done so far."

"I'll be looking forward to that, lass," he said earnestly. "I'm fair impatient to see Product X on the market."

CHAPTER II

When Gareth Dunskirk returned from his honeymoon I rang him up and was able to get from him a cautious statement to the effect that Product X was a compound of leaf oils, bergamot, and citrus oils, with a touch of peppermint, some ginger-grass, some terpene esters, and a few other things that he preferred to keep secret.

"When can we have a firm date to start shooting, do you suppose?" I asked George, who had been down to the works again.

We had roughed out a campaign, TV commercials and colour pages in women's weeklies and monthlies; I was impatient to have it okayed by client and get it into operation.

"They have to leave the new batch another week to clear, till it has adjusted to its final osmical level," George said, looking knowledgeable and pleased with himself.

"Oh yes?" I said sceptically.

"There are a few undesirable top notes, apparently."

"Sounds like infiltration in the Bach Choir." I was pretty sure George hadn't any more notion what those technical terms really meant than I had.

"Suppose we call a client conference for Friday week," he suggested.

In spite of the usual hold-ups and snags—the osmical level didn't adjust as fast as it should, Jimmy came down with shingles, there was a one-day printing strike, and my secretary had a poisoned finger—we actually did hold our meeting on the Friday, and it achieved even more than we expected.

In the end we had decided on the name *Avalon* for the perfume. Amazingly, everyone liked it, even old Dunskirk, who said he didn't know what it meant but it had a nice classy sound. We also got him to okay our plans for packaging and merchandising: a neat, plain, gilt-mounted flask was chosen, the same at each price level; by strenuous tactics we managed to head old Dunskirk off pink or blue bubble-glass in chianti-bottle shapes. Then I made a little speech to introduce the campaign, and Jimmy showed a series of storyboards to give an idea of the TV commercials, with romantic queens in barges and gothic castles dreaming up out of the mist. Tom had done some really inspired artwork for the colour pages, and if Jimmy was heard to mutter that it was by Burne-Jones out of the Pink Fairy Book, that was merely envy, and because his shingles were fretting him.

Gareth was not at the conference. A crisis had arisen at the lab, and he had to be there, his father explained. Between the lines, I gathered that Gareth wasn't so happy about the osmical level as old Dunskirk, and, in fact, thought his father was hurrying matters on too fast. It was hard to discuss Product X with Gareth; he seemed strangely reluctant to talk about it. Surprisingly enough, though when his father was out of earshot Gareth made little secret of his scorn for the cosmetics industry, he was really quite knowledgeable about perfumes. I am no expert—I can tell Blue Grass from Je Reviens, and know what I like, but Gareth, apparently, was somewhere near absolute pitch in perfume recognition, and his father used to say hopefully that when the boy learnt to lay off the booze and the fags he'd be a sort of Grade-A World No. I. This was one of the many annoying things about Gareth—he despised his gift, and minimised it; he would far rather have been able to play a brilliant game of bridge. Anyway, I was glad he couldn't come to the meeting; we were far more comfortable without him.

Old Dunskirk was delighted with the whole campaign, okayed it without hesitation—if only all clients were like that!—and asked when we could begin shooting the commercials.

"As soon as possible," Jimmy said firmly. "It's nearly April, it's essential to have them finished and through by June. We ought to start next week or the week after at the latest. It's just a matter of finding a suitable castle."

He traced a design of battlements in the air and old Dunskirk looked hopefully at me, as if he expected me to ring a bell and summon a butler with a tray of keeps and bastions.

"Well there are plenty," George said comfortably. "Did you have any special one in mind when you wrote the copy, Martha dear?"

"N-no, not particularly." I was lying, of course, but my mind sidestepped at that point. "It ought to be on the coast, naturally—"

"Warkworth, Bamburgh?" Mimi had spent her last holiday in Northumberland.

"Rather a long way *off*, Mimi dear."

"Pevensey?" Susan said doubtfully.

"Not exactly a stern and rockbound coast, my love."

"Tintagel?"

"It's a little too well *known*," George said fastidiously. "And it is such a repulsive place."

"There are lots of castles in Wales," I suggested. "Cardiff, Caernarvon, Harlech?"

"I bar Wales," Jimmy announced. "There's *no* light, and it rains all the time. We'd have the film unit kicking their heels day after day at ruinous cost, probably getting drunk and insulting the natives in some utterly unforeseen way. No, Wales is out." He sank his chin on his chest in a final way.

We all sat silent, racking our brains. I noticed, glancing out of the window, that the day, unseasonably warm for late March, had clouded over; the sky looked like thunder, dark as a lid in the middle and pale round the rim.

"Come on, Martha love, be constructive," George said after a while. "This is your campaign, it isn't like you not to have a suggestion at your fingertips. Surely you must have been thinking of *some* castle, however vaguely, when you wrote the copy?"

"Well—as a matter of fact—"

"Cough it up, lovey."

"There is a castle, a bit farther along the Cornish coast beyond Tintagel," I said lamely. It was odd how reluctant I was to mention, even to think of, Trevann, even now, nearly eight years afterwards. I wonder if everyone feels that way about the place where they spent their honeymoon—as if it should be put in a box, locked away, never seen or spoken about again. Perhaps that's why people honeymoon on yachts; my mind wandered briefly to Gareth Dunskirk, drifting idyllically through the Mediterranean with his Italian beauty (whom we had not yet been obliged to meet).

"You don't mean Boscastle?"

"Farther on. It's called Trevann."

"Who owns it? National Trust? Ministry of Works?"

"No, it's privately owned—or was, eight years ago. It's on an island, just a stone's throw from shore. It's ruinous, not lived in, but rather nice. *Very* picturesque."

"Can we get permission to shoot there, d'you suppose?" from George.

I didn't know about that. "Depends who owns it now."

"Oh, people are only too pleased, as a rule. And it's much better if it's private," Jimmy said, looking slightly happier. "Then we shan't have a lot of bananas wandering round while we're shooting, getting in the picture and tripping over cables and asking damfool questions."

"Right, that's fixed." George suddenly became quickfire and executive. "Susan dear, you'll get permission to use Trevann castle. Jimmy, you've got the unit laid on—who are you using, by the way?"

"Mid-Century, Harry Kodor. He's very good, you remember he did the mountain films for Fairweather and he's doing their Picnic Soups. With any luck, we can combine the locations."

"Yes, yes. Excellent. Now about the casting."

Jimmy began to look mulish. Casting was something he liked to keep strictly to himself; he couldn't stand what he called George's amateurish outlook.

"It's getting rather late," I said hastily. (It was; it was also dark as if a monstrous crow were flying overhead.) "Perhaps we'd better leave that for now—"

George opened his mouth to speak, but old Dunskirk's voice here made itself heard.

"Maybe I joost ought to mention here that Mr Salmon kindly agreed to let my daughter-in-law take the main part in the commercials."

Jimmy's jaw dropped. For once, he was stricken to silence. So were the rest of us, in varying degrees of stunned horror, imperfectly concealed. However marvellous, legendary, and romantic a setting we managed to cook up for the commercials, the whole effect would be ruined if the actress were unsuitable; and what possible chance could there be that Gareth's wife would do for the role?

Zero.

George had sold the pass, and our beautiful campaign, which was supposed to make advertising history, was shot down before it had even taken off.

"Cara's doon soom fashion modelling in Savona, so I don't anticipate any awkwardness," old Dunskirk went on serenely.

"Probably won a beauty contest at Little Solferino on the Po," I heard Jimmy mutter to himself.

"In fact I'm sure you'll all be more than satisfied with her. She's waiting in the reception hall now, as a matter of fact, for she's having a bite of loonch with Mr Salmon and myself after this little meeting, so I'll joost take the liberty of calling her in and introducing her to you all."

That was one of the most uncomfortable three minuteses I've ever sat through. Nobody dared say a word. George scanned some media charts in a lofty and preoccupied manner, Jimmy whistled through his teeth, Mimi looked as if her thoughts were amusing her, Susan took notes. I sat miserably staring out at Paris Garden (where thin rods of rain were beginning to fall on the plane trees) and wished I could be somebody else, somewhere else, a long way off.

By the time I've finished a campaign I'm always so wrought up in it that it's agony if the final result has to differ even in the slightest degree from my original conception. And I would have been prepared to lay a thousand to one in gilt-mounted perfume flasks that Gareth's choice would not be my idea of a stately Arthurian queen.

Which shows what a snob I am, I suppose.

Tom caught my eye and gave me a comforting, brotherly grin. After a moment I felt better and was able to smile back at him.

The door opened and Cara Dunskirk came in. I heard Jimmy draw in his breath with a little hiss, and old Dunskirk chuckled in a satisfied way.

"Ladies and gentlemen, this is my daughter-in-law," he said, and then he took her round, formally introducing her to everybody in turn.

It was pretty dark by now, and Tom had put on all the lights; in their dusty, pinkish, fluorescent glow her white skin really did look like alabaster. She had a long—immensely long—neck, a cloud of fine dark hair, dead black, not blue-black, and a rounded, heavy jaw, like Rossetti's models. Her eyes were big and black and mournfully appealing and her nose was short and straight. She looked like Circe, as she moved slowly round the circle. When she reached Tom, who was next to me, she gave him a little wistful smile.

"Gareth has spoken of you—I am so glad to meet you," she said in a low voice.

Tom made some conventional, polite rejoinder.

I wondered where Cara had learned her English—she spoke hesitantly, with a bit of an accent, but what came through strongest, with slightly comic effect, was a Mayfair drawl, a sort of modish weariness. Then they moved on to me, and old Dunskirk drew me forward.

"This is Miss Gilroy," he said warmly. "I've told you all about her, my dear; Miss Martha is the clever yoong lady who's written the commercial pieces, and in my opinion they're as good as anything Tennyson ever composed. I joost hope you two will be great friends."

"I'm sure we shall," I said, smiling at Cara. She raised her eyes and I was surprised at the look of frank hostility she gave me. She had smiled at the men; Mimi and Susan had been greeted with cool indifference; why was I singled out for dislike? She soon moved away from me and talked to George and Jimmy; George

25

See p. 36.

Fleet Street; we turned to look at one of the best views in London, Ludgate railway bridge and the complicated hierarchy of buildings, some old, some new, marshalled up Ludgate Hill with St Paul's soaring above them.

Then Tom said, "Don't you think it's time you told me about it? After all, we've known each other more than a year."

I pulled my ringless left hand out of my pocket, where I had it clenched.

"Really there's nothing much to tell. It's a long while ago. It's over."

"Then tell, and get it out of your system."

"Forceps, please!" I laughed shakily, and drew a deep breath. "All right.... But be prepared for a lot of anticlimax, which seems to be my speciality."

Even so, it was hard to get started. Tom said, to ease the way,

"What was his name?"

"Lucian. Lucian Ferguson. I married him when I was nineteen. Honestly," I said with passion, "people shouldn't be *allowed* to marry so young. When I think what a callow, unfledged chick I was— Of course than it all seemed so wonderful."

"Didn't you have any family to advise you?"

"No, they were divorced. Father had remarried and gone abroad, Mother died the year before. I had quite a good job in a publishing firm; Lucian was one of the editors. He seemed to have a tremendous career ahead of him, he was intelligent and full of original ideas; very sensitive.... We fell in love. He hadn't any family either. His mother died giving birth to a dead baby when he was ten, his father had had lung cancer. He'd been brought up by a grandmother. We got married almost at once. Thinking each of us would supply all the other needed.

"For a short time everything was perfect. I suppose just the same I should have been warned by small things, but I was so ignorant.... We went to Cornwall for our honeymoon; Lucian adored the sea, he was a wonderful swimmer. We were so happy; but even then once or twice he seemed queerly abstracted. And then—we'd found a flat in St John's Wood—I remember one evening after we'd been there about a month he suddenly said to me coldly, 'I wish you wouldn't leave messages for me, Martha. If you have anything to say to me, come out with it straight.' I said, 'Messages? What *do* you mean?' He said, 'That book you left lying on the floor.'"

26

"I bet you she *can* add two and two, just the same," Jimmy said.

And in fact she could, as we discovered later.

We came to know her better in the next couple of weeks. She called at the office for conferences several times, and Mimi and I took her out to lunch. Away from the presence of males she turned out to be harmless enough; not a great deal to say for herself but what there was, perfectly pleasant. It still seemed fairly evident that I wasn't her favourite person, but she was civil to me. Old Dunskirk didn't even try to conceal his pride and satisfaction in Gareth's wonderful prize; he was touching about her. "But," he said, "cooming from abroad she naturally feels a bit strange in London, not knowing anybody. If a nice lass like you, Miss Martha, that knows all the ropes, would have time to take her about a bit—you know, show her the shops and the sights—you're joost the sort of company I'd like for her—"

Well, I supposed Gareth was very busy with his osmical level, though you'd think he'd have a little time for taking his new bride about. But I obliged a bit, and Cara was faintly surprised at this, though gracefully acquiescent; I felt like a giraffe with a gazelle in tow as, with languid lack of interest, she gazed at the Mall and Temple Bar and St Paul's. I soon found she liked Marks and Sparks and the boutiques best, so we concentrated on them and abandoned sightseeing. In the course of these trips I learnt a bit about her; parents were dead, killed in a train crash, she had no relatives living except for a cousin at Bergamo, she'd had a secretarial job in a factory at Savona—she seemed totally vague as to what kind of factory but I finally concluded that it had been pharmaceutical products—and, as Jimmy had guessed, she had won a local beauty contest, decided to become a mannequin and gone to evening classes in modelling. Astonishingly, no one had snapped her up; she'd never even gone to Rome. Perhaps it was because her face lacked animation; it was almost totally inexpressive. Whatever her thoughts—if she did think—her face gave no clue to them. Probing a little further I discovered that her sole ambition, apparently, had always been to make her way either to England or to America; I couldn't help wondering—uncharitably —if marriage to Gareth Dunskirk hadn't been merely a practical step towards the realisation of these aims.

Jimmy discovered that the Mid-Century film unit wouldn't be free for a couple of weeks owing to weather delays on another schedule. Meanwhile we'd decided to kill two birds with one stone and, while we were on location in Cornwall, make a batch of commercials for the Faireweather pilot project. Mimi and I were hard at work bustling them through.

Faireweather, as I think I've said before, were an American firm who manufactured foods with an accent on sporting, carefree, out-of-doors consumption. There were various different barbecue products, frozen salads, the prefab kebabs, smoked fish rings (The Fun Food That You Can Use for Pitch'n Toss) and now their latest, Picnic Soups. These were an adaptation of a k-ration device: they consisted of a tin of soup with a flip-top lid, and a small chamber of solid fuel under the tin. When you flipped the top of the soup can it automatically started a chemical reaction in the fuel compartment, and in a couple of minutes your soup was boiling hot. There were disadvantages, of course—the things were rather fiddling to operate, and fairly expensive. Also I gathered that, like the makers of Product X, Faireweather hadn't quite disposed of the teething troubles yet; the soup tended to get into the fuel chamber or something. That was why they were trying the stuff in a small way in the U.K. first, before launching a major campaign across the American continent. On account of this we felt free to be fairly light-hearted in our approach; Faireweather rather went in for light-hearted advertising anyway.

Mimi, who had a terrific talent for food copy, had done a series of scripts combining dotty situations with mouthwatering descriptions; she had devil-may-care adventures falling out of helicopters, pausing on their *pitons*, arresting bronchos in mid-buck, meanwhile heating and quaffing cans of Picnic Soup with appropriate comments. Cornwall was a good, varied locale for shooting such antics, and luckily the film unit could spare the time to make both lots concurrently. This plan would have many advantages: we could do a lot of dovetailing, the unit would be used to maximum capacity while we had it, and, since half the staff of Salmon and Bucknell would be out of the office for ten days, it was only economic to fit in as much as possible while we were at it. Furthermore, the two sets of commercials were so different in character that there wasn't the faintest chance of a link-up.

So Mimi and I were up to our ears in work getting everything ready before we took off for Cornwall, and making sure that, if anything unforeseen did occur while we were away, Susan was well briefed to deal with it.

Four days before we were due to leave, George Salmon threw an office party. He was rather pathetically prone to do this sort of thing. A childless man, he had strong paternal feelings about the staff, when not distracted by his constant succession of wives. (By now we gathered that Eloise had vanished off abroad, probably for good. George was pretty well to pieces over this, so organising the party gave him something to think about.)

We all attended, and there was a good deal of the rather hectic gaiety that brews up at such times between people who see each other every day anyway. A grudgingly small further supply of Product X—we hadn't yet got into the way of calling it Avalon— had been released to us, and Mimi and I had sprayed each other lavishly. It really was a remarkable perfume and lived up (I thought) to the creative genius we'd spent on it.

Luckily there were quite a few clients to leaven the party besides us all. Old Dunskirk came, and Cara, and the regrettable Gareth (who annoyed me by bringing his two friends, uninvited; spare men are supposed to be always welcome at a party but I would automatically except any friend of Gareth's; I was confirmed in my view of them when I noticed that, evidently finding the pace too slow, they very soon left). Franz Oesmacher drifted in with an amazing debutante, who looked as if she had been carved out of scrolled paper. And witty little Harry Kodor came, and several people from the Faireweather London office. My favourite of these was Barnstable Soglow, who had had a lot to do with the production of Picnic Soups; he looked like a stork, was always frantic, did the work of ten men, and could have afforded to retire and live anywhere in the world, only he would have died of boredom in a week. The Emir of Turkinistan turned up too, he had flown over for somebody's coming-out dance at the Dorchester and looked in for an hour. That made the evening, of course; in his robes and turban, with his sweeping moustaches and goatee, he was a stunningly picturesque addition to S & B's sedate board-room. He paid flowery compliments to all the ladies and insisted on dancing an old-fashioned waltz with Mimi, who twirled round him like an elegant monkey, unblushingly exchanging red-hot repartee.

I was feeling rather strung-up. I wouldn't admit it to myself, but the thought of going back to Trevann depressed me terribly; over and over again I cursed myself for ever having mentioned the place. I had once been ecstatically happy there, and the happiness

29

had proved such a total fallacy that I felt it would be like a second meeting with somebody who had played me a particularly cruel trick.

However, apparently these feelings didn't affect my unremarkably fair-haired English outward appearance.

"But you are so beautiful tonight!" the Emir said, giving me a whole series of flashing Middle Eastern smiles. "This is the night Mees Gilroy has come into her own. She is like a half-open rose, full of sweetness and promise."

"Like Turkish Delight, don't you mean?" I looked down at the top of his turban (I was a good five inches taller but he made up for it in width and agility) wondering if the ruby securing it could possibly be a real one. It was as large as a bantam's egg. But then the Emir's income, from oil, was reputed to be over £10,000 a day.

"And the perfume—ahhh!" He left go of me for a moment as we danced to raise his hands to heaven in ecstasy, and then clamped down in a firmer grip. "I am bound to say that, on the more buxom beauties of my own country, I prefer a perfume with a little more ethyl phenylacetate and a good deal more ethyl cinnamate, but on you fragile English woodnymphs—ravishing!"

"Oh, Excellency, you do say the prettiest things," I told him happily. "No one has ever called me fragile before."

Indeed, since the advent of Cara Dunskirk I had been feeling my inches particularly; she had a wonderful knack of making me see myself as a big, blonde half-back.

Tom came up and said, "You haven't danced with me all evening. Don't welsh."

"I'm not welshing. But I must find the Emir another partner. Who can I introduce you to, Excellency?"

His eye roamed round the room with a harem collector's practised virtuosity.

"How about Mrs Dunskirk?" I suggested. "Over there in dark red."

I owed her some civility anyway.

"Aha! Yes indeed," the Emir agreed cordially.

I led the way across the boardroom with Tom and the Emir close behind.

"Is that Product X you've got on?" Tom said in my ear. "Heavens, it's potent stuff, isn't it? Do you suppose it has any insecticidal qualities?"

"Well, there, Miss Martha!" old Dunskirk greeted me. "All the family's here, as you see, enjoying ourselves."

"I'm so glad," I said, smiling at him. "Cara, I've someone here who particularly wants to meet you. May I introduce his Excellency the Emir of Turkinistan—"

Cara's eyes widened at the title, she opened her mouth to reply, but no sound came out. Her face became completely blank. She was always fairly pale, but now she slowly whitened to a sort of dead-fish colour, gave a little choking moan, and began to keel over.

"Here, hold up, lass!" old Dunskirk exclaimed, and grabbed her arm. I got hold of the other one and we half led, half shuffled her to a chair.

"I fetch a restorative drink!" the Emir exclaimed, and whisked away with his usual rapidity. Tom, old Dunskirk, and I stood round Cara exclaiming and commiserating. For a crazy moment I wondered if it could have been the Product X that had upset her; by now I had learned from my background reading that perfumes can have a strong psychic influence, that some illnesses are treated by smells and others caused by them. In no time, however, the Emir was back with a glassful of liquor which had such a lightning restorative effect on her that I couldn't help thinking he must have slipped an oriental pick-me-up into the firm's nondescript claret cup; Cara's indisposition, whatever the cause, was soon dispersed.

"I am so sorry—I am all right now," she said, raising her huge eyes to smile at the Emir, but still contriving to look pathetically appealing.

"What's the matter, luv?" old Dunskirk asked concernedly. "Eh, you should niver ha' come if you were feeling poorly."

"Oh, it is nothing—only the heat," she said quickly. "I apologise *so* much—it was most stupid of me. I will sit here quietly a minute, then I will soon be quite better."

"Sure you wouldn't rather go home, dearie?"

It struck me that Cara's father-in-law was showing a lot more concern than her husband; Gareth was at the other end of the room talking to the Faireweather crowd. He glanced round at the commotion, shrugged, and evidently decided that it was not worth regarding. The Emir, however, sat down beside Cara, all solicitude.

"I have my Daimler outside—are you sure, Mrs Dunskirk? It would be a pleasure to drive you home."

31

"But I do not want to miss the party!" she said with a pretty, childlike air.

"She'll do now," said Tom drily in my ear. "Come and dance." He dragged me away. I went willingly enough.

But we had only made one circuit of the room when Gareth came up to us.

He looked his very worst in evening clothes—like something out of a B film, too glossy to be true. Actually he was extremely handsome, with a sort of blond Nordic good looks, quite different from his father—he must have been a throwback to some Viking ancestor who'd stepped ashore at Bruddersford. He had thick fair hair, carefully brushed, and superb teeth which he often bared in a big, false smile, and a smooth synthetic-looking skin, putty-colour all over, like frozen pastry. People said he and Cara made a lovely couple, but it had already occurred to me that her novelty was wearing off for him even faster than if she had been a new hi-fi or a new car. When people praised her his look of complacency was beginning to corrode. Annoyingly, he had reverted to a habit of casting admiring looks in my direction, a tribute I could happily have forgone.

"I s-say, Martha—" he had a slight stammer which at first gave a misleading impression of diffidence—"is anything the matter with C-Cara?"

"Why don't you go and ask her yourself?" I snapped.

"She came over faint," Tom, more charitable, said. "Because of the heat."

"She l-looks all right now." Gareth's intonation was noticeably sour; craning round I saw that Cara and the Emir were getting on like humming-birds. He was sparkling and chatting away, nineteen to the dozen, while her mournful appeal was trained on him like an arc-light.

"She was all right when we started this evening," Gareth said irritably.

"Is she pregnant?" I asked.

Tom frowned at me disapprovingly, but I believe in plain dealing. Gareth fluttered his eyelids and gave a deprecating smile.

"N-not that *I* know of," he said.

"I hope she'll feel all right by next week," I said. We were going down to Trevann on Monday, and shooting was due to begin on Tuesday, weather permitting. Jimmy had gone ahead with part of the film unit to arrange about locations—his shingles were making him too tetchy to endure the thought of an office party.

If Cara were to fall ill now it would certainly complicate our schedule.

"C-can I have a d-dance, Martha?" Gareth said.

I was trying to think of excuses when I noticed old Dunskirk making his way towards us. I turned to him with relief.

"Cara's decided to accept his Excellency's kind offer after all, Miss Martha," he said. "So I'll joost say goodnight and thanks for a wonderful evening on behalf of us both. I expect yoong Gareth will want to be staying on a bit longer, eh, Gareth?" Gareth gave a surly nod "—but I'll be running along with them. Old bones—"

"I'm sure it's very sensible of Cara," I said. "She needs to take care of herself—"

"Ay, that's what I told her, so's to get right before we leave for Cornwall."

"Are you coming too, Mr Dunskirk?" I said, rather startled.

"That I am!" he said comfortably. "It's a long time since I was in those parts, but Moother and I used to stay at Par Sands when we was yoong. So I thought I'd joost give myself a couple of weeks off and coom down with the family to see the foon. I've rented a house at Polneath, that's only ten miles from Trevann."

"How—how nice." I collected my manners and smiled at him. The shooting of commercials was the one time at which we did try to discourage even our favourite clients from sitting-in because their ideas at such times were apt to be devastatingly disrupting and expensive. But I could see that in the Dunskirk family we had met our match. Maybe the old boy wanted to keep an eye on his daughter-in-law. And maybe that wasn't such a bad idea, I thought, observing one of the languishing looks she gave the Emir.

"Will you be coming too?" I asked Gareth. To my relief he shook his head.

"Someone's got to do the work," he said, sounding martyred. "I'm s-staying to keep an eye on things at the lab." But he added that he might fly down to Plymouth and drive over at the week-end.

"And little Laureen's cooming too, she can do with some sea-air," old Dunskirk went on. Who the devil's little Laureen? I wondered. "She's Gareth's little girl by his first marriage," his father explained to my look of inquiry. "You'll joost love her, Miss Martha, aye, she's a lovely little girl."

By rights the heavens should have opened and rained down lightnings at those words, but in fact I didn't even have a premonition; I just said what fun I was sure it was all going to be, and urged Mr Dunskirk to see that Cara had an early night and took it easy.

Seeing them to the door and accepting the Emir's farewell embrace I hoped I'd managed to give Gareth the slip, but he bobbed up beside me again the minute they had left.

"H-how about that d-dance now, eh, M-Martha?"

I couldn't in politeness refuse, so I glumly went with him.

"That's P-Product X you've got on, isn't it?" he said. "It suits you. You're a g-good-looking girl when you dress yourself up, you know, M-Martha." He eyes me appraisingly—he had greyish-yellow eyes, oddly flat and opaque.

"Thank you," I said coldly.

"And P-Product X is a bloody good perfume, isn't it? Real f-first-class quality. Trust me to think up a winner," he said with odious self-satisfaction. "It'll really put D-Dunskirk and Son on the map."

"What do you think your father's hard work for the last twenty years has done?" I said acidly.

"Oh, most of Dad's lines are trash, everyone knows that. No class to 'em at all. I've often tried to get him to s-sell out and start up in some other business, but no dice. Dad's got n-no idea of prestige or appearances at all. Honestly! F-fancy expecting us to live over the factory still. C-Cara could hardly believe it. No, it's a ropey old firm, I'm afraid."

"I notice you don't despise the money it makes."

"Easy, d-darling! You don't have to bite my head off every t-time you speak! Little spitfire you are!" He smiled down at me patronisingly—he was quite tall—and I could have socked him. I contented myself with saying,

"Don't call me darling, please. I'm not your wife."

"Wish you were!" he said. "Cara turned out to be a bit of a washout, I'm afraid. B-But I think you and I would get along fine. Well-m-matched couple." He looked at himself complacently in the long glass at the end of the room. I maintained a chilly silence.

Luckily the dance ended fairly soon; it always seemed as if nothing could prick Gareth's happy belief that he was irresistible, but I was sometimes afraid that one day my irritation with him would drive me too far and I'd say something that was bad for business.

34

"C'mon, how about an-nother one?" he said when the music stopped.

"Sorry, I'm having the next one with Mr Toole," I said. Tom, bless him, was right behind, and expeditiously whisked me away.

"Now," he said, "let's get out of here. This is the first time I've had you to myself all evening and I don't want any more inter-ruptions."

I glanced round. The departure of the Emir with old Dunskirk and Cara had started a general trend of leave-taking.

"You've done your duty quite sufficiently," Tom urged. "Come and have a drink somewhere."

I knew that I ought to go home and work, but the prospect of Trevann was weighing on me like a ton of lead, and I agreed.

"That's the girl. I'll get your coat."

I found it restful to be organised by Tom. The only person in the office taller than I, he was large and loose-built, with an untidy mop of brown hair and a crooked nose acquired in a school boxing-bout. Although he seemed to take nothing very seriously, he was effortlessly efficient at his job, and I knew him to be a passionately keen spare-time photographer. He travelled huge distances and took endless pains over his shots; he had won a number of international medals.

He dragged me off now, after a quick whisky, insisting that he must show me a superb view—it turned out to be a fig-tree grow-ing on a bombed site—and then, instead of sensibly going home to bed, we somehow progressed on to a long moonlit walk about the City. I love wandering through London at night; it is such a beautiful city in the dark, even the hideous buildings are tolerable, the good ones are stunning, and the streets are clean and bare, looking as they were designed to look. One can walk along them at a good clip, which is seldom possible by day—I hate dawdling. The whole experience is liberating.

"What's the matter, Martha?" Tom said after a while.

He sounded as if he really cared, and that threw me.

"I'm having the most frightful premonitions about Trevann," I blurted. "Oh, it sounds unutterably stupid when it's put into words —you'll think me a moonstruck fool—"

"It's something about your husband, isn't it?" said Tom quietly.

"Yes. How did you guess?"

"Radar."

We walked a few blocks in silence. We were going west along

35

Fleet Street; we turned to look at one of the best views in London, Ludgate railway bridge and the complicated hierarchy of buildings, some old, some new, marshalled up Ludgate Hill with St Paul's soaring above them.

Then Tom said, "Don't you think it's time you told me about it? After all, we've known each other more than a year."

I pulled my ringless left hand out of my pocket, where I had it clenched.

"Really there's nothing much to tell. It's a long while ago. It's over."

"Then tell, and get it out of your system."

"Forceps, please!" I laughed shakily, and drew a deep breath. "All right.... But be prepared for a lot of anticlimax, which seems to be my speciality."

Even so, it was hard to get started. Tom said, to ease the way, "What was his name?"

"Lucian. Lucian Ferguson. I married him when I was nineteen. Honestly," I said with passion, "people shouldn't be *allowed* to marry so young. When I think what a callow, unfledged chick I was— Of course than it all seemed so wonderful."

"Didn't you have any family to advise you?"

"No, they were divorced. Father had remarried and gone abroad, Mother died the year before. I had quite a good job in a publishing firm; Lucian was one of the editors. He seemed to have a tremendous career ahead of him, he was intelligent and full of original ideas; very sensitive.... We fell in love. He hadn't any family either. His mother died giving birth to a dead baby when he was ten, his father had had lung cancer. He'd been brought up by a grandmother. We got married almost at once. Thinking each of us would supply all the other needed.

"For a short time everything was perfect. I suppose just the same I should have been warned by small things, but I was so ignorant.... We went to Cornwall for our honeymoon; Lucian adored the sea, he was a wonderful swimmer. We were so happy; but even then once or twice he seemed queerly abstracted. And then—we'd found a flat in St John's Wood—I remember one evening after we'd been there about a month he suddenly said to me coldly, 'I wish you wouldn't leave messages for me, Martha. If you have anything to say to me, come out with it straight.' I said, 'Messages? What *do* you mean?' He said, 'That book you left lying on the floor.'"

"What was the book?" Tom asked.

"It was *An Ideal Husband.* Lucian said, 'I suppose that's intended as a dig at me, is it?' I was utterly astonished, I thought at first he must be joking. I said, 'Don't be silly, I just happened to leave it there.' But I could see he didn't believe me; he was fearfully tidy himself, he'd never just leave something lying. That blew over, but it frightened me terribly—to have been so completely misunderstood! And there were other incidents. He kept saying I was trying to *get at* him somehow.

"Then he began giving things up."

"What sort of things?"

"Oh—at first we'd gone to a lot of concerts. He stopped doing that, stopped even listening to music on the radio. He said it wasn't necessary. He gave up drink, cigarettes, even coffee.... As soon as he detected himself enjoying anything he'd give it up, that seemed to be a sort of test. Of willpower, I suppose. And all the time he was turning away from me and in on himself. By the end of six months we weren't going to bed together any more...." My voice wavered as I navigated past a particularly searing memory; I went on quickly, "By the time we'd been married a year he hardly ever spoke to me."

"What about at the office?"

"His work was all right. But he looked thin, and years older. Of course I can see now, what I hadn't the wit to realise then, that he was ill, that I should have had a psychiatrist to him. But I was too hurt and ashamed to think of calling in outside help. And when we had been married a year, he just quietly vanished. One day I got home and he wasn't there. Wh-when I finally swallowed my pride and rang his office—I was working somewhere else by then —they seemed surprised, told me he'd given notice and left. They didn't know where. I've never seen him since."

"You tried to find him?"

"Yes, in due course when I was too miserable to be ashamed any more I got a private inquiry firm to look for him. It was squalid—as far as I could make out, all they did was search through shady seaside hotels. They didn't find him. I used to wonder if perhaps he'd gone abroad, to the far east. Otherwise, how could he vanish for so long without a single trace? And he was always interested in eastern religions. At the end of seven years I got a divorce for desertion—that was last winter, just before I came to Salmon and Bucknell."

"Do you think he could be dead?"

Tom's words sounded so cold and final. I had often thought them to myself, never said them aloud. I said quickly,

"No. No, I'm sure he isn't. I've always had a feeling that he's *somewhere*—"

"You're still in love with him, aren't you?" Tom said quietly.

A knife-blade turned in my heart. I stood still and put my hands over my face, remembering those early days, the sunshine and the primroses on our Cornish honeymoon, the foolish jokes of early marriage. Tears cataracted out between my fingers.

It was a long while since I'd cried. I had gone through some pretty dark times during the early part of those seven years. I'd felt, of course, that there must be some terrible flaw in my own personality which Lucian had discovered too late. So I'd thrown myself into work—there's always one's job, thank heaven—and kept well away from the male sex. I didn't intend ever to risk another letdown. And for the last three years or so I'd been on a pretty even keel.

"Handkerchief," Tom said, pushing one between my fingers. We had turned left, down on to the Embankment; the Thames ran still and black below swags of lights on the other side; Tom put an arm round me and steered me to a bench, saying, "There, there," and "Now you'll feel better," until my deluge had run dry.

"I *don't* feel better," I said weakly then. "I can't think why I'm crying in this stupid way and it doesn't help a *bit*. I feel rotten! This would have to happen just before we start shooting."

"Shooting!" he growled. "Can't you think of anything but work? You wrap yourself in it as if it were chain-mail. The trouble is, you've never grown out of your calf-love. You're just hugging a romantic memory."

"You know nothing whatever about it! You never met him." I was suddenly angry. "I think—I think I'd better go home, or we shall start quarrelling."

"Okay, my dear," Tom said equably. He hoisted me to my feet. "We'll go up to Charing Cross and find a taxi. You think I'm badgering you and being unfair, don't you? And you know what the point is, don't you? You know I'm in love with you?"

We were passing a big, dark shop-window with nothing in it except some opened books propped on stands. Our lamplit reflections moved slowly across the glass.

"Oh, Tom," I said miserably.

"It's no use, you've got to face it. I love you and I want to marry you. What have you got to say to that?"

"I can't think why you should want to," I said, hedging. "I—I'm not a good person to marry."

"Rubbish. Just because you had bad luck the first time—"

"But it may have been my fault." This was the thought that had haunted me through wakeful nights and days of silent, bewildered agony as Lucian went about the flat ignoring me. What was wrong with me that I didn't know about? There had even been a relief, I remembered, in the different quality of the silence in the flat after he was gone.

"My darling, it wasn't your fault. He was a schizo. It would have been the same with anyone. Marriage maybe accelerated it, that's all."

"I'm not going to risk it a second time."

"You can't keep clear of other people for ever. That's just pride and sulkiness. You aren't really self-sufficient—you're warm-hearted, you're a mixer. It's good for you to be chased out of your shell—you've got to join the party again sometime."

"Can't we just go on as we are?" I said weakly.

"No we can't," he said. I had never seen Tom so near angry. "I'm sorry, but that's just not possible."

"What if I say no?"

"I'll get a job in Munich. If you won't have me—well, I'd rather get right away where I don't have to bump against you all the time."

"Tom!" I was appalled. "Leave Salmon and Bucknell? Leave George? Just when we've got this new account?"

"Blast George!"

With a selfish pang I realised how much I should miss the warmth that Tom radiated about the office, his companionship and sense of humour and dry good sense. A chill feeling of desolation came over me.

"Oh goodness," I said unhappily.

"Hold it—there's a taxi!" Tom shot off round the corner, whistling like a maniac. I waited on the kerb, shivering and uncertain. In a minute the cab reappeared; Tom sprang out and opened the door for me.

We travelled for some distance in silence, well away from each other in our separate corners. Then Tom said ruthlessly,

"You believe you're going to find Lucian in Cornwall, don't

you? Don't you think that is rather a childishly romantic notion to be harbouring?"

"Oh *blast* you!" I snapped. "No I don't, and it's not romantic. It's only that—when I remembered about the castle at Trevann, another thing came into my head that I'd clean forgotten—"

"Yes?"

"The castle belonged to a peculiar sort of Brotherhood, you see, some oddbody order. I don't think they were Christian. I suddenly remembered how, when we were walking on the cliffs one day, I noticed Lucian looking up at the monastery. The monks didn't live in the castle, they had a big house on the headland opposite. Lucian didn't say anything, he just looked—as if he had an almost irresistible impulse to go up there—"

"And you'd forgotten that all this time?"

"I suppose it never seemed important."

"Or was it that you didn't *want* to remember it? You didn't really want to find him?"

"Of course it wasn't!"

"And now," Tom went on implacably, "you've remembered it at last because now for the first time you've got free of him."

I was thoroughly annoyed, the usual reaction when other people analyse one's motives.

"That's not it at all! It's just that it seems such a likely place for him to be, if the Brotherhood is still there—"

The taxi pulled up outside my block, and Tom paid it off.

"I'm not asking you up," I said crossly.

"Wouldn't come if you did ask me." He put his arm round my shoulders and gave me a quick hug. "Relax, darling! Don't distress yourself to death. I won't wave an axe at you. We'll wait till you get back from Cornwall, okay? If you *do* find your ex, well, maybe it will prove a salutary shock. And if you don't—when we get back I'll ask you again. Agreed? Have a hot drink now, and go to bed. See you in the morning."

He walked off down Stamford Street with his long slouching stride. I went up to my flat, had the hot drink, and crawled into bed. My mind was a racing muddle of emotions, mostly indignation at Tom. What right had he to badger me so? It was unfair, when I needed all my concentration for the Product X commercials.

Just before I went to sleep I remembered Cara Dunskirk and her queer turn at the party. What had come over her? It could scarcely have been the heat, as she had said—the boardroom was far from overheated, downright chilly if the truth were told. She had seemed quite all right until I had led the Emir up to her. What had upset her then? Had she recognised him?

Weaving an enjoyable fantasy in which it turned out that Cara was an escaped member of the Emir's harem who had persuaded Gareth to smuggle her out of Turkinistan in Brad's yacht with a load of heroin, I fell at last into a distracted doze.

Next day I asked Susan whom she'd applied to for permission to film at Trevann.

"Oh," she said, "the castle belongs to some peculiar Order—they were pretty cagey about it at first but when they finally realised it would mean a bit of money they gave grudging agreement, provided we don't go anywhere near the monastery itself. Here we are, I knew I had it somewhere: The Brotherhood of the Pierced Stone."

"Of course," I said. "How could I have forgotten that?"

CHAPTER III

So there we were in the train going down to Cornwall: Mimi, Tom, Cara, and myself. Susan had offered to lend me her car, but I love train journeys. Besides, I wanted to work during this one: a requisition had just come in marked *Most Urgent*—Midinette scripts for commercials on Canadian TV—and I had to do them right away. Mimi, likewise, was working on copy for Picnic Soup display material. Tom had left his car in Cornwall when he went down before with Jimmy for a preliminary survey; he said it wasn't worth doing the nine-hour drive twice in such a short interval.

Cara, unexpectedly, had asked at the last minute if she could join us instead of driving down with old Dunskirk. I wondered vaguely if this had any connection with the apparent worsening of relations between her and Gareth. But she said,

"I get very easily car-sick. It will be such a long ride—my father-in-law he drives so slowly! And there will be also the housekeeper and Gareth's little girl and much luggage—I do not like to travel with children—"

Of course we said we'd be delighted to have her with us. And she made someone to talk to Tom, as Mimi and I were obliged to work.

Tom and I had met without embarrassment on the day following the party. Firstly, one couldn't be embarrassed with Tom; he wasn't that kind of person; and furthermore, we were both up to our eyes in work. Advertising is really a frantic profession; just when your spirits are at their blackest nadir you may be sure you will be whisked into some dotty but essential operation such as trying to assess the relative merits of two different raspberry ice-lollies, or canvassing your men friends for dirty socks to try out in a new washing-machine. This is often jolting to the system but it has many good points.

When we were clear of London I fished out a batch of depth questionnaires and statistical charts showing why Midinette washing machines enjoyed higher sales among the professional classes and Income Groups A to C than among other social categories. The reason for this was nothing to do with price, for once. Midinette was a toy-sized gadget, relatively inexpensive, intended for washing a small load of half a dozen garments at most. It had been put out experimentally, but was doing rather well, as it proved such a blessing for bed-sitter dwellers afflicted with dud drip-dries. We'd even thought of using the slogan "For the white-collar wash" but George vetoed that; he was deadly sensitive to any copy with a flavour of snobbery.

"Midinette, the bachelor's pet," I wrote, and chewed the tip of my ballpoint while I gazed out of the window at the regimental mascots carved in white along the sides of the downs. Army, navy, medicine, law, I thought, and scribbled down,

"Barrister, minister, vicar, vet,
Dunk their smalls in Midinette."

What occupational garments pertained to the male professional classes? Wigs and gowns, but these, presumably, like uniforms, were sent to the cleaners. Dentists' white coats, choirboys' ruffles, painters' smocks. Chancellors and judges wore bands, whatever those were. Lord Mayors had chains. Monks had robes but never washed them, so I had heard. . . .

Monks.

I glanced sideways at Tom. He was telling Cara about the pre-historic monuments in Cornwall, while she listened wide-eyed, her exquisite head turned sideways on its long neck and tilted up to him; uncharitably I wondered if she had heard a word he said. She seemed quite recovered today from her dizzy spell at the party, looked dazzling, in fact, in a mustard corduroy coat that would have turned me into a boiled parsnip. Tom was being extremely nice, making sure that she didn't feel an outsider among us, or become bored by the journey. Kindness was such an integral part of Tom's nature; suddenly it struck me how really forbearing he had been with me the other night about Lucian. Anyone else would have said, "If you *do* find him again, what use will it be? He can't want to see you or he'd have been in touch long ago. And in any case he must be an entirely different person now from the man you married; what is the point?"

Tom had said neither of those things.

"Midinette—the toy-sized washing machine with a king-sized action," I wrote. "Takes up no more room than a brief-case." And I drew a squiggly picture intended to represent a little man in a bowler hat carrying his washing machine in one hand. I felt singularly uninspired and, after I'd churned out half a dozen paragraphs which would all have to be done again, I switched over to copy for a counter-card, window bill, and wraparound for Bom, the Meat'n Milk Drink. Bom was vile stuff, a gluey-brown dram that contrived to be both salty and sickly, but contained, according to its makers, a higher proportion of calcium than milk, plus enough other useful ingredients to maintain life almost indefinitely. Luckily no high level of inspiration was called for in drafting display material; I simply wrote *"Two-way goodness with Bom"* and drew some little diagrams with measurements.

"Think of an adjective for peas," Mimi said.

"Tender."

"I've used that already for asparagus."

"Sweet juicy."

"Mmmm ... I meant to keep those for corn."

In no time, it seemed, the dining-car attendant was thumping past with his chant, "First lunch! All sittings for first lunch, please."

"Come on, let's eat," Tom said. "I'm starving."

He opened the door for Cara, who got up with alacrity.

"Just a moment while I put all these charts away," Mimi said. I waited for her while the others went on ahead; by the time we reached the dining-car they had settled at one of the only two double tables left. Mimi and I took the other and did her *Times* crossword. After lunch we all more or less slept until we arrived at a godawful little station in the middle of bleak nowhere called Doynen Road, which was the alighting-point for Trevann. Mercifully Jimmy was waiting with Tom's Rover and drove us swiftly over a wrinkled ridgy landscape adorned with corrugated tin sheds, piles of slate, and poverty-stricken breeze-block dwellings. All the trees leaned in one direction. Nothing looked how I remembered it. But I consoled myself by thinking there was probably a long way to go yet.

"This is like the Bad Lands," Mimi commented with distaste. "There ought to be names on the signposts like Poison Peak and Dead Man's Gulch and Alkali Flats.... In heaven's name what are *those* things?"

"China clay tips," Tom said.

"It all looks so different from how it was when I came here before," I murmured nervously. "Is the castle all right, Jimmy?"

"Oh, the *castle's* all right," he replied with gloom. "But everything else is like a waking nightmare. Just wait till you see the hotel. There—look!" Wrenching vindictively at the handbrake he brought the car to a shuddering halt.

"We can't be here already? I remembered Trevann as quite a big place ...?"

However when I climbed out and looked around in the chilly dusk I saw that it was in fact the same place which, I suppose, the previous visit had bathed in a rosy glow of honeymoon happiness: a few cottages, a few Victorian villas, a pub, and the Trelawny Hotel, all grouped round a hairpin bend in the coast road at the top of a narrow ravine with a stream in it which ran down to the Atlantic. An evening mist had come down so no sea was visible, but it could be smelt, and some gulls floated past with doleful cries. The hotel was built of mud-coloured roughcast and decorated with terra-cotta woodwork. A blasted palm tree grew out of the granite chips in the courtyard, among some little rusting tables and chairs.

"Unlicensed?" I said, looking at the sign in horror. "But I'm sure I remember—oh, no, of course, we didn't stay here, we stayed at the pub."

"Pub's become a roadhouse now. No accommodation, " Jimmy said with morose triumph. "But at least one can get a drink there, and it's only just round the bend. Where we'd be otherwise."

"Let's try and board out at a farm," I said, when Mimi and I had taken stock of the inadequacies of the room we had to share because the film unit and actors for the Picnic Soup commercials had already strained the hotel's accommodation to bursting point. "There must be several farms round about, and the tourist season's hardly begun yet."

"Tomorrow at the latest," agreed Mimi, coming back from an incredulous survey of the hotel's upper floors. "Do you know there appears to be only *one* bathroom in this entire establishment?"

"Probably no bathroom at all in a farm but at least we'd have it to ourselves."

"Nonsense, mon cher, all farmers now have Jaguars and central heating because of the farming subsidies. Where's Cara?"

"I invited her to come to our room and freshen up but she elected to wait in that gruesome lounge. Papa Dunskirk's coming over to collect her."

"Is she all right, d'you think? I thought she looked a bit tense. She's not pregnant?"

"Gareth said not."

"He should know."

"Maybe has nerves about her acting."

"Nerves? That one? Impossible. She's nothing but a peasant," said Mimi, who has fine atavistic fits of aristocratic Russian snobbery. "Besides, she doesn't have to act. Only has to sit and gaze about like a giraffe."

"Come now, Mimi—"

"And furthermore she has all a peasant's cunning," added Mimi vindictively. "She's the sort who needs to be watched and kept down all the time. I wouldn't hire her as a scullerymaid; she'd be sure to make off with the teaspoons. You keep an eye on her, my girl."

An old lady who was probably the proprietress, as there didn't seem to be any chambermaids, here popped her head round the door and asked if Mrs Dunskirk was with us; her father-in-law had called for her.

"Was in the lounge."

"She isn't there now, madam."

Cara seemed to have vanished from the hotel; she was finally discovered to have gone down to the pub for a drink with Tom.

"Oh, I am so sorry," she said when run to ground. "Tom

45

thought we should tell you where we were going but I thought you looked so tired I did not like to disturb you. And you and Miss Dourakin always seem to have such a lot of office matters to discuss together—"

She gave a mournful little left-out smile, turning her head to look from one to the other of us.

"Espèce de chameau," said Mimi coldly when arrangements for tomorrow had been made and Cara had departed with old Dunskirk.

Then we all went in to Camelot to find somewhere for dinner, as the prospect of the cuisine at the Trelawny Hotel was even more depressing than its beds.

The next day, by some miracle, was celestially fine. It seemed a privilege to be up at eight in the morning, making our painful way down the steep rocky path to the cove. Blazing sunshine warmed our shoulders. The sea ahead shone translucent green, turquoise to emerald. Primroses were splashed all about with a lavishness unimaginable in the Home Counties; bluebells, hardly open, showed more green than blue; larks sang; it was all, astonishingly, just the way it had been before.

The gully was exceedingly deep; by holding your first and second fingers as far apart as they will go, you can get an idea of the angle at which its two sides met. Higher up they were grassy, scarred across and across with sheep tracks; then the bracken began, this year's croziers uncurling through last year's dank brown rags. Lower still the valley walls were cloaked with a growth of windswept trees, little hardy oaks, hawthorn, sloe, and rhododendron and fuchsia run wild from some nineteenth-century planting. A stream rushed chattering down between tilted slabs of rock and spread in a silver fan over the clean, washed sand of the cove, where Jimmy had boats, equipment, and manpower already waiting.

A quarter of a mile out, neatly framed in the V of the valley as one descended, a small rocky island tilted up out of the sea like the tip of a wedge of cake, iced with grass. On it were a few bits of castle—an old, outer wall built of small stones laid in slanting courses, all that was left of a twelfth-century fort, and inside this a turreted Victorian folly, admirably suited for our purposes.

The monastery, perched above us on the headland, was not visible from the cove. A sort of pier, made, incredibly, from what looked like a vast concrete boat, stuck out near the tip of the headland and sheltered a couple of dinghies which presumably belonged to the monks. Otherwise, nothing had changed; apart, that is, from the helicopter in a field (one of the Picnic Soup props), and the mess of other gear, cameras, lights on tripods, microphone booms, trolleys, cables lying everywhere like a tangle of boa-constrictors, and a muddy track down across the headland which showed the route by which all these things had been brought from the road.

Jimmy was down by the sea, arguing with Harry Kodor, a small pale bald man with eyes like drills and an incisive manner. I noticed Tom wandering up and down the beach, taking readings with a light meter; he was going to get some shots for magazine use. Boatloads of stuff were being ferried back and forth to the island, where there was another concrete jetty.

I looked about for Cara and found her sitting disconsolately on a canvas chair with a white cloth round her neck while a make-up girl did things to her face; she was in costume but looked as if she felt she were a long way from the centre of activity, so I went to keep her company.

"Doesn't it seem odd to find all this bustle going on down here," I said. "Nobody would guess it from the road."

She looked at me rather blankly; small talk was outside her repertoire.

"Tell me, who is that man, the bald one?"

"Talking to Jimmy? That's Harry Kodor."

"Oh; is he married?"

"Yes, he is," I said rather shortly. "So's Jimmy."

She nodded reflectively. "And George Salmon, he is married, I think, too? In England men marry very young."

"It's the damp climate."

"Please?"

"Never mind; it was a joke."

"So:" she pursued, ignoring this. "Tom Toole? He is not married yet?"

"No." I wondered what was in her mind; already disillusioned with Gareth, was she looking for a successor?

"How much money does he get a year?"

The amount of everyone's salary is common knowledge at S & B so I told her with a certain amount of wry amusement and indeed the sum made her look thoughtful.

"That is not much."

"No; he could get four times as much elsewhere," I said truly. "He likes this firm because he's given his head."

"Given his *head*?"

"Tom is a creative genius; elsewhere he might not have so much freedom. He'd rather have that than money."

"Ah; a genius; I see." She pondered, chin on hand. She might have been Morgan le Fay working up a good spell. "You think he will have a great career, this Tom?"

"He certainly might."

"Cara! Martha!" Jimmy yelled. "Come along, we're going across to the island now."

I helped Cara down to the boat. She was wearing a white medieval dress with a square neck and low-slung girdle. Over this was a black cloak, and she had one of those pointed headdresses with a veil; I must say she looked marvellous. We'd laid in six different headdresses for the six films we were going to make which went by the code-names of Window, Tower, Boat, Swords, Archery, and Staircase; this one was my favourite; it suited her Belle Dame Sans Merci looks to perfection.

For the first film (Staircase) they'd fixed up a throne on the rocks, low down near the tidemark. Behind it were the winding rock steps leading up to the castle. A machine on a launch round the corner of the island was busily churning out fog, which drifted gently down in layers like pampas-grass seed. Out of it bloomed the ruined castle on its crag above.

I found myself a seat on a reasonably dry rock and watched the cameramen trying to get a low-angled shot from the water level so as to include Cara with the castle behind her. They had to wait till the tide went down a bit, but ultimately made it with a tripod clamped to some underwater rocks.

It was a perfect day for filming out of doors; cloudless and practically no wind; the sort you hardly ever get. By the law of probabilities, I reckoned, it would almost certainly start to rain tomorrow and go on for a week. . . . Arranging myself more comfortably, I looked across to the monastery. Only its roof was visible from here, over the top of the headland. On this side of it, a large walled vegetable garden sloped down to the cliff edge. A tiny black figure was visible, working among the neat beds. I wondered how one approached a monastery. Were they on the telephone? Could one ring up and say, Is my husband there? The whole idea, now that I was at close quarters with it, seemed a major impossibility; quite unthinkable; I went on thinking about it.

My presence was required only in case some unforeseen event necessitated adjustments to the script. None did. Shooting went well for two or three hours, so I baked happily in the sun, and brooded, and even wrote quite a lot of Midinette copy.

Just before noon, however, a brisk wind sprang up, which kept dispersing the artificial fog. Also a huge flock of gulls decended, hoping for food; time after time they swept across the camera just at the crucial moment, flapping and clamouring.

"Flaming things!" growled Jimmy. "Why didn't I think to bring a shotgun?"

"I don't suppose the monks would like it."

"Thank god we don't have to worry about sound, at least."

"You wouldn't like the gulls in, Miss Gilroy?" Harry suggested.

"No. Wrong emphasis," I said firmly.

A thin, clear bell sounded from the monastery. We decided to knock off for lunch, ferried back to the mainland, and all went up to the pub.

After lunch the wind was stronger still and fluttered Cara's draperies in a hopelessly undignified way; no good at all.

By this time, however, Tom had set the scene for the first of the Picnic Soup films; a bit of wind didn't matter in the least here, in fact it added to the liveliness.

Jimmy told Cara she could go home if she liked, there was hardly a chance that we'd be able to do any more Avalon filming today and if we did we could always phone for her. But she didn't choose to go; her mouth drooped like an unwanted child's and she said plaintively that her father-in-law was *supposed* to be coming for her but he hadn't arrived yet. If she hoped someone would offer to drive her home, she was disappointed; everyone was too busy just then. So she disappeared into the make-up girl's little tent and came out again in skin-tight trews and a shaggy sweater. Having surveyed the scene of operations with care she strolled over and sat by me.

Picnic Soup was Mimi's charge, so I was compiling a Midinette Instruction Brochure and enjoying the hugger-mugger with a relaxed mind. Harry was trying to arrange a family group consisting of mother, father, dog, and baby on the beach (dogs and babies always go over well in commercials, you can't have too many of them, but they are hell to pose). Tom was rushing about making marks on the sand which next minute were obliterated as the cameramen manhandled their trolleys around, hunting the most suitable point for a shot. Meanwhile the property helicopter drifted up and down between the island and the shore, drowning even the wails of the gulls with its staccato putt-putt-putt. I wondered if the monks wouldn't object that it was distracting them from their meditations.

"What a lot of money must go to making such a film," said Cara, whose mind seemed to run a great deal on finance.

"Thousands. But the makers of Picnic Soup don't mind. It's a huge firm."

"Bigger than my father-in-law's?"

"Heavens, yes. But," I added quickly, "Gay Gal is an up-and-coming firm, doing very well."

She let that one go by.

"You do not find this Trelawny Hotel comfortable, I think?"

"No, it's terrible," I said. "Mimi and I have found a farm up on the hill behind the village which will take us from tomorrow."

"What is its name?"

"Trewithian Farm."

"Do you think it will be better?"

"Couldn't be worse," I said, faintly surprised by her interest.

Mimi approached, tearing her hair, shaking her fists at the heavens, and perched herself on a rock beside us.

"What's the trouble now?" I asked.

"The baby got sand in its mouth and started yelling. Now the father's lost his pipe. What a mob! The dog's the only trained actor among them."

"Babies do introduce an element of risk," I said. "I know they're a sure-fire draw, but that's why I always avoid them."

Oh, how soon I was to remember those rash words!

In due course the sand was extracted, the baby pacified, the pipe recovered, and the helicopter drifted over the group. A stunt actor slid down a rope towards them, holding something in his hand.

"How's the script go, Mimi?"

"It's the same in all of them. Voice over: *Hot Picnic Soup completes the treat! For sun, wind, and holiday appetites, hot Picnic Soup*—caramba, what happened?"

The actor on the rope had suddenly given a yell and tossed his can of Picnic Soup from him; next moment it exploded like a mortar in mid air and showered boiling lobster bisque over a radius of twelve yards. Luckily most of this fell in the sea rather than on the expectant family group, but enough spurted their way to make them leap from their carefully prepared positions with shrieks and oaths.

"*Teething troubles*," Mimi said. "You know, I wondered if Barney Soglow really had that process taped."

She darted away from us into the group.

"This is not meant to happen?" Cara said, turning great wondering eyes to me. I shook my head.

Jimmy and Michael, the stunt actor, were shouting recriminations at one another, few of which, luckily, could be heard, because of the row the helicopter was making up above. At last Jimmy waved it furiously away and it dropped, with a defeated, tail-between-the-legs appearance, back to its field, first slinging Michael down on to the beach.

"For Christ's sake, Michael," Jimmy said, "what did you *do* to the can?"

"Bloody nothing—I just followed the instructions," Michael said angrily.

"Here, let's try another one—Sam!" shouted Jimmy. "Bring over that crate of soup, will you?"

While Michael went to have his burns dressed, Jimmy tried half a dozen more cans, one of each kind of soup. They all exploded.

"We'll have to use dummies," Jimmy decided. "Mike, you'll just have to hold a cigarette clamped against the back of the can for steam."

"Yeah?" Michael growled, coming back. "Ever tried dangling from a rope with one hand while you hold a can of soup and a lighted fag in the other?"

"Oh, I'm sure you will be able to do it, Michael," Mimi pacified him. "You are so extremely clever."

While she went on soothing him, Jimmy said to me, "Martha, be a sweetheart and run up to the pub and ring Barney and ask him to get another crate of soup down here the fastest way he knows how. And while you're up there, get hold of a couple of cans that are about the same size—baked beans would do."

Barney, needless to say, was horrified to hear of our little mishap. "How in god's name did they manage to send you *that* batch?" he kept saying.

"Don't give it a thought, Barney. Nobody's hurt. Only, could you let us have some that *won't* explode, rather fast?"

"Yes, yes, I'll put them on the next plane to Plymouth. I'll come with them myself. Heads shall roll for this," he said darkly.

"Never mind about the heads, Barney darling, just so's we get the soup. It's marvellous filming weather down here, we mustn't waste it, and it can't last; destiny wouldn't let it."

"I'll be there. See you, Martha."

"See you."

I bought two tins of baked beans at the village shop—they were rusty, pre-World War I at a guess—and took them back to the beach, where matters seemed to have calmed down.

The first person I ran into was old Mr Dunskirk.

"Ee, I'm right sorry to hear that Avalon filming is over for the day," he said to me. "I brought little Laureen along too, I made sure she'd enjoy it."

"Never mind, there's still plenty to see," I consoled him, and gave the cans to Jimmy, who slapped Picnic Soup labels round them. "Have a chair," I invited Mr Dunskirk. "They're going to try this one again."

Mimi's cajoling and Jimmy's bullying had persuaded Michael into going aloft again. The helicopter pottered off round the island and returned down wind. But this time, before Michael had even begun on his rope-trick, an angry commotion burst out among the family group.

"Cut!" shouted Harry Kodor through a loudspeaker. "Now! What's the matter *this* time?"

The actress who was playing mother strode furiously across the beach.

"Who's in charge of this child?" she demanded. She was dragging by the hand a little girl of five or so who remained studiously indifferent.

"Isn't she yours?" Jimmy said, looking baffled. "God knows, then. Where did she come from?"

"She certainly is *not* mine! That's the third time she's sneaked up and poured sand into the baby's mouth. She's asking for a good tanning!"

"Eh, good heavens, that's yoong Laureen," old Dunskirk exclaimed, turning agitatedly from a conversation with one of the cameramen. "Laureen, Laureen, coom here, dear. Ye moostn't get in the way when they're making a film. Coom here now."

"It isn't even as if the baby were mine," the actress was saying indignantly to Jimmy. "I borrowed my sister's—I don't know what she'll say—"

Mimi soothed her, and old Dunskirk led little Laureen back to me, keeping a firm grip on her hand. She retained her remote, disdainful expression and made no reply while he lectured her. In fact she did not seem to be listening.

She had colourless fair hair, rather longer than shoulder length. Her blue eyes were large, pale, and contemptuous, and her doughy-looking skin was so covered with freckles that you couldn't have squeezed a match-end between them. Although she bore no identifiable likeness to Gareth, I think I would have been able to guess that he was her father; she was a most unattractive child.

When the actress and baby had been pacified and the original poses restored, filming began again. Old Dunskirk found it highly absorbing; by degrees he slackened his hold on Laureen, who slipped herself free of him and began slowly inching her way once more towards the Picnic Soup group.

"I shouldn't do that," I said.

She turned sharply, stared at me, then flicked her hair off her shoulders with a careless, nonchalant air, as if that were all she had intended, moved back, and began throwing pebbles, artlessly getting them as close as possible to a large, elaborate make-up box that was lying nearby.

I wondered if Cara knew that her stepdaughter had arrived. Looking round for her I saw that she and Tom had wandered off together to the far end of the cove. She was posing on a rock while he took pictures of her, presumably for pleasure, since she no longer had her Product X costume on.

"That's my dad's new wife. I wish my dad was here," a voice croaked beside me. I turned round, startled. I could hardly believe that such an extraordinarily harsh, nasal sound could emanate from so small a child. But there was nobody around except little Laureen, who had abandoned her stone-throwing, since no one objected to it, and now squatted by me like a gargoyle, with her pale eyes fixed on mine. "Who's that with her?" she went on.

"A man called Tom Toole, from our office."

"What's he doing?"

"Taking her picture."

"Why?" she demanded in her corncrake voice.

"I suppose because he likes doing it. Why did you pour sand in the baby's mouth?"

"I hates babies. Stupid things."

"You were one once."

Disdaining this essay in the obvious she eyed me up and down. Then she said,

"What's your name?"

"Martha Gilroy."

"Is your hair natural?"

"Yes it certainly is. What about yours?"

She ignored that one too.

"I don't like dark hair. When I'm a lady I'm going' to have a hairstyle like yours. What are those beads you got on?"

"Jade."

"Can I look at them?"

"No. You can have a piece of chocolate if you like."

She took it without thanks and ate it without apparent enjoyment. Why do we try to placate children? She was certainly a dire specimen. I wondered how she and Cara got on. The whole Dunskirk menage seemed remarkably ill-assorted.

Jimmy called me for a consultation about the next day's Avalon filming; as the wind was expected to rise still more, he was wondering if it would be better to go out of sequence and take the shots in the castle (Window and Tower) which would be relatively sheltered. I agreed, and was arranging for the necessary costumes and props when I noticed little Laureen making back with obvious baneful intent towards the baby; a moment later there came another outburst of howls and of commination from its aunt. Old Dunskirk hastened over, red-faced, and dragged Laureen away; as before she remained impassive, coldly detached from the consequences of her crime.

"What a poisonous child," Jimmy remarked. "Where did she come from?"

"She's Gareth's; a chip of the old block."

Old Dunskirk announced that he was taking Laureen home, which was a relief; I thought Cara would go too, but when he called to her—she was halfway up the cliff by now, having her picture taken beside a little cascade—she shouted back that Mr Toole was going to drive her to see some famous view.

I could see old Dunskirk was not pleased. However he said, "Oh, well, there's no denying it'll ease things if Mrs Oldcastle gets

54

yoong Laureen to bed before Cara cooms home. To tell you the truth, they don't get on too well together."

I could well understand this.

Laureen showed a tendency to whine, grumble, and drag as she was led away, demanding why couldn't she be in a film?

"Maybe you will, soom day," her grandfather said. It seemed highly probable.

After shooting had ended for the day Tom asked me if I'd like to drive to Land's End with him and Cara.

"But, Tom, it'll be dark by the time you get there."

"Oh, not quite. Cara's never seen it."

"Well, I don't think I'll come, thanks Tom. I've seen it before."

I'd had visions of a quiet evening in some tiny village pub, just Tom and me, perhaps, and then early to bed. For the moment I'd given up thoughts of phoning the monastery; for one thing they weren't in the phone book.

In the end Mimi, Michael, Sam, Harry, Jimmy, and I, and the rest of the party, all went to see a very old, very bad film at the Camelot Odeon, and had a Chinese meal. And so late back to the Trelawny Hotel. And dog-tired to bed. Tom and Cara still weren't back.

CHAPTER IV

Next morning Susan rang me in a frenzy, at eight o'clock, before we'd left the hotel. There had been a crisis over Faireweather Pitch'n Toss Rings; they'd had to change an ingredient, and at the last minute all the copy in three articles for the catering trade press would have to be rewritten.

"Oh heavens, Susan," I said. "I can't dictate those over the telephone, it would take all day. Besides I haven't the originals here."

"No, George thinks you'd better come back for a day. Mimi can cope down there, can't she?"

"Yes, of course. But wouldn't George prefer her to come back?"

"No, he says you, because then you can receive your Monaco Award at the same time. The ceremony's tonight, had you forgotten?"

55

"Oh, blister it," I said with feeling. "Wouldn't he rather Jimmy came for that?"

But I knew that Jimmy could not be spared from the filming; it was another good day, bright and not too blowy.

"George says you must come and do your bit by the firm."

So I told Mimi, who gave a sympathetic groan and said she'd keep an eye on Avalon for me and please bring back her other sunglasses.

"And make George give you a decent dinner before the ceremony."

Jimmy cackled with delight when he heard what I'd landed in, and asked me to bring his binoculars back with me as he thought he'd spotted a buzzards' nest on the cliffs. Tom wasn't about; he had gone down to the cove early, probably to get still shots of Cara in costume.

I went off very unwillingly to Plymouth in the village taxi, caught a plane, and was in the office before lunch. It took most of the afternoon to rewrite two articles because the previous approach wouldn't do, and anyway my mind wasn't very co-operative; it kept speculating about what was happening at Trevann.

After I'd gone back to my flat (only a stone's throw from the office, luckily) and changed, George took me out to dinner; he was very nice about the award, which was more Jimmy's than mine really; it had been for a Midinette film we made last winter. The ceremony was at the Arundel Hotel and took hours, because there were about a hundred other awards, and speeches, and films, and drinks, and conversation, and more drinks. George could really have represented us by himself, but I could see he was feeling bereft and wanted support.

Halfway through the evening I sneaked away to a callbox in the lobby and rang Mimi at Trewithian Farm.

"Hallo, duck. How's it going?"

"God, we've had a time today," she said. "You haven't missed a thing, not a thing."

"Not more explosive soup cans?"

"No, they're all right, for a wonder. Barney arrived soon after you'd left and he's staying on for a few days to make sure everything's all right. No, it was when we were shooting the water-skiing sequence for Picnic; everything nicely set and then one of those old Brothers came prowling along and said would we mind doing it elsewhere because the girl water-skier in her bikini was visible from the Brotherhood House and she was upsetting their meditations by short-circuiting the wave-lengths or something."

"Oh dear."

"You can say that again. He was full of fire and brimstone—I'd forgotten they still came like that."

"Wh-what did he look like?" I asked, trying to subdue a ridiculous inner trembling.

"Oh, about ninety, with a long dirty beard that kept getting tangled up in the straps of his sandals. Then the sight of him in his black robes scared little Laureen and she started having hysterics."

"Oh lord, is she back again."

"Is she *back*?" I was surprised Mimi's tone didn't splinter the telephone. "Twice she nearly murdered the property baby, once she knocked over a camera, five times she got in the way of shots, accidental-done-on-purpose—that child ought to have been drowned at birth. She's even worse than the little terror we had for filming Chocka-Blocs, remember, who ate all the sample bars before shooting began and we had to use wooden dummies. And Jimmy says the same."

"Can't you drop a tactful hint to old Dunskirk?"

"It's a bit awkward, dearie. He obviously dotes on her. And he's got worries enough; apparently Product X is giving more trouble at the lab, Gareth rang him up in a taking saying they were behind schedule; and he's thoroughly anxious about Cara, too. She went off with Tom, exploring a cave this afternoon, they were gone hours, and the old boy obviously didn't like it a bit."

"Oh."

"So you'd better hasten back, to protect Gareth's interests," Mimi said tactfully. "How soon can you make it? How was the award?"

"Terrible. I ought to be finished by tomorrow lunchtime. I'll get the afternoon plane."

"Honey do you think you could rustle up a *car*? It would be terribly convenient for getting to and from the farm."

"Okay. I'll borrow Susan's and drive down. How is the farm, by the way?"

"Very nice. Blissful food—I've put on pounds in twenty-four hours," said Mimi, who could eat Christmas pudding for breakfast every day and not put a millimetre on her 23 waist. "There's a

57

back way you can get here across the moor without going into Trevann; after you leave Launceston take a turning off the Camelot road to Brameloe Downs."

"Hold on while I write that down."

I did so, but somehow, even from Mimi's clear and explicit directions, some grain of doubt came through.

"You're sure it isn't simpler to go into Trevann and come back?"

"Oh no, cherie, this way cuts off miles."

"Anything else you'd like brought?"

"Hot-water-bottle—nights are chill at the farm. I almost asked that cross old Brother if I could borrow one of their nice black robes," Mimi said with a chuckle. "I'd look much better in it than he does."

"I wonder how many Brothers there are."

"Twelve, Mrs Tregagle at the farm said."

"You haven't seen any others?"

"Only Crossface who objected to the bikini. I wonder what they do all the time?"

"Read, work, meditate, I suppose."

Suddenly I recalled, as if it were yesterday, Lucian standing on the cliff-path; a visual memory opened in my mind like a camera shutter: the heather-tufts, the leaping, turquoise-coloured sea, and Lucian turning his head to look at the monastery and say, "I wonder what they do there, I wonder what they think about?" I could call up the very tones of his voice, half hostile, half envious. How blind, how blind I had been on that honeymoon.

"Everyone else okay?" I asked.

"Fine. Poor Jimmy has a new tantrum every half-hour. The weather's holding. Harry Kodor's a darling, I must say. Oh, *who* do you think called up? Old Ibn Abdullah al-Fuad!"

"The Emir?"

"Himself. He's coming down to visit his aunt at Torquay and proposes to give himself the pleasure of dropping in on us."

"*Aunt at Torquay?*"

"Everybody has an aunt at Torquay, you know that cherie."

"Well he ought to add to the gaiety, I suppose.... How's Tom?" I asked, wishing she'd say without my having to ask.

"Fine. He's taken enough pictures of Cornish scenery to paper St Paul's. Mostly with Cara in them. Oh, just listen to this, here's a piece of scandal that you won't have heard—"

At that moment the pips went and drowned her. "Th-r-ree minutes," a voice said. "If you wish to continue, please put another two-and-sixpence in the box."

"No more change," I said. "Tell me tomorrow night."

"Okay cherie. Take care driving."

After that I didn't, somehow, feel like any more celebrating. It was already quite late in any case. I found old George, pleaded tomorrow's long drive in a borrowed car as my excuse for leaving, overrode his offers to see me home, and took a taxi back to the flat. I felt very churned up, and glad there was no inquisitor to ask me why.

Next day I worked like a beaver on the last article, settled one or two other little matters that had come up, gulped a hasty sandwich, and set off hell-for-leather down the M.4 in the Admiral, Susan's aged little Hillman. It was a well-behaved little car—all things considered—but stiff to drive. Susan warned me that the battery was a bit low and mentioned that if I had occasion to stop for any reason, better choose a place where males were about, in case cranking was necessary.

As a matter of fact, not having started till about 3 p.m., I didn't stop at all. When I am driving on my own I tend to do this, just go blinding on and on, wrapped up in my thoughts, ignoring hunger, fatigue, and the calls of nature; I am always so anxious to get to my journey's end.

This time I was even more anxious. I drove extremely fast, for hours and hours, through Berkshire, Wiltshire, and Somerset. But then, in Devon, the fog came down.

I slowed, because I take fog seriously, particularly when driving a borrowed car. I went slowly through Devon and got to Launceston well behind schedule. Then I began looking out for Mimi's left turn to Brameloe Downs, being by now tired enough to welcome the thought of a short cut that would chop seven or eight miles off my journey.

Luck was with me in that I found the Brameloe turning while traversing a thin patch—though maybe, if I'd passed it by, this story would have had a simpler conclusion. No matter; I found it; I turned; into a narrow lane with high banks so close together that a horse and rider could easily have jumped clear across from one side to the other over the top of the old Admiral.

By now it was well dark. I'd hoped that a three-hundred-mile drive would have had a beneficial effect on the battery, but the headlights were like candle-beams; they showed up nothing but a V of wavering, swirling, smoky stuff that seemed to swing to and fro, receding and approaching as I inched up the lane.

At this point I did think of turning back on to the main road and going by the longer but easier route—the lane was beginning to give me claustrophobia—but there was no place to turn. The horrible little track wound on and on, twisting about, until my sense of direction was completely conked. I only hoped that some happy tractor-man, who knew where he was to a nicety, didn't come thundering down the lane on his way home to supper, because I knew who'd get the worst of the encounter. There wasn't room to pass a paper cut-out. Furthermore the fog deadened all sound; the first intimation I'd have of anybody coming would be his snout through my windscreen.

The car had no fog-lamp, but I'd brought a big flashlight with me (having forgotten to ask Mimi if the farm had outside sanitation I thought it wiser to be prepared for the worst) so I switched this on and held it jammed with my right elbow, pointing out of the window. It illuminated tufts of fog-spangled grass on the bank for a while; then not even that, unless I opened the door and craned out. The reason for this was a deep ditch at the side of the road, which didn't make me any happier. Whichever way I looked, fog engulfed me; I might have been alone on the moon, if they have fogs up there.

I began to realise how tired I was. Realise is an understatement; every hour of the last thirty-six came back to thump me like a sandbag. I seriously started to wonder if I could drive that hard-mouthed old car another mile, even half a mile, up this creepy blind lane, without having a rest first.

Mindful of Susan's warning about the battery I halted, leaving the motor running, tied my blue scarf over my hair, and got out to prospect forward with the flashlight. I hadn't gone half a dozen yards when, thank god, there was a negotiable gateway on the left, leading into a field. It would be possible to pull the car in there and take ten minutes' rest; if I couldn't start it up again afterwards, well, Mimi had said Trewithian Farm was only three miles up the lane, and I must have done a good two and a half, even at my snail's pace. There couldn't be much farther to walk. The car would be all right in a field overnight; no doubt some farmer would revile me in the morning, but at least that was better than abandoning it slap in the middle of a seven-foot track.

I went back to the car, drove into the field, switched off engine and lights, and slumped back in the cosy little bucket-seat which seemed to fit me like a shell, like a sheath, like a shroud, like a cloud.... I fell asleep.

How long I slept I don't know; maybe quite a short time. Discomfort woke me; my feet were freezing, I was ravenous, droplets of fog were running off the scarf and down my neck. Outside the car, darkness and silence lay like thick black felt.

Cursing myself for a fool I pushed the starter. Nothing happened, not so much as a whisper. None of the lights worked, nor the wipers, nor the horn. The poor old car was dead as a doornail, dead as Queen Anne.

One thing, I thought, no one's likely to steal it. However I locked up, shivering in the raw, choking murk, buttoned up my suede jacket, slung my shoulderbag round me satchelwise to leave my hands free, shut the field gate, and set off up the lane, edging along the left bank and probing every inch of the ground in front of me with the torch. The ditch on my right, although narrow, seemed to have deepened to the dimensions of a junior crevasse.

I hoped devoutly that it was going to be possible to make somebody hear when I reached Trewithian. Farm people, I knew, kept early hours; still, perhaps Mimi would have sat up for me, or at least seen that a door was left unlocked. If it hadn't been for Mimi and her bright ideas, I thought crossly, I should have been there long ago, curled up in a nice warm bed instead of plowtering about on the moor in the fog.... Perhaps she would be waiting up with a bowl of soup. The hard-boiled egg sandwich I'd eaten about nine hours ago seemed very remote. And I could swear that I'd walked more than half a mile since leaving the car.

That was the moment at which I rounded a sharp corner and saw the upended pram in the middle of the lane. If I'd been driving, I'd very likely have hit it.

Could that have been what somebody intended?

It was tipped forward, leaning on its handle. Rather weak at the knees, I had a look inside. It isn't often, after all, that you find an upside-down baby-carriage in the road, feathery blue blankets spilling out, in the middle of a cold April night. It was a nice glossy pram, not a scratch on its lacquered surface, moist drops of dew conglomerating to rivulets on the thick waterproof hood. There were huge tangly spidery wheels and a lot of suspensions—touch of the perch phaeton—the sort of pram proud young mothers push on Council estates, and will still be paying for when the occupant has graduated to football boots and rocket guns. Examining it I wondered vaguely why we feel obliged to spend such a lot on containers for babies and corpses—the two members of the family who honestly don't give a damn what sort of casket they lie in.

Kneeling down I felt among the blankets with—I won't deny—shaking hands to see if there was an occupant in the warm tangled nest. There wasn't. But judging from the warmth there had been recently. In the cocoon-like hole that had been left I found a sheet of stiff writing-paper, best quality bond. I shone the torch on it and saw words printed:

WE WON'T HURT THE BABY IF YOU ARE A SENSIBLE GIRL

At this juncture my cumulative exhaustion took a hand. Fog, hunger, fatigue, this inscrutable frightening message—to whom? from whom?—were all, suddenly, too much for me. My knees buckled, the fog sank over me like a collapsing tent, and I rolled sideways into a cavernous pit, deep as the crater of Popocatapetl. Time slowed down and stopped.

It didn't stop for very long. When I came to I was still lying in the ditch among some damp tufts of what felt like heather, and it was still pitch dark.

I spent a moment or two wondering where the devil I was, *who* the devil I was, in a weak and lackadaisical way. It didn't seem to matter very acutely. I felt dreamy and a bit light-headed; was half inclined to go right on lying there. My mind wobbled about like a half-set jelly, full of unrelated fragments: the address of a man I'd meant to write to about detergents before coming down to Cornwall, lines from Twelfth Night, the fact that my library subscription needed renewing, a series of slogans for Bom which I'd been trying to hatch on the way down. Whether you're coming or going, mending or mowing, scything or sewing, reading or rowing ... you need Bom, the meat'n milk drink, made from pure fresh milk and lean juicy beef. Bom, tiddly, om, BOM! I can't, offhand, think of any nastier beverage than Bom, but at that moment I felt hazily that I might even have accepted a cup of the stuff if someone had offered it to me, hot.

It seemed much simpler to go on lying in the ditch, thinking about Bom, than to give my tired body the task of climbing out and fumbling on up an unknown lane to a problematical farm. If

I spent the night in the ditch, I wondered, would I die of exposure? I had a vague notion that people caught pneumonia from such experiences, so I decided, reluctantly, that I had better move. If this were a romance, a hero would be at hand to rescue me; as it was, even if the alternative were merely rheumatism for the rest of my life, I had better stir myself. Product X needs me, I thought. But I decided I wouldn't move just yet, not till I had counted up to fifty, or perhaps sixty. Besides, I had to find the torch, which I had dropped in my fall.

I had reached thirty-seven when I heard the two whispering voices. They seemed to come from directly over my head.

"Funny thing, I could have sworn I heard foosteps."

"Must have been mistaken. Anyway she'd be in a car."

"She's late. Suppose she's decided to stop the night at the hotel?"

"She's been as late before. She'll be along."

"Think this'll really scare her into coming through?"

"God, yes. Any woman's chicken where a missing kid's concerned."

This remark shot me back to reality. I'd been wondering vaguely if they were talking about me. Now I suddenly remembered the empty pram and the ugly little note among the warm blankets.

"S'pose she decided to clear out? We'd look like a couple of charleys left holding the baby."

"Well what would you suggest? Thumbscrews?"

"I reckon something like that would be better."

"Shut up—listen! Is that a car? Better get back out of sight."

Someone's foot scraped on a stone, right by my ear it seemed. I heard the sputter of a match and smelt cigarette smoke. The sharp whiff of sulphur and tobacco brought all my wits together just in time to stop me from calling out "Chuck us one too, will you?" Instead I began to move cautiously on all fours along the bottom of the ditch. Heaven knew who these men were, but plainly they were the people responsible for pancaking the pram and removing its occupant and I felt hostile to them; firstly their actions had caused me to faint, which was shaming; secondly, children should be in their beds at night, not dragged about in the fog. Thirdly, some poor woman must be in for a horrible shock. I wondered if it would be possible for me to intercept and warn her, if I crawled back along the gully and then climbed into the road. Though what form my warning should take, I couldn't imagine. "Excuse me, madam, but a hundred yards farther along are two men who appear to have kidnapped your baby. No, I'm afraid I don't know their names...."

I had gone, I suppose, about three yards when my left hand bumped into the torch; I clutched it with a prayer of gratitude and a desperate hope that it hadn't broken in the fall. But the feel of its well-balanced heaviness gave me a little more confidence; it would do as a weapon if need be. I didn't like the sound of those whisperers in the road.

It seemed imprudent to try the torch right away; there was still plenty of fog which protected me adequately enough down here, but a torch beam would be sure to show up. I crawled on.

The ditch had been dry at the point where I fell in; dry for a ditch, that is; but after about twenty yards it changed character and I found my wrists and ankles sinking in cold, clammy, oozy mud.

Mud has never been my favourite crawling medium. I decided that the ditch had served its turn, and began feeling my way cautiously up the bank on the side away from the road. It was set about with lopped-off stumps, easy enough to climb; I worked higher and higher, finally found myself up against what felt like one of those scrubby little half-hedges that Cornish farmers perch on the tops of banks round their fields in the hope of retaining their chamois-like cattle. The hedges are seldom very thick; I struggled through this one without much difficulty, trying not to make a noise, and lowered myself down a steepish slope beyond.

There were now three courses open to me. I could follow the hedge downhill, going back the way I had come to the main road, well over two miles; or I could follow it uphill past the two men in the direction of the farm. Or I could walk straight away from the road into the pitch-dark unknown.

I decided on the third course. According to my vague recollections of the map, this lane ultimately passed Trewithian Farm on its left-hand boundary, after crossing a ridge and bending to the right. Therefore, I reasoned, if I cut away across the field to the right, and then worked round in a leftward direction again, I ought in the end to rejoin the lane above the point where the two men had their ambush. Or I might come to the farm itself. The main thing was to keep going uphill. At the farm there was a telephone and there must, surely, be some sturdy dependable male who would explain, no doubt, that the whole business of the men

64

and the pram was just a couple of village lads playing a harmless practical joke, one of those laughable, frolicsome old local customs called Hunt the Nipper, celebrated on Saint Barnabas's Eve.

Crouching down, I cautiously pointed the flashlight into a tussock of grass and switched it on. Thank the Lord it was still working, and illuminated a little circle of bedraggled greenery. Much heartened by this, I smothered all but a blink of light with my hand and set off quietly across the field, holding the torch low down and being as sparing of its beam as I dared. I hoped there were no livestock on my route; a noisy encounter with a startled cow at this point would be disastrous.

For the first time it occurred to me to wonder whether I myself would be in danger from the two men. It hadn't been logic that had driven me so far, but a sort of female unreasoning instinct that said, Don't let them know you are there. Clear out and get help, get this untoward business tidied up, before it is too late. Now I began to speculate on what the men would have done if they had found me: an auditor, if not a witness, to something pretty queer, pretty nasty, probably illegal. And I wondered about the *she* they had mentioned. Who was *she*? The farmer's wife? Or someone staying at the farm? Someone with a child? Not Mimi, obviously. Mimi, a born spinster, detests all children. Perhaps Jean, the Picnic Soup actress, with her sister's baby? She had come over from Exeter, but perhaps she'd decided to stay because of the fog.

Occupying myself with these thoughts I had accelerated to a fair pace, but now my leading foot sank calf-deep with a disconcertingly loud squelch. I went into reverse hastily, guessing at a concealed stream creating a bog in the centre of the field, and bore away to the right. Presently I came up against a thick bramble hedge and was forced to go right again, feeling my way along until I came to a gate.

Another field—and this one, to my horror, contained large, invisible, breathing, cud-chewing Presences. I bumped one and almost let out a yell of distress. Mercifully the cow, bullock, or whatever it was, possessed a phlegmatic disposition—it backed hastily away, stepping on my foot and spattering me with mud, but made no outcry at being rammed so unexpectedly in the foggy dark. I almost laughed, then, thinking of Mimi and how horrified she would be when she heard of my adventures; Mimi just despises cows.

Now I collided with a hard obstacle which proved, on cautious inspection with the torch, to be a dilapidated drystone wall. When I tried to climb over, the rocks of which it was built began to topple and slither alarmingly, so I gave up and bore right again. The wall led on and on. Presently it turned back on itself at a sharp angle. Still no gate. I was beginning to be deeply discouraged. A lot of time seemed to have passed since I had left the lane; by rights I should have been quite near the farm by now, but I began to fear that I had miscalculated and aimed in a completely wrong direction.

At last I found a gate and thankfully climbed it. On the other side, to my joy, was a hard-packed stone track, the continuation, I desperately hoped, of the lane I had left. I had only to follow it one way or the other and I was certain to reach civilisation. But was it the same lane? Which way should I go?

The last thing I wanted was another encounter with the baby-snatchers.

I decided to try uphill, remembering the map. By now the sky was faintly lighter, though the fog was just as thick. I peered at my watch by the light of the torch: 4.30 a.m. About three-quarters of an hour to hypothetical daylight. Hell of a lot of work I shall be able to do in the morning, I thought, after capers like this all night, and then comforted myself with the recollection that, unless the fog lifted, nobody would be able to do any filming.

As I bore uphill the fog lightened somewhat. Impeded by a skirt that flapped wetly against my knees, and stockings so encrusted with mud that they felt like hockey-pads, I walked forward as fast as I could. Into my mind had swum a celestial vision: hot bath, hot drink, hot-water-bottle, a downy, sagging, comfortable farm bed.... Almost certainly those two men were just playing a light-hearted trick on a wayward girlfriend or wife, weren't they? Or were they? I wished I could really think they were.

But those were not Cornish voices.

The birds were beginning to stir. I heard a long bubbling call —curlew? snipe?—my ornithological knowledge is of the scantiest —and then a thin, plaintive cry which I completely failed to identify. It came again, woebegone, halfway between a gull's call and a lamb's bleat.

Suddenly I stepped into a clear patch in the mist and saw a shoulder of heathery hillside above me to my left. Following the track, which curved sharply round the hill, I found a small disused quarry, with steeply shelving sides and a floor of velvet-green moss. My first feeling was angry disappointment because I had walked half a mile in the wrong direction; then I saw the car in the quarry and my heart lurched up against my windpipe. It was a Crespina convertible; not the sort of car one expects to see in the middle of the moor at four-thirty in the morning except in rally country. There seemed to be nobody in it but as I hesitated in the quarry entrance I heard again, from the back seat apparently, that forlorn wailing cry.

I loathe the sound of babies crying. It strikes some exposed nerve in me and I get all steamed up full of impotent rage, and want to bash somebody—I suppose because I feel something ought to be done about the crying, though I gather Dr Spock now says that's not necessarily so any more and that once again babies get along just fine on a good healthy yell. Babies, along with birds and a few million other everyday things are among the blank spots in my repertoire; I try to give them a wide berth.

So it says something for the oddness of this whole situation that I went instantly forward, opened the car door, which made a light come on inside, and looked in.

The baby was on the dusty floor in the back of the Crespina, thrashing its arms and legs about in the intensity of its rage and despair. I picked it up, with the faint hope that human contact might cheer it, but no such luck; it yelled louder than before. Its face was dahlia red, and shiny as polythene; tears kept spurting out of its tight-shut eyes and one tiny fist hit me on the jaw. It was frantic. I could see that it was a fairly young baby by its smallness, though it had a fine thatch of black hair on top of its head.

Almost without taking any conscious decision I found myself walking away, out of the quarry. The track led on, I now saw, and I followed it, with the baby howling and squirming in my arms. Judged rationally, I was behaving in an odd, irresponsible, if not utterly insane way; but then, I told myself, to dispel faint protests from my superego, there must be something decidedly wrong with people who leave an unwrapped baby lying on the floor of a car in the small hours while they play dubious tricks with its pram. That this was the rightful occupant of the pram I didn't for a minute doubt. I felt it was my plain duty to report the whole affair to some proper authority such as the N.S.P.C.C., and, as soon as possible, to get the baby to a place where it could be fed and tended, so I hurried on at a good pace. The fog was patchy here, thick where the road dipped, thinner where it climbed, and the track itself twisted about disconcertingly; after ten minutes' walking I wasn't sure in which direction the quarry lay behind me.

But presently I had a pointer: I heard the roar of a car's engine and the quick angry zoom as it accelerated into third and came in my direction.

I looked quickly round. Just as this moment I was in a clear patch, where the track ran across unfenced, heathery moor. On my left the land folded up sharply to a little tor, beyond which lay a dense pocket of fog. Leaving the decision to the autopilot who seemed to have taken charge, I ran like a rabbit up the uneven slope and down the far side, into the fog. None too soon; as I dropped behind a jagged outcrop of rock the Crespina flashed into sight between the two banks of fog, roared past, sounding startlingly close, and was gone.

I sat up, feeling hollow inside. Whether I had acted rightly or wrongly, I was now committed, out on a limb, stuck in the middle of a moor with an unknown baby of incalculable potential, which was still crying at the top of its lungs. Quite providential, I thought, that the Crespina had made such a noise; otherwise the driver—presumably one of my two whisperers—would have heard the howling of his purloined prey. The crying was beginning to make me desperate, and I decided that I must, before going any farther, see what I could do to make the baby happier. I took off my suede jacket and spread it on the ground.

"Come on, Shrubsole," I said, trying to sound businesslike and confident, "let's have an inventory of you," and I put the baby on the jacket. Unexpectedly it stopped crying and opened two smoky-dark eyes to look at me. It was rather a nice-looking baby, as they go: small, but with a fine, thoughtful forehead, delicate features, and beautifully articulated little hands. It wore a striped blue and white knitted jacket over a sort of nightie, waterproof pants, and nappies. Blue-and-white-striped football socks were on its legs. Even I, amateur that I was, could see that the nappies were sopping wet and in this chill air must be hideously uncomfortable for the poor little wretch. With many a qualm I undid a couple of safety-pins, removed all the underwear, and discovered a. that the baby was of the female sex, and b. that wetness, luckily, was the worst of its troubles. It seemed relieved to be rid of the sopping mass and waved a leg at me amiably enough, but I felt that it ought to have some protection from the cold and mist. I took off my brushed-nylon waist slip, folded this into a rude triangle, and pinned it round as best I could.

Then for the first time I remembered the vacuum flask in my handbag: hot milk with a dash of coffee and a dash of brandy. Susan, bless her, had pressed it on me at parting. Probably not very hot by now, as it had been in there at least twelve hours. Not the most suitable tipple for a baby, either; but in an emergency perhaps better than nothing. I was pretty sure the baby must be hungry from the way in which, between yells, it feverishly sucked and mumbled at its fists.

I uncorked the flask and poured a little of the lukewarm brew into the plastic cup. Now of course came the question: could the baby drink from a cup or was it still at the sucking stage? in which case we were sunk because I had nothing on me that could be adapted to this.

The baby solved the problem. I decided that if it had never drunk from a cup before it was a remarkably quick learner. After a few preliminary splashes and misfires the milk went steadily down and in about five minutes the whole cupful was accounted for. Instantly the baby began to cry again, so I tipped out the remainder of the milk, my hands shaking with haste, and fed in a second cupful.

Then, with vague recollections of Rosemary, Tom's married sister, and her methods with the younger members of her large brood, I up-ended the baby over my shoulder and rubbed its back in what I hoped was a soothing manner. This treatment seemed acceptable; beyond a sleepy hiccup or two it made no further noise, its head rocked about perilously and, peering round into its face, I saw that it was fast asleep. Small wonder really: there must have been at least a teaspoonful of brandy in the flask. Hoping fervently that the ill-effects of the brandy, if any, would not offset the good effects of the milk, I adjusted us both to a more comfortable carrying position and started back towards the quarry, deciding, now the men were gone, that my most sensible course would be to back-track down the lane and collect the pram. There might be some clue as to name and address in it, besides those nice warm blankets; also the baby was surprisingly heavy for such a small member of the human race.

Now I began to notice again how weak and tired my legs were, how hollow and shaky I felt; it was lucky that I'd been too much concentrated on getting the drink down the baby to feel envy at the time; I could have done with a good nip myself.

The track was bordered by turf and I kept on it because it made smoother walking and my shoes, soaked through already, weren't primarily intended for hiking over flints. By sheer luck therefore I was going along pretty quietly when I reached the lip of the quarry and this was just as well for, when I looked in, there was a man standing on a hummock and staring about. He had his back to me and his clothes weren't right for a farmer.

I began edging noiselessly backwards, went half a dozen yards, tripped in a draining-ditch, and fell. The baby woke and let out a whimper. Mercifully we were out of sight by now. I took to my heels and plunged off the track into the mist, running blind. I heard a shout from the quarry but dared not turn my head to see if I was being followed.

Running through the mist with no idea where one's feet were going to land was an eerie business. I half tripped a couple of times but righted myself through sheer speed and blundered on, wondering whether the regular thud-thud that I began to hear was pursuing footsteps; after a while I realised that it was my own heart.

A little grassy dell, hardly more than a hole in the ground, opened before me; I lurched into it, almost head first. Tall, bushy heather, growing right up to its lip, seemed to offer a scanty shelter, and I crouched there, obliged to stop a moment because my legs were collapsing under me. My mouth was dry and my breathing had gone into reverse; I couldn't seem to get enough air in to make the process worth while. Huddled against the shallow bank, I wondered what I could do if the baby began to cry again. Her face was puckered ominously, and she was looking about in a dissatisfied way.

"Oh, Shrubsole," I muttered, "however did we manage to get landed together in such a dotty situation?"

Rummaging in my bag I found two battered squares of chocolate. I broke off a tiny corner and popped it into her mouth; probably most unsuitable but she accepted it graciously; presently I had a bite too, my exhausted metabolism was ravenous for sugar; meanwhile I strained my ears for sounds of pursuit but could hear none. In any case, if the Hound of the Baskervilles himself had been after me, there was nothing more I could have done; I had shot my bolt.

I don't know how long I stayed in that little dip; it must have been about an hour. I had a doze, and so did Shrubsole, tucked against me inside my jacket. Really, she was a good baby. When, stiff with cold, I finally moved and stood up, a pale silvery sun like a segment of lemon was peering dimly through the fog. That was fine; if I went straight forward, keeping the sun on my right, going roughly north, I ought presently to hit the main Launceston-to-Camelot road. I resolved to have nothing more to do with the track—and it was a good thing I did for after a while I heard the Crespina again, coming slowly, no doubt returning to collect its second passenger who was supposed to have been hunting for me. I walked steadily and silently ahead, trusting the fog to protect me. After all, two men couldn't comb every inch of the moor.

By degrees the sound of the car died away in the distance.

After about an hour's downhill walking I hit the main road and turned west, towards Trevann, resolving to flag any car that passed. It was still not much after half-past six. The first thing that came along was a pickup truck crammed full of workmen. They waved to me with derisive cheers as it hurtled past, but plainly there wasn't room in it for a skinless sausage. Then a bleary-eyed Jaguar whipped by, going towards Launceston and bed at eighty. At last an aged Ford, with a trailer full of straw, rattled to a halt beside me.

The driver, who looked like Rip Van Winkle, put his head out of the window.

"I'm only goo'n half a mile down road, midearr," he said. "Be that any good to ee? You'm welcome if 'tis."

"It's better than nothing," I said cheerfully.

"Eh?"

"Better than nothing."

He shook his head. "I'm mortal hard of hearing," he apologised, gesturing towards his ears in case I was too. Abandoning the idea of trying to tell him my story, I climbed in and sat down for one of the most bone-shaking rides of my life. Shrubsole woke and started to cry again. I had an uneasy feeling that she needed changing once more.

The old boy pulled to a halt.

"Ere we be midearr," he explained.

He opened a gate and drove the Ford into a field where some bullocks came purposefully towards him.

"Are there any houses round here?" I asked. My main objective now was hot water, soap, dry towelling, and a telephone.

"Eh?"

"*Houses?* Where I could wash the baby?" I made appropriate gestures.

I wasn't sure at first if he'd got the message, but he broke into a chuckle and said, "Oh, arr. Bear 'ee on thataway, midearr, and goo up the liddle lane yonder. The friends'll help'ee for sure."

This seemed conclusive enough so I thanked him and went on along the road towards the entrance to his little lane. Behind me I heard another car coming. Should I try for a lift on to Trevann? Or was it better to go for immediate help to the old boy's friends? Still undecided, I turned, wearily hoisting Shrubsole on to my shoulder, to scan the approaching car. And it was the Crespina.

I had just enough sense left to dive into the little lane, which was right beside me. Had I been recognised? Or the baby? I ran gaspingly uphill, wondering how long I'd be able to last at this game of hide and seek. The lane had a sharp right-hand bend. Beyond, a gate led into a field. I staggered through, stopped, listened—a routine which by now seemed drearily familiar. Shrubsole began to whimper and, rather desperately, I adminis tered another crumb of chocolate.

With a roar, and a screech of brakes as it rounded the bend, the Crespina passed the gate and shot up the lane, leaving a powerful whiff of exhaust. I felt glad I'd hidden; there was a sense of savage rage, of uncontrolled destructiveness about the way that car was handled; I didn't like it. As strongly as the smell of blood it con veyed one thing: violence.

I began to plod diagonally across the field, biting my lips to keep from tears. Help had seemed so near. And now to find myself in flight again like this, in full daylight too, knocked the bottom out of my sense of rightness and confidence. What was I doing, chasing about the country like a madwoman, with a stolen baby? If its parents caught up with me, I should most likely be jailed, and it would serve me right for my harebrained behaviour.

Momentarily I hesitated, so low had my spirits sunk. Should I go back to the lane, wait for the Crespina which would have to come back—the sign had said *No Through Road*—and give in?

I was within an inch of turning. But then I looked at the baby, gazing dolefully about with those intelligent dark eyes, and I re membered how she had been lying in the grit and dust on the car floor without even a blanket to cover her. I thought of the pram, and the note, and the two men. People just don't treat their own children like that.

And it was simpler to go on the way I was heading than to turn back uphill. I passed through a gate, dragged myself across another field, saddle-shaped, this one, with a dip in the middle, and then realised that the sound I could hear now was the murmur of the sea, somewhere below me out of sight in the mist.

Next moment I was startled by the sight of a building looming out of the fog just ahead. It was big and looked vaguely familiar—late nineteenth century, with a lot of needless pinnacles and turrets. The Trelawny Hotel? No such luck. Same period, though—and thank heaven it seemed prosperous and inhabited, the sort of place that would have running h. and c. Smoke came from a chimney. A donkey grazed peacefully in the meadow. A flight of fantails wheeled down from the roof.

Moving like a puppet I ambled stiffly across the grass, unlatched a little wicket-gate in a high brick wall, and found myself in a neatly kept kitchen garden. Then I saw what the old boy with the Ford had meant by "friends".

A tall man, who had been planting potatoes, straightened himself and came rapidly towards me. He was wearing a black hood and a long black robe.

CHAPTER V

The black-robed man strode towards me, making shooing gestures as if at an intrusive child or animal.

"Get away! Clear out!" he hissed, when he was near enough to speak in a low voice. "This is private property, what are you doing here—can't you read? Be off with you!" And he pointed to a notice that said STRICTLY PRIVATE—BROTHERHOOD OF THE PIERCED STONE—COMMUNITY MEMBERS ONLY.

I was so taken aback that for a moment or two I could only gape at him. Viewed from near to he was a strange, tatterdermalion figure. His thick black robes were threadbare and frayed, his sandals were tied by bits of string. A long yellow-grey beard emerging from his hood looked decidedly grubby, and the skin of his face, hands, and bare feet was dark with a mixture of weathering and dirt. But what really threw me was the arrogant upper-crust accent issuing from this antagonistic old scarecrow. "Be off!" he said, fixing me with a cold blue eye, making me feel like a trespasser in some sanctified St James's club, or as if I'd been caught poaching his hundred-pounds-a-yard salmon water.

The accent had its effect, too; I'd begun an automatic retreat when the baby started crying again and recalled me to a sense of my urgent need.

"Please—I've got to have help! I'm sorry to—to put you out, but the baby—"

"Yes, yes, I can see the baby, I'm not blind!" he said irritably. "That makes no difference. You know very well that women aren't allowed in here. Take it round to the east doorstep, that's the place to leave babies—if you must. Why didn't you think of all this nine months ago? You ought to support it yourself—should be ashamed of yourself. Cigarettes and permanent waves, I suppose. Aren't you married?"

"No I'm not," I said, disconcerted, as his hostile eye fell on my ringless hand. "Though what business it is of yours—"

"Now, my good woman, don't stand here arguing with me. I have more important things than you and your infant to think about, I assure you."

Turning from me with finality he took up his spade again, but at that moment a bell began its thin warning chime somewhere overhead in the mist; I recognised it at once. The old monk gave an impatient exclamation; quite evidently checked an impulse to hurl down the spade, and instead stuck it carefully into the soil. Without taking any further notice of me he hurried off along a cinder-path and disappeared among some bushes, heading towards the house.

Shrubsole was now yelling with an intensity of despair that echoed my own feelings. Were they all the same in this unfriendly place? Would no one give me any help?

It was the first time I'd ever been treated, not as a person, but merely as a member of a thoroughly undesirable class of objects, and I found the experience strangely demoralising. Retreat seemed the only dignified course, and I was moving wearily towards the gate when a whisper from the bushes surprised me.

"Hey! Psst! Psst! Over here!"

I saw an agitation of the branches; a black-robed arm was beckoning me.

"This way! This way! Come along! But don't make a sound."

It was hardly possible to comply with the last part of this instruction, since Shrubsole was still yelling her head off, but I showed willing by tip-toeing; I'd have gone down on all fours for anyone who seemed to promise succour. Circling the bushes I found a path on which stood my beckoning figure—another monk, short and stout, with a cheerful wrinkled face, who nodded at me vigorously, laid a finger to his lips, and set off at a fast pace round the corner of the building, making gestures of exaggerated caution. I hurried after him, hoping that the incessant tolling of the bell overhead would drown Shrubsole's howls; luckily nobody seemed to be about. I could hear voices chanting from a high window.

"Quiet, Shrubsole!" I whispered. But she was beyond soothing.

My guide led me past a couple of outbuildings, across a paved yard with a water-butt, along a cement-floored passage with a glassed-in side giving on to the yard, and finally into a sort of utility-room which might at one time have been a dairy; it had a wide slate shelf round three of its walls.

The first thing that struck me was the heat, which came from a big old circular iron stove; hungry, cold, and exhausted as I was, it hit me with a sort of wonderful shock, making all my pores yawn blissfully together.

"Now, now, now, then! You are in trouble, I can see, but we don't talk about that yet, eh? First we look at the little one, isn't it?"

With amazing speed and dexterity my guide scooped a bundle of newspapers off the floor, fanned them out over a big old-fashioned kitchen table in the middle of the room, flung a large piece of old but clean towelling on top of the paper, and invited me to lay Shrubsole down there, which I thankfully did.

"Ttt-tt-tt-tt! Poor baby, she *is* in a state, no matter, we soon have her all to rights, isn't it? *You* sit down for a little minute, I can see you are hardly able to stand—" he pulled out a broken old basket chair for me—"while I make this little one comfortable. *There's* a poor little one, so patient and good!"

At this last, thoroughly undeserved tribute, Shrubsole opened her smoke-dark eyes wide and gave him a long look, perhaps of astonishment; she seemed quite silenced, or soothed by his confident handling, and allowed him to finish his wonderfully quick divesting operations without any trouble. As if by magic he produced warm water, soap, cottonwool, vaseline, more towels, and with practised skill soon had her swathed in a new set of underpinnings.

"Now she'll be a happier baby, eh? You hold her then so, while I fetch milk—"

He whisked away and returned almost at once carrying a medicine bottle full of warm milk with a rubber teat. I was past being surprised by this time, quite confident, in fact, that this extraordinary monk would be able to produce anything that was needed. Shrubsole seized the bottle with frantic enthusiasm and sucked away at it, staring at us over the top with an expression of utter concentration.

"Aha, she likes that, the little one! Now we put her in here—"

He had lined up another of his makeshift but efficient arrangements: an orange-crate wadded with more newspapers and old sheets; Shrubsole was transferred to it and lay peacefully swigging while the monk turned to me.

"I think you too would like a wash, perhaps, my child?"

His brown eyes took in, without dwelling on any one particular, my draggled skirt, soaking shoes, mud-caked stockings and jacket, my torn scarf, my generally dishevelled appearance.

"Oh, I should, bless you!" I said gratefully. "I'd like it above anything!"

"In here, then." He opened a door by the boiler and showed me a cement-floored cloakroom with pegs on the walls, a sink at ground level, evidently for washing gumboots, a tap, a tin basin, and a WC.

"So; here is soap, here is towel. You are hungry, too? While you are washing I get you some food."

The water was boiling hot; heaven! I could have stayed in there for hours if it hadn't been for the beckoning vision of a meal.

When I came out I saw that the traces of Shrubsole's toilet had been tidied away. The room was still pretty chaotic, though; there were seedboxes, sacks of animal food, dangling strings of onions, an old wringer, several battered prie-dieux, a stone birdbath or it may have been a font, a hand sewing-machine, and a small organ. On the whitewashed wall pictures of Christ and Buddha hung companionably side by side.

My host had dragged another orange-box up beside the basket

chair and had arranged on it a plate and knife, butter, honey, a round brown loaf, and a cup of hot milk.

I have never eaten anything better. The bread was hot too, straight out of the oven; the butter and honey were both home-made.

"You like?" he beamed, when I was on about my third slice. "Our own bees. Our own cows. The only thing we cannot grow enough of is corn for flour. So: now I think you tell me about the baby? I do not think it is your baby?"

"No, it isn't. That other monk—"

"Ah yes, Brother Lawrence. Is a pity you first meet him. He feels ill at ease with strangers. He is a saint, you see. Saints occupy themselves with holiness; they are sometimes difficult. But now all is well and you tell me your trouble."

I picked up Shrubsole, who had just finished her milk, and patted her on the back. She let out two splendid belches, worthy of the Emir of Turkinistan, sighed deeply with repletion, and then gave me a long, radiant, conspiratorial smile. It was the first time she had smiled at me and I felt it like an accolade.

"Well," I said. Where to begin? "It was like this, you see, Father—?"

"Brother Stanislas, my child."

"Brother Stanislas. I found the baby up on the moor last night— two men had taken her out of her pram and left the empty pram in the road to frighten somebody—the mother, I suppose—into doing something, giving them money, perhaps. So when I came across the baby I just ran off with her. Then they chased me—"

"Aha!" he said. "Two men in an Italian sports car, very angry?"

"Why yes! Did they come here?"

"Not twenty minutes ago, asking if anyone had recently left a baby. I was able to say no. Now was not that the good working of Providence?" He beamed with satisfaction, like a kind, wrinkled monkey.

"Oh, what a piece of luck," I breathed. "And of course they'd be bound to believe you, so they'll have gone away sure that where-ever else she is, she won't be here."

"In the meantime, what do you do, my child?"

"Ring up the police—if I may use your telephone? Find out if a lost baby's been reported yet."

I saw a doubtful, negative look cross his face. "What's the trouble?" I asked.

"Firstly, my child, we have no telephone. Brother Lawrence does not approve of electrical devices. That is one objection. Secondly, are you so sure that the loss of this little one—what do you call her?"

"*I* call her Shrubsole."

"The loss of this little Shrubsole will have been reported? Consider: the mother no doubt believes the kidnappers have her child. She may be keeping quiet; frightened to death in case they do it a harm."

"Yes, I can see that, but as they *haven't* got it, surely it won't hurt to tell the police? They'll be able to trace the mother much faster than I can. And those men ought to be punished, surely?"

Brother Stanislas looked more doubtful still. "The police are a clumsy instrument, my child. They often drive the wrongdoer deeper into his wrong; they bring on the very violence that should be prevented. They are accompanied by evil. Here in this community we do not too much value the police."

Unbidden, the idea sneaked into my mind that perhaps some of the brothers had a particular reason for avoiding the law. After all, no one in the neighbourhood seemed to know much about the community, and it would make a perfect place for a criminal to lie low in.

"No, we have no crimes to conceal." The monk smiled kindly, reading my thought with embarrassing ease. "But some of our members have entered your country in a somewhat unorthodox manner and would not welcome publicity. Your immigration laws are so strict! I myself—where I come from, in eastern Europe, the very name of the police can strike terror. But that is not to the purpose. Understand, we are all men of peace in this quiet house, but we believe that law is of God, not of man; physical enforcement will do more damage than good. You see? Once this matter is in the open, moreover, the kidnappers will know where to strike a second time, is it not so? No, I think it better to make careful inquiry first, to find out a little bit more about this matter, before we call in the police."

It would be only fair to take his advice, I supposed. After all, he had been extremely kind with his unquestioning help and hospitality.

"If I don't go to the police, what would you suggest?"

He answered my question with another.

"What do you plan to do with this little one?"

Shrubsole, after a spell of wide-eyed wakefulness in which she had reclined against my shoulder looking intelligently round the monks' utility room as if memorising its miscellaneous contents, was gradually drowsing off to sleep, her head wobbling more and more until it came to rest under my chin.

"Well—I'm not exactly sure. It's obviously too risky to go carrying her round the countryside. And my car's miles from here. I don't know if they'd have her at the farm where I'm staying—"

"Why not leave her here?" he said tranquilly.

"Here? At the monastery?"

"Why not?" He gave a benevolent smile at my surprise. "You think we do not know how to look after infants? But you would be surprised at the number of foundlings that are left on our doorstep—even in this remote part of the country!"

Then I remembered Brother Lawrence's curt instruction: Take it round to the east doorstep, that's the place to leave babies. Much was now explained, including Brother Stanislas's startling ability with bottles and nappies.

"Ha—have you any at the moment?"

"Two—so you see your little Shrubsole will not lack company."

Finger on lips, he opened a door at the end of the room and allowed me to peep through. With a queer pang I saw another room as bleak, functional, stone-floored and whitewashed as the one we stood in; but some loving hand had stuck brightly coloured pictures from grocers' calendars and seed catalogues round the walls, and two more orange-crates each held a small, sleeping occupant.

"How long shall you keep them?" I whispered when he had shut the door.

"Oh, the Camelot District Council will find a place for them, in foster homes or orphanages, as soon as possible. But meanwhile, unofficially, they are quite glad if we will keep them for a period while these arrangements are made. So I care for them. To tell the truth—" his smile broke out again—"I am always sorry to see them go. It is the part of my work I enjoy most."

Carefully, so as not to wake her, he gathered Shrubsole from me and restored her to the box, where she settled deeper into oblivion.

"Well—in that case—if you're sure it's all right—"

"We are glad to help you, my child. And meanwhile you make some inquiries for the poor mother—discreetly—and let her know the baby is in safety. Tell her to come here, to the east door, ring

79

the little bell, and ask for Brother Stanislas. She may even think of coming here herself; people often do, with their troubles.'

"Will you be able to let me know, if she does come here?"

He reflected. "I can arrange. We take turns going to the village for paraffin and necessities—I can send a note. Where do you live, my child?"

I wrote my name and address for him on the back of an envelope, explaining my connection with the film unit.

"Aha!" he chuckled. "This terrible filming! Some of the brothers do not much like it—they say it disturbs the vibrations in this peaceful place. Myself I have no objection. Besides, the money will buy us two cows and a secondhand cultivator."

"Brother Stanislas—please don't think me rudely inquisitive— but what exactly is your religion here? Nobody I've asked round about seems to know."

"My child, it is complicated. A lifetime would be hardly long enough to explain."

"But—?"

"Our doctrine brings together all religions, takes the essence from each, and shows a way through confusion to enlightenment. That is the symbolism of the pierced stone. You see?"

I nodded dubiously.

A piercing yell broke out in the nursery.

"Forgive me," he said, "but I must not delay any longer."

He led me quickly along another passage to a big arched doorway, evidently the entrance where foundlings were to be deposited. I badly wanted to ask him if Lucian was a member of the community, but while I was trying to frame my question another bell began ringing and two extremely elderly and doddering brethren came shuffling out of a doorway.

"Brother Lawrence was asking why you weren't at devotions?" one of them said to Brother Stanislas. Neither of them took the slightest notice of me.

I hadn't the strength of character to put my question in front of this additional audience, and so merely thanked him again. He murmured a blessing—at least I suppose it was—in what sounded like Greek, made a circular sign over my head, and shut the door gently but swiftly behind me.

I found myself back in the lane, outside the high wall, and hurried down towards the main road; it seemed odd not to be carrying the baby, I felt quite bereft without her warm weight on my arm and had a pang for other girls coming away from that door, empty-handed and full of anguish. But having found a safe resting-place for Shrubsole certainly made matters simpler. On neither of the two brief occasions when we'd encountered one another did I think the baby-snatchers could have had time for a recognisable glimpse of my face—I certainly hadn't seen theirs, the car was the only thing I had to go by. Of course they would have seen my blue headscarf and suede jacket; I tucked the scarf into my bag and, taking the jacket off, rolled it so that the lining was outermost, and carried it over my arm. Now, without the baby, I was just any anonymous girl. Or so I hoped.

When I reached the main road I glanced warily both ways; nobody was about. There was still a good deal of fog; no filming till it clears, I thought.

Nothing passed me as I walked the stretch of road between the monastery lane and the Trewithian turning. This proved to be no great distance, not much over a quarter of a mile. I knew it was the right turning when I came to it because of the weatherbeaten scarlet letterbox at the foot, let into a granite gatepost. It carried a notice: TREWITHIAN Coll. 2.30 Not Sats, Suns, Christmas, Boxing Day or Bank Hol.

The track to the farm, which cut straight up the seaward side of the ridge, was pretty steep going, and I had to slow down. Brother Stanislas's breakfast and company had put a wonderful heart into me, but I was still short of a night's sleep, and stiff from all the unwonted exercise; besides, I wanted time to think. What would be the best way of locating the baby's mother discreetly? It was plain that sticking up a FOUND notice in the post office would not meet the case, but whatever I did must be done fast; the poor woman must be nearly crazy with worry.

It was also needful somehow to account for my late arrival; the truth seemed inadvisable.

However this problem was easily solved. When I reached the farm—a cluster of whitewashed, slate-roofed buildings with a big, pleasant, Queen Anne house, set among windblown trees at the top of the hill—I was greeted by a placid, elderly couple, the Tregagles. Mrs Tregagle said,

"Ah, you'll be the other lady that Miss Whatname was expecting. She thought likely you'd got caught in the fog somewhere and decided to bide the night, was that what you done? Very sensible too. Now she left a message to say Don't hurry yourself down to the shore because they won't be working till dinnertime, 'count of the weather being so thick. Your room's all ready for you and there's a fire in the parlour, and would you like a bite of breakfast? Say the word and I'll pop the kettle on."

I thanked her and declined breakfast but said I'd be glad of a wash and change, so she showed me up a breakneck flight of stairs with hunting prints on the walls, and into a spacious comfortable farm bedroom. It was at the back of the house, overlooking an orchard full of daffodils. Beyond the orchard I could dimly see a sweep of moor through the thinning fog; somewhere out there must be the track I'd taken last night and my deserted car.

When I'd tidied, and changed into sweater and slacks, and bundled my muddy clothes into the suitcase which Mimi had brought over from the hotel for me, I went out exploring. A cart-track led out of the farmyard towards the moor, and fifteen minutes' walking down it brought me to the point where I'd left the car; it was exasperating to think by how little I must have missed the farm in the foggy dark.

On the way down I passed a left fork; another track led away over open moor, presumably the one I'd struck which led to the quarry.

The pram had gone, there was no sign of it, but I found the car where I had left it, garlanded with gossamer. Gloomily I got out the starting handle and started tugging it round. However I had not been at this distasteful occupation very long before Mr Tregagle came chugging down the lane with a tractor and a load of reeking straw. When he saw me wrestling he climbed off his driver's seat, leaving the tractor to roar, and had the Hillman started in two turns of a brawny arm.

"Battery a bit low, is she?" he yelled cheerfully above the tractor's row.

"She died on me when I stopped for a rest," I explained without saying when.

"I've a spare a-charging in the shed you can borrow, and my son Ken'll take yourn to be recharged if you like; he'm going upalong to the garage at Trevann presently."

So that was fixed; but I asked Ken, a silent, friendly, red-faced giant, to get me a new battery; I reckoned the old one was past resuscitation.

While I was talking to Ken Mrs Tregagle put her head out of

the back door and called, "Ken! Coffee's ready! Wouldn't you like a cup, Miss Whatname?"

The thought of coffee was irresistible, and I decided I might pursue some cautious research at the same time. In the big untidy farm kitchen with its stone-slabbed floor and rag rugs I found, as well as Mrs Tregagle, a dark-haired pretty girl introduced as Lily, Ken's wife. Lily and Ken, I gathered, lived in the farm cottage across the orchard. And had they any children? I asked. Yes, three, Lily said sighing, and home didn't seem the same now even the youngest went off to school every day.

I told her, truly, that she didn't look old enough to be the mother of three school-age children, and crossed her off my list; nobody who had lost a baby could put on such a good act as that. Then a Co-op grocery van drove into the yard; both Lily and Mrs Tregagle hurried out for the gossip which was even more important than groceries. I followed and, pretending to inspect the Hillman's aged little engine, eavesdropped for any word of a missing child, but heard none; it seemed extraordinary that an obviously well-cared-for baby like little Shrubsole could drop out of sight so casually.

Finally, after having polished the windscreen and checked oil and water, I ran out of pretexts for loitering; anyway conscience told me that I ought to go and see how my colleagues were getting on. So I drove down to Trevann cove, following the well-marked track over the headland from the main road that had been made by the camera crews.

A thin veil of mist still lay over the beach but the sun was rapidly melting it now; cameras were being set up and people were moving busily about. Somebody was exercising a horse, presumably the one due to have a can of Picnic Soup heated on its back. I hoped the new lot of non-bang tins had been duly delivered by Barney.

"Oh, hallo!" Jimmy greeted me. "Did you remember my binoculars? The mist's lifting, but we shan't be doing any Avalon shooting today."

"Why not?"

"Cara's got a migraine," he said sourly. "Or so *she* says. Hangover, more likely, after all that pub-crawling with Tom. How was the Monaco do, frightful?"

"Frightful."

It all seemed very normal and reassuring, like returning to

another life. I looked round for Mimi and saw her sitting on the big concrete boat that served the monks for a jetty, talking to Barney Soglow. She broke off to wave to me vigorously.

"Cherie! *There* you are! Did you sensibly spend the night at Exeter or somewhere?"

"Somewhere," I said. "How are things going?"

"We did all the castle filming for Avalon yesterday, and got some beautiful piton-sequences for Picnic Soup, didn't we, Barney?"

"They were great," Barney assented. "Oh, excuse me, that guy's going to get thrown if he doesn't tighten his girths."

"It's so useful that Barney knows all about horses, the actor has obviously never stepped outside riding school," Mimi said as he rushed away, and added without a pause, "Have you heard about that miserable Cara?"

"She has a migraine, Jimmy says?"

"Migraine, schmigraine!"

"What would you call it?"

"Family trouble."

"How do you mean?"

"Well, you know how, for the last four days, ever since we've been down here, she's been living in Tom's pocket. With a few spare glances for Barney Soglow if Tom happened to be busy. Good grief, you'd think the girl was Garbo the way she's been queening it. Real saturation technique—languishing looks, deep, deep confidences, the whole barrage."

I looked round uncomfortably for Tom, but he was nowhere to be seen.

"So," Mimi pursued, "not surprisingly, old Dunskirk didn't like this much. He couldn't help noticing, and his upright north-country soul was disturbed. He's got worries enough without his daughter-in-law letting down his precious son and making a scandal of herself in front of the entire film unit. The evening before last he evidently felt the time had come when it was his duty to give her a good lecture—she was proposing to go off with Tom and have her picture taken on top of Brown Willy. Dunskirk scolded her—at least that's what it looked like from the other end of the beach—of *course* did more harm than good, she went in spite of him, and furthermore was apparently so mad at all this supervision that she upped sticks, moved out from his rented house, and came over to stay at the farm."

"At our farm? At Trewithian?"

"Yes, she's in the cottage where the son and daughter-in-law live. Her pretext is that it's handier for the filming, but it was plain as a pikestaff that that wasn't the real reason."

"In the farm cottage," I repeated slowly. "Is she there now?"

"Very much so," Mimi said drily. "Plus trunks full of clothes, plus her cousin from Italy and the baby."

"*Baby?* Oh, you mean little Laureen?" Reminded of the awful brat I looked for her, and saw her grandfather disconsolately leading her up and down by the edge of the sea; he appeared far from his usual cheerful self.

"No, not Laureen—oh, I forgot; that's another piece of gossip you hadn't heard. Yes, apparently just before they came down to Cornwall Cara's cousin arrived from Italy with a baby she hadn't thought to mention before."

"Whose baby? Who hadn't thought to mention?"

"Cara, you goose," Mimi said impatiently. "She had this baby in Italy—"

"Gareth's?" I was still bewildered, half a lap behind. Lack of sleep was making me slow-witted.

"No, no, somebody else's."

"She'd been married before?"

Mimi shook her head. "Just a slight lapse, I gather. And then either the cousin had grown tired of acting as foster-mother—I bet Cara didn't pay her—or Cara had a sudden impulse of maternal longing, which was what *she* said—or wanted to annoy Gareth—suddenly, presto! cousin arrived with baby. Old Dunskirk was unburdening himself to me about it all yesterday, lacking your hand to hold. I suppose Cara thought her position was now secure enough to be able to produce the baby, but I gather it was a miscalculation; the Dunskirks, père et fils, weren't very pleased."

"Good heavens," I said faintly.

"Well then yesterday Gareth suddenly appeared."

"I thought he was safely in London?"

"He was, but he flew down and gave Cara a ticking-off. At least it was more of a stand-up fight, really. They were in the farm orchard. I heard a lot of it from my bedroom window—they were fairly yelling at one another. I gathered old Dunskirk had rung Gareth and told him that Cara was being altogether too oncoming and promiscuous with the opposite sex, and Gareth told Cara that

85

if she didn't behave herself she could just send her unwanted brat back to Savona. And she was coming right back at him with the fact that he wasn't altogether perfect himself—'Suppose I tell your father what *you* did in Savona?' I heard her say."

"Wonder what she meant."

"Oh, probably just that he slept with her before he married her," Mimi said carelessly. "The old boy's got such an obsessively high notion of Gareth's virtue that I daresay it would upset him to think his white-headed boy capable of such conduct."

"Must be something more than that," I speculated. "I've always suspected, for instance, that Gareth slipped back a bit of contraband with him from those innocent buying trips. Drugs, perhaps. Isn't this all fascinating! What a drama."

"So in answer to that—"

"You seem to have gathered plenty. Were you wearing your ear-trumpet?"

"No, but I have *very* good hearing," said Mimi, unabashed "—Gareth threatened to send her packing too, back to Italy bag and bastard, and she just laughed at him and said, 'Don't forget that I'm the model for your precious perfume that you can't even *make*!' and then Gareth got *really* mad. They were at it for ages longer, but I became bored with listening," she ended virtuously.

"More likely they moved to the far end of the orchard where you couldn't hear."

"Then Tom arrived—"

"*Tom?*"

"He and Cara had a date to go to the pictures in Camelot, apparently. Would you *believe* it, she flitted out, gay as a lark, jumped into his car and off, leaving Gareth to fume."

"Wasn't that a rather feckless thing to do, if Gareth was in such a rage?"

"She is feckless. I tell you, she's peasant."

"Is Gareth still here?" I asked, apprehensively glancing behind me.

"No, thank God. They've still got trouble with Product X—something won't jell—that was what Cara meant. Even now they can't fix it the way the first batch came out—seems extraordinary to me, they must have a formula. But I suppose it's a question of heating or cooling or one of those bits of know-how. That's another thing that's making old Dunskirk worried and tetchy. So Gareth had to catch the last plane back to town."

"But my God then," I said aghast, "what about our beautiful campaign?"

"If you ask me, mon ami, our beautiful campaign is hanging on the knees of the gods along with the sword of thingummy," Mimi said calmly. "But we might as well go on and finish it now we've done so much. Provided Cara doesn't crack up on us with all this domestic brouhaha. I heard Jimmy delicately asking old Dunskirk if her migraines tended to be very frequent and might it be wise to get a stand-in? I think he was really sounding to see if the old boy wanted to cancel the whole programme after these developments."

"And did he?"

"Not a bit; quite affronted at the idea, and almost threatened to take the account elsewhere. We had to soothe him down. No, whatever her defects as a wife and daughter-in-law, he's still dead keen on Cara as a model. So, migraines or no, we're stuck with her."

"Migraines," I said slowly. "I wonder ... Have you *seen* her baby, by the way?"

Mimi shook her head. "I avoid infants, as you know. Anyway, I gather it has a cold today and is incommunicado. Or d'you think it has bubonic or smallpox and she's keeping it dark?"

"No, it's just a thought I had. I'll tell you later. If there isn't going to be any Avalon shooting I think I'll go back to the farm for a bit."

"Yes, why don't you? You look rather tired. How was the journey?"

"Mixed. Tell you later."

"Did you bring the car?"

"Yes."

"Thank heaven," said Mimi fervently. "That was the most useful deed you ever performed. And you did yourself a good turn too—just think, if you'd come back by plane you'd probably have had the seat next to Gareth. So count your blessings."

"I'll count them," I said, and yawned.

"Take a nap!" Mimi called after me. "You'll need all your strength. Old Ibn Abdullah al-Fuad called up and he's going to take us out tonight."

"Oh goodness." I halted at the foot of the rock-path. "I'm not sure if I can face an evening with his Excellency."

"Nonsense; well, see how you feel when you've rested."

As I drove back to the farm I reflected that, in their usual way, our clients seemed to be catching up with us. Barney, old Dunskirk, and now the Emir—what other distracting old acquaintances were due to arrive? But my chief interest at present was in a new arrival—I was mightily curious to see Cara's baby, if it was indeed at the farm.

My knock at the cottage door produced a long pause; at last the door was opened by a black-haired sulky girl who wore the most improbable clothes I have ever seen on a Cornish farm in the chilly spring.

"Mees Tregagle not here. Over at other house," she said grumpily.

"I don't want Mrs Tregagle. I'd like to speak to Mrs Dunskirk."

"Mees Dunskirk she see nobody."

"She'll see me, I'm sure. It's very important. Where is she?"

She shook her head, but I moved past her. From an open door across the small entrance-hall Cara's voice called an inquiry in Italian. I walked through, and found myself in a ground-floor bedroom, furnished simply but pleasantly with Co-op Contemporary, Numdah rugs, and India cotton quilts. Over everything was strewn a rich top-dressing of Cara's clothes; she herself was disposed, Recamier-fashion, one one of the twin beds, against a pile of pillows. A voluminous white terry robe cascaded around her in classic folds, and she looked wan and pathetic; Tom sat by the bed. I couldn't see if he was holding her hand.

When I came in he jumped up with a smothered exclamation and walked over to the window, where he stood with his back to the room.

"Oh, Martha," Cara murmured languidly. "It is kind of you to come but really I am better without visitors. Thank you so much for thinking of me but I think you should not stay."

Tom turned, as if about to say something; she raised her brows at him in mute, mournful inquiry, and he shook his head.

"I just wanted to ask you something; I won't stay more than a moment." As usual she made me feel thoroughly awkward and intrusive. "I'm sorry you're so under the weather."

"It is nothing; it will pass," with a small suffering smile.

"How is the baby?"

"But, asleep?" Cara raised her brows again. "In the other room." Her gesture as she pointed to a closed door caught my attention; it was superfluous. Why should she need to tell me where the baby slept?

88

"I'd love to see her," I said, moving gently towards the door.

"No! Certainly not! No, you might wake her, she has a cold, she needs to sleep."

"I really think, Cara," Tom began.

"No!" she snapped at him. But in spite of her protest I had already opened the door.

The first thing I saw was the pram, with its huddle of blue blankets now spilt on the floor. Beyond: an empty carry-cot, an unmade single bed, and a litter of baby equipment. The girl, Cara's cousin, darted angrily past me and began tidying the bed. I came out, and shut the door again.

"How dare you go in!" Cara stormed. "How *dare* you?"

"I knew she couldn't be there," I said composedly. "Because I know where she is."

"*You?* You *know* where she is?" Cara sprang upright off the bed and faced me; in the intensity of her surprise she sounded angry rather than relieved; questions poured from her. "How can you know about it, you? Where is she? Did you take her? Where is she?"

"She's at the monastery. The monks are looking after her."

"At the monastery? How can you know this? You must be crazy."

I heard a slight movement from Tom, behind me.

"Sit down," I said, "I'll explain."

"Well, please do! Can't you see that I am in torture? Oh, my *head*!"

She sank back on the bed, with a hand pressed theatrically to her brow; Tom moved forward with a glass of something but she waved him back.

"I found her up on the moor. In a quarry," I said, abridging the story to essentials. "I left her at the monastery—as I didn't know whose she was—the monks there look after foundlings, they said they'd keep her till her parents were located. Of course I'll go and get her right away."

Glancing past Cara at Tom I saw on his face an expression of unbounded relief that suddenly made him look ten years younger.

"Did you tell the police?" he said quickly.

"Not yet, I—"

"Oh, what does it matter, as she is found?" Cara interrupted.

At that Tom shrugged and, throwing me a curious look—wry, apologetic, baffling—he walked out of the room.

"Tom!" Cara extended an arm in a graceful gesture to detain him, but it was too late. So she turned to me.

"Oh, you cannot *know* what I have been through since last night," she said, with a dying fall.

"Why didn't you tell the police?" I said bluntly.

"How do you know that I did not?"

"It's obvious. If you had they would have been all around, asking questions. But you kept it secret. Nobody knows the baby wasn't here."

"But don't you see? I was afraid—afraid of what he would do to her?"

"Who?"

"Gareth, of course!" She opened her eyes very wide. "Don't you see—he is crazy with jealousy of her because she was not his. They all, all hate my poor little Giovanetta—Gareth, his father, even that dreadful Laureen, who loses no chance to torment her."

Something to that, I thought, beginning to understand Laureen's attitude to babies.

"When did you find that she was missing?"

"When I came back last night with Tom. We had been to the cinema and then to view some Standing Stones—very boring. Agnese had gone to have her supper at the farm, leaving the baby asleep here—stupid girl—when she came back she never even noticed the cot was empty. Tom and I find the pram—oh, Gareth is a monster! Sometimes I think he must be mad."

"But wasn't it a bit tactless to bring Giovanetta to England so soon?" I suggested.

"But, do you think I am made of stone?" She spread out her hands. "I was breaking my heart to see her. She is only four months! Besides," Cara added more practically, "my cousin was not willing to look after her any more and there is nobody else."

Born in January, I thought. Gareth went to Italy in October—

"Did Gareth really not know of her existence?"

"Gareth is not observant in that way," Cara said candidly. "Besides, I am so slim that I hardly show, until the very birth."

Feeling that as I had been flung into the middle of the situation I had a right to know a bit more, I said,

"What about the baby's real father? Who is he? Wouldn't he like to have her?"

A strange, guarded expression came over Cara's face.

"He is dead. He was killed in the autumn, in a fire."

"Oh, I'm sorry. I see." Poor Cara, I thought, feeling more sympathetic; no doubt marriage with Gareth had seemed a sensible solution towards providing for her fatherless child. And, if it had been rather disingenuous not to mention the baby beforehand—well, events had proved, perhaps, that his reaction would not have been very favourable.

"I'll go and get her, shall I?"

"Oh, wait," she said quickly. "I do not think you had better, for a while. You say the monks are good, kind men? Oh, I think it will be better if she stays there, just for a little. My cousin goes back to Italy tomorrow, you see—and Gareth is *so* jealous. But if he does not know where she is—"

"You'll just leave her there?" I was thunderstruck. "Your own baby?"

"Oh, not for ever, of course," Cara said hastily. "But, you see, Gareth—"

"Cara, there's one thing that puzzles me. Who were the two men in the Crespina?"

Her jaw dropped. For a moment she gaped at me in silence. Then she said,

"Two men? Where did you see them?"

"Up on the moor, when I was carrying the baby. They chased me, but I got away."

She gave me a narrow look.

"What made you think the baby is not theirs?"

"Oh, it was obvious. Who are they?"

"They must be Gareth's friends Tigger and Mait."

Thinking back, I supposed they could. I had not heard their voices because their talk had been conducted in whispers; and of course I had not been expecting to see Tigger and Mait in the middle of a Cornish moor, so I had never thought of them. But the man whose back view I had seen in the quarry might easily have been Mait.

"How in heaven's name do *they* come into this? Surely even Gareth wouldn't get his friends to snatch your baby? Just because he was jealous?"

"Oh, very easily he might," Cara said scornfully. "He *worships* those friends of his! Everything they do, he must copy, and they all do things for each other; it is like some little boys' club. Mait lends him his yacht, now his car, and Gareth listens to all they say; I am sure they think it a big, fine joke to steal his wife's child."

"But, Cara, what will you do now? You can't lodge the baby in the monastery indefinitely."

The wary look returned to her face.

"I will see, I will see. Perhaps I divorce Gareth—we do not suit. He is too unkind. But you will wish me to wait for that until we finish the filming? I would not like to cause you inconvenience. And divorce might make an awkwardness with Mr Dunskirk—it is he who so greatly wishes me to be in these films. Maybe he does not wish me to have the part any more if he knows I divorce Gareth," she said simply.

"Oh, I don't think he'd do that."

But I saw her point. No doubt she'd need the fees, if she proposed to leave Gareth, who would probably be highly reluctant about settlements.

"I suppose the monks won't mind having the baby for a little while. What will you do then?"

She shrugged, disingenuously. "Who can tell? Maybe someone offers me another job?"

Or maybe someone offers to marry you, I thought. Whatever happened, it seemed likely that Cara would fall on her feet.

"Well, all right—I expect you'd like me to tell the monks? Do you want to come and see for yourself? It's a bit rough and ready —but they seem very kind."

Cara looked dismayed.

"But *I* could not go to the monastery! Gareth, or those two, might see me and guess she was there! Could you not go? Just to make sure she is all right and ask them to keep her a little longer? You could take some more of her clothes."

"Yes—all right. And I expect they'd be glad of some money for her keep."

"But I have hardly any! Gareth is so mean! Could you lend me a little, Martha, you must have a good salary and are, after all, only a single girl with few expenses."

It was wonderful how even in the midst of her crisis she managed to loose these winged words.

"All right."

"And you will go to see her again? Often? Every day? I shall break my heart wondering how she is getting on among all those queer old monks," said Cara, who looked more and more cheerful as she saw her problems sorting themselves. "You are such a reliable person, Martha—like some nurse or teacher. You will go to see her regularly?"

I was on the point of saying that I couldn't spare the time, but I thought of little Shrubsole and my heart melted.

"Oh, very well—so long as the monks don't object. And so long as they don't start thinking I'm her mother—"

She laid a hand earnestly on my arm. "Please! Could you not let them think that?"

"No, I could *not*, Cara! It would probably get back to the film unit."

"But that would do no harm—if they thought that you had been a little bit gay! After all, you have no special man friend to consider."

"Just the same, no."

She looked unconvinced, but said, "In any case, you will not mention my name? You promise?"

I couldn't help it—I burst out laughing. Cara looked at me, faintly puzzled.

"What have I said that is funny?"

"Nothing, really." I couldn't explain that I was tickled by her calm exploitation of whoever was at hand. She was so single-minded that it was almost endearing.

"I'd better get back to the monastery straight away," I said, "before *they* start making inquiries. Besides—" I had to keep my flag flying a little—"Mimi and I are going out with the Emir later on."

"The Emir of Turkinistan? The one I met at your party?" Cara showed a wan interest.

"Oh, of course he drove you home, didn't he? Well—I'll be off. See you later. I'll tell you what the monks have to say."

"I think I get up now," said Cara, struggling off the bed. "Agnese!" she shouted. "Where did you put my sandals?"

As I left the cottage I looked around, just in case Tom was still there. But he had gone; probably conscience-stricken at all the working-time he'd spent with Cara.

I started on foot, thinking it would attract less attention than driving a car up to the monastery. It wouldn't take long to get there and back; and then, I resolved, I'd have a good long nap. I was beginning to have that removed-from-this-world feeling that comes from losing a night's sleep.

Halfway down the lane I met Barney Soglow.

"Fog's getting thicker again; had to pack in filming," he explained. "Thought I'd call by and inquire how Cara was getting on."

"Getting on nicely now," I said.

"Oh, that's great! Do you suppose I could persuade her to come down to the pub for a bit of food?"

"I shouldn't be a bit surprised," I told him, and plodded on, feeling a martyr.

But at heart I knew that I was glad to have an excuse for going back to the monastery.

CHAPTER VI

Brother Stanislas did not seem in the least surprised to see me back again so soon with a bundle of superior baby-clothes, nor to hear that my friend, the baby's anonymous mother, was asking if Shrubsole might remain in the care of the monastery for a little while longer.

He smiled his unfathomable smile, and only remarked,

"Poor old Brother Stanislas! Cows, goats, hens, a donkey, and now, three babies to care for! I shall soon wish there were forty-eight hours in the day!"

"I'll help with the babies a bit if you like," I offered impulsively, forgetting my resolve to take a nap. "You'll have to tell me what to do."

His smile broadened. "I shall be happy! Sometimes the Health Visitor comes to assist me with the baths, but she is on holiday at present. So; come in; I am just about to give the bath now. You shall do it while I prepare the milk."

Well, it's nice to feel wanted, I thought wrily, as he escorted me into the nursery room and fetched a can of hot water and a large battered papier-maché tureen which was used apparently for the babies' full-scale immersions.

"The little Shrubsole she still sleeps, she is tired, you leave her till the last."

"I'll probably drop them or do something awful," I mentioned. "I'm ignorant of these matters."

"So? Then it is time you learned," he said imperturbably, and proceeded to instruct me.

When it came to Shrubsole's turn I hesitated to wake her, so deeply and peacefully did she sleep, with one minute fist curled into her cheek. Brother Stan had disappeared in search of goat's milk or I'd have asked him if she shouldn't be left. But the others had seemed to enjoy their baths and routine was routine—I hoisted her gently out of the orange-box and on to my lap. She yawned, stretched—absurdly like an adult in her sleepy reluctance —looked up at me and, as before, gave me that mysteriously radiant recognising smile, as if she and I shared a secret undreamt-of by the rest of the world. She let out a little murmuring sound, like the chirrup of a sleepy canary.

"You funny little object!" I whispered, charmed as if a wren had come to perch on my finger.

We were still studying one another when I heard footsteps.

"Heavens, here's Brother Stan coming back with the milk and I haven't even undressed you yet!"

Sitting her up, I began undoing the strings of her nightie. "Do you know," I said without turning, "I believe Shrubsole recognised me."

Brother Stanislas neither moved nor spoke; in a moment, puzzled by the silence, I looked up.

"Aren't I doing it the right way...?"

My voice died. For the black-robed figure in the doorway was not Brother Stanislas at all, but my former husband, Lucian.

"So you *were* here," I said slowly, after what seemed like a seven-year pause.

Lucian made no answer to this inane remark, just went on looking at me; how well I remembered that withdrawn, inimical stare; slightly moving and compressing his lips as if trying to swallow something bitter. Oh, god, I thought, what possessed me to come here and risk this? Why didn't I stop to think? Why don't I ever?

Then he turned on his heel with such violence that the black woollen material of his robe slapped against the door, and strode off; I heard his footsteps die away down the passage.

One of the babies began to cry hungrily; Shrubsole thrust a warm, woolly-socked foot against my shaking hand; I finished undressing her somehow and had reached the last lap of the wash-dry routine by the time Brother Stanislas reappeared with three bottles of milk.

"Here we are, then, for three poor hungry children," he said beaming, and dealt them round. "You wish to hold the small Shrubsole while she drinks, perhaps?—What is the matter, my child?"

"It's only that—Brother Stanislas, I shan't be able to come here again."

"Not so? A pity; I had hoped you might visit every day at this time to help me," he said placidly. "You have seen your husband and it has upset you, is that it?"

"Seen my—how did you know?"

"Why, because Brother Lucian, who is the youngest of the Brothers, helps me with the animals; he saw the envelope you left, with your name on it, and asked me where it had come from. I knew, of course, that he had had a wife and had left her."

"Brother Stanislas—can you tell him, please, that I'm not here to try and make him come back to me."

"Then why, my child, did you come here?"

"I came because I wanted—oh, what did I want? To know he was all right, I suppose."

"Of course I will tell him this, my child," he said kindly.

"I've divorced him, as a matter of fact," I went on, anxious for it to be clear that I wasn't there to claim conjugal rights.

"Then what need to worry? I will tell Brother Lucian this; he will understand that you are not pursuing him. So then all will be well, will it not? and you can continue to visit in your lunch-hour and bath the little Shrubsole, and poor old Brother Stanislas will be lightened of his labours."

"But Lucian would *hate* to have me coming here."

"In my opinion," said Brother Stanislas calmly, taking its bottle away from a hiccuping baby, "hating something might be just what Brother Lucian needs. So you see," he gave me an encouraging nod, "you may be useful to him."

"Brother Stan—"

"Yes, my child?"

"Have you known Lucian for long?"

"Ever since he came here—which is now more than seven years."

"You must know him better than I did—how queer it seems."

He waited, looking at me kindly. I up-ended Shrubsole over my shoulder and rubbed her back. Finally I said,

"His mental state—would you say it was normal?"

"He has had an illness for a number of years; without a doubt. But he has been emerging from it. Now, I think—" Brother Stanislas rubbed his chin, absently replaced one baby in its orange-box and picked up another—"now, I think, very soon, he may, perhaps, recover."

When I got back to the farm I found old Dunskirk's Wolseley incongruously parked in the yard, and little Laureen trying to garotte a timid farm-cat which she had cornered by the cowshed.

"Don't do that," I said automatically.

"Why not?" she demanded in her strident croak.

"Because it'll scratch you, for one thing. And cats should be treated kindly."

She stuck out her lower lip, then demanded,

"Do you live here?"

"Yes, just now."

"Can I come to tea with you?"

"No."

"Why not?"

"Because I'm going to bed."

"To *bed*? After *dinner*? That's like a baby," she said scornfully.

Old Dunskirk appeared from the cottage. He looked drawn and harassed, but seemed pleased to see me.

"It's grand to have you back, Miss Martha! We've missed you, haven't we, Laureen? Yoong Laureen's taken a great fancy to you, I can tell you!"

I didn't tell him the fancy was not reciprocal.

"I was looking for my daughter-in-law," he explained. "You wouldn't know where she's gone, I suppose?"

"I believe she went off to have lunch with Mr Soglow."

"Eh, dear." He gave a distressed sigh. "If she isn't off with one yoong fellow, then it's another. Poor Gareth's clean distracted with worry, but he can't keep leaving his work to chase after her. What would you do if you were me, Miss Martha?"

"Oh, heavens, Mr Dunskirk, I expect it's all harmless enough really. She's young and gay, that's all. I think I'd leave them to battle it out for themselves, anyway. There's never much a third party can do."

Laureen let out a wail; the cat had scratched her.

"Now look what you've doon," he scolded her. "Coom along, we're wasting Miss Martha's time, she's a busy lady."

"Why can't we have tea here?" she whined.

"We'll have tea at a café."

"Can I have cream cakes?"

"Yes, if you're a good girl."

Their voices died away in the distance. I went up to my room, blind with weariness, drew the curtains, pulled back the white honeycomb counterpane, and flung myself down on the bed. I was asleep before my head hit the pillow.

I suppose it was about half-past two when I fell asleep; when I woke I found myself in the dark and lay dazed, for a moment, wondering where I'd ended up. Someone had covered me with an eiderdown as I slept and I felt warm and relaxed and cocoon-like. Slowly I ruminated over all the events of the last twenty-four hours, the baby, and Brother Stanislas, and Cara, and Lucian. I wondered what Lucian was feeling now and vaguely pitied him; I hoped Brother Stanislas had found time to reassure him that he wasn't in for a series of harrowing come-home-Bill-Bailey scenes. Oddly, now that I had rested, I found myself quite calm about Lucian; it suddenly came to me with a feeling of slightly shocked relief that it didn't matter to me *how* he felt; he could look daggers at me all day long if so inclined. The tense, anguished girl who had suffered under his ostracism seven years ago existed no longer; I was another person, and free. I had grown up, I supposed.

Feeling quite benevolently towards Lucian for making me aware of this fact, I began to wonder about Cara. Could she be thrown by Gareth into such a panicky, trapped frame of mind as I had been by Lucian? I doubted it. Cara, as Jimmy had said, was no greenhorn; could add two and two. In fact, now I came coolly to consider the story she had told me, I was pretty sure there must be a lot more behind it; the version I had been given was as leaky as an old sieve. Firstly, Gareth: Cara had represented him as a creature of wild passions and jealousies, who had persuaded his friends to snatch Shrubsole because he was so enraged at Cara's infidelities. That didn't jive with my view of Gareth's character; I found him cold, wary, calculating, and bone selfish. I didn't think he had ever been enough in love with Cara to rise to such heights of jealousy, and he certainly wasn't now. Shame, at being made a fool of in front of people who knew him might move him, but then, surely, he'd simply want to get rid of Cara the quickest way.

98

No, there must have been some further reason for the snatch beyond pure spite; any other motive would seem more plausible. Perhaps some discreditable secret which Cara possessed about Gareth's activities in Italy, I thought, remembering what Mimi had overheard, and the note. WE WON'T HURT THE BABY IF YOU ARE A SENSIBLE GIRL. That didn't sound like jealous rage, far from it.

So: not jealousy but pressure.

And Tom—where did he come in? How deeply was he already involved with Cara? I had hardly seen him since we came to Cornwall; certainly never had a chance of private conversation with him. He seemed to be avoiding me. "We'll wait till we get back from Cornwall," he had said in London—perhaps he was being scrupulous about not trying to influence me. Rather *too* scrupulous. With a queer ache at my heart I wondered if Cara had Tom cast as second string in her tidy plan for when she had finished the filming and left Gareth. It seemed horribly probable. The thought of Tom married to Cara made me feel all hollow inside; then it occurred to me that some of the hollow feeling and despondency was probably physical; I hadn't eaten since Brother Stan's wonderful breakfast at about eight o'clock this morning.

After searching vainly for a bedside light I got up and bumbled around until I found the switch by the door. Looking at my watch I was thunderstruck to see that it was half-past eight; I'd been asleep for six hours. Panic! Weren't we supposed to be going out with the Emir? I shot across the passage to Mimi's room, opposite, but she wasn't there; returning to my own I found a note on the dressing-table.

You looked too tired to disturb, cherie, so Abdullah and I took Cara instead as she seemed rather at a loose end. His Excellency sends love and says he'll see you tomorrow. Meal ordered for you at pub at 9.00 Mind you're there! Mimi.

Mixed with my relief—I still felt too tired, really, to be able to face the Emir's exhausting notion of a lively evening, which invariably went on into the small hours—was a slight indignation. Did Cara have to annex all our escorts? Still, the Emir was more Mimi's flirt than mine, and Mimi was more than a match for Cara; so was his Excellency, for that matter.

I tidied up quickly, put on a jacket, ran downstairs past the farm parlour—where the whole family were watching television—and drove down to the pub. Much to my surprise I found Tom there; he seemed to be expecting me.

"Do you feel better now?" he greeted me.

"Oh, fine; all I needed was sleep."

I felt tongue-tied, oddly shy of Tom; too much lay between us. Luckily almost at once the pub produced an enormous steak and I applied myself to eating. Tom, too, was rather silent. Presently, under cover of the conversation from a hilarious party on the other side of the dining-room, he said in a low voice.

"Did you get Cara's business settled?"

I glanced round. No one we knew was in the room.

"Yes," I said, "the child is going to stay at the monastery for the time until—until Cara's domestic affairs have sorted themselves. She seemed to think that would be wisest. And the monks don't mind."

"Is it a nice baby?" Tom said unexpectedly.

"Yes, very nice."

"Not like little Laureen?"

"No no, not in the least."

I gave him a cautious look. Was he considering the baby as a possible stepchild? But he went on, "Do you know what that vile child did today? She found those explosive cans of Picnic Soup and swapped one of them for the working can in the bucking broncho scene; we only just missed mayhem. The horse bolted, of course, when the can went off; luckily the actor had the sense to turn its head out to sea instead of straight among the cameras. I had to lock up the cans in my car or god knows where she'd have planted one next. She really is a case for smothering. I'll be thankful when we've finished the Avalon filming."

"How many more days should it take, do you think?"

"Say three more, if Cara's all right and the weather stays good. Saturday tomorrow—we'll work in the morning—if everything goes to plan we should be through by Wednesday."

"With luck."

"Do you think Cara will be fit to go on by tomorrow?"

"Oh yes, I'm sure of it. She's just as anxious as we are to hurry up and finish the filming."

"She's certainly got guts," Tom said.

"Yes."

I thought we had better get off the subject of Cara; I didn't want to invite confidences or betray them. So I asked him about the pictures he had been taking, and the conversation wandered away to work. But there was still constraint in the atmosphere;

we were being unnaturally formal and polite with one another.

When I'd finished my steak we went into the saloon bar for a nightcap. It was a large, dimly lit room with a lot of phoney fishing-nets and glass balls dangling about, and an air of being ready for some festive occasion that never arrived. Apart from a couple of men with their backs to us in a far corner we had it to ourselves. We sat at a horrid little composition table by the fire and Tom ordered whiskies; when the barmaid had come and gone he said,

"So you managed to get into the monastery."

"Yes," I said. "Yes I did."

"And did you find your—what you were hoping for?"

I looked up and found his eyes fixed on me gravely. All of a sudden I couldn't speak. My throat seemed to have seized up. I managed a nod, and took a gulp of my whisky, enraged with myself. Where was the mature, independent Martha Gilroy that, not an hour since, I had congratulated myself on having become?

"Yes. Lucian was there," I said when the whisky had done its heartening work.

"You must be glad you acted on your hunch."

"Yes I am of course."

"So—what happens now? Are you going to see him again?"

"I suppose I may. Cara's asked me to go along there every day to keep an eye on Sh—things, as she daren't go herself. So there's at least a chance of seing Lucian some more, I suppose." Pride prevented me from revealing how very unwelcoming Lucian's reaction had been.

"How convenient." There was a dryness about Tom's tone that unnerved me; it was so unusual.

"If you'll forgive me," I said, "I think I'd better go back to the farm and get some more sleep; I'm still feeling the wear and tear a bit."

"I'm not surprised," he said. "Finding Cara's baby *and* your ex-husband." He still had that flat, rather chilling intonation.

I went along to the Ladies (which was gaily labelled Memsahibs) and took some long, shaky breaths while slapping on a lot of powder and thickening my eye-shadow. I had almost nerved myself to return when I heard a man's voice coming through the wall, which apparently was made of nothing thicker than fibreboard.

"Well, it was a chance, wasn't it? It was well worth taking. It didn't work out, that's all; wasn't our fault. Christ, Gareth, you don't sound very grateful. How the hell were we to know some damn girl would come along in the middle of nowhere and muck things?"

I froze, my hand halfway to the doorknob.

"Not a clue," the voice said sulkily. "Cornwall's full of girls. Ah, can it, we're trying to help you, aren't we? No we *don't* know where it is right now, but Mait's got a hunch. Blasted girl musta gone down to the beach, don't you see? We couldn't follow her in the car—she might have walked round Penrose Head to Instow. Yeah, all right, but we got to get Cara to open up somehow, haven't we? And *you* haven't been so goddam sublime at it, have you? Ask me, she just laughs at you, she's certainly having herself a ball down here. Wants teaching a lesson. Yeah, well, okay. See you tomorrow. Yeah, we'll meet you with the old hearse."

There was a ting, as the unseen speaker rang off, and the sound of footsteps on a stone floor. I waited another five minutes in the dimly lit cloakroom, giving him time to get well away, and then left myself, glancing at the pay phone on the wall just round the corner. Thank goodness he hadn't been there when I passed the first time.

Nipping out by a side exit into the pub's little carpark I dropped my suede jacket in the Hillman before rejoining Tom; just as well I did for when I went back to the saloon he was talking to Tigger and Mait who had paused by our table.

They looked as usual: Tigger about as trustworthy as a stoat, and Mait like a turf accountant who'd decided to stand for parliament: Vote for Big Brad Maitland, the Punter's Friend.

I nodded to them and said, "You on holiday?"

"Yeah," Tigger said. "Putting in a coupla nights here. We promised Gareth we'd keep an eye on his old woman while he was working; date her up and see she didn't get lonesome. But seems we're a bit behind the times."

"I'm going home to bed," I told Tom.

"I'll see you back," he said.

"No, honestly, thanks, don't bother. I've got the car. It's only five minutes up the lane."

"Sure? All right, see you tomorrow. Didn't you have a jacket with you?"

"It's in the car," I said, and left fast. But I was uneasy. I'd noticed Mait giving me a long, queer, speculative look, his attention focused apparently on my left shoulder. When I got into the car I had a look in the driving mirror and cursed; on the wool of my sweater was a small but unmistakeable—to anyone who knew —splash of milk from one of Shrubsole's belches.

I saw the Crespina car in the car park, near the exit, so I started up and drove the short distance to Trewithian as if I had the devil on my heels.

Next day was cloudlessly beautiful after a slight morning haze had cleared; we were certainly being lucky with our weather.

I managed to catch Cara alone on a secluded corner of the island before shooting began, and tell her that I was afraid Mait might have recognised me or guessed me to be the girl who had made off with the baby.

"I don't know that I ought to go to the monastery, Cara; if either of those two spot me going back there, they'll be sure to suspect."

Cara gave me one of her tragic looks.

"But you promised you'd visit my poor little Giovanetta! Supposing she were to fall sick! All alone in that strange place, oh, I can hardly bear to think of her. I can see that Tom does not approve of my leaving her there, and if you do not keep an eye on her, what would he think?"

"What the devil does it matter what Tom thinks?" I asked irritably.

She opened her eyes very wide.

"Surely you care what Tom thinks? Can you not be extra careful? For my sake? Please? Otherwise Tom will say that I ought to take her away from there. And Agnese has gone back to Italy this morning—I do not know what I should do with her!"

"Oh, very well."

"Thank you, dear Martha!"

Cara gave me an angelic smile and arranged herself harmoniously on a bit of battlement. A man in archer's costume knelt in front of her in a heroic attitude, aiming a drawn-back arrow in the general direction of Ireland. I suppressed a wish that someone would jog his elbow and deflect his aim through Cara's abdomen.

"Shoot!" yelled Jimmy, and the arrow whistled off into the Atlantic. I hoped we were provided with plenty of replacements.

Out of patience, I stomped off to find Mimi, noting out of the corner of my eye that old Dunskirk and his granddaughter had arrived.

"Hallo, what's with you, mon vieux? You look as martial as Brünnhilde—are you cross because I didn't wake you to go out with Abdullah?"

"No, not a bit. I'd never have stood the pace. What time did you get back?"

"About four—that's why I missed breakfast." Mimi gave a chuckle. "It was a riot—I'm sorry, really, that you missed the fun. Our Cara played up to his Excellency for all she was worth, and he thoroughly enjoyed it. She didn't for an instant realise that he sees straight through her—he really *appreciates* Cara."

"I'll bet he does."

"He's coming to take you out for a drink at lunchtime."

"Oh, curse, I shan't be able to make it. I have an errand."

"Can't it wait?"

I thought of little Shrubsole, and Brother Stan expecting me.

"No, it can't really, Mimi; tell his Excellency how sorry I am. Give him my love. I'll explain later."

Unfortunately as the morning drew on, little Laureen showed a tendency to dog me about, asking questions and clamouring for attention.

"What's that book for?" she demanded in her carrying whine.

"I write notes in it."

"Can I have it to draw in?"

"No you can't, but you can have a page if you like."

She received the page, but then said, "*You* draw something."

"Oh, heavens, I can't draw! You ought to ask your grandpa, or Tom," I said meanly.

"Grandpa keeps telling me to run away and paddle, and Tom's always cross. *You* do something."

So I drew a bed, and then she drew a baby in it, and then she bombed her drawing with sand and stones. At least there were no dangerously repressed emotions in little Laureen, I thought; all her feelings were right out in the open.

At half-past twelve I walked along the beach to the concrete jetty. A path ran up from it, through the tangle of sloe and fuchsia and rhododendron, straight to the monastery. It was much quicker to go that way, besides being far less noticeable than if I went round by road. But I'd reckoned without one snag; little Laureen came whining after me.

"Where you goin'?"

"Oh, Hades," I said. "Look, I'm going on an errand and you

can't come this time, so run along back to your grandfather."

"He's talking to that man with glasses and says don't plague him. *Why* can't come with you?"

"Because I'm going to walk very fast—too fast for you to keep up."

She stuck her lip out and began to cry in a put-on and unconvincing manner at first, but as she gathered momentum real tears trickled out.

"Make a lovely big castle on the beach and I'll look at it when I come back," I suggested.

"Grandpa left my spade and bucket at the house, oh, wah-wah-wah, wah!"

"Well, here, for heaven's sake, use a Picnic Soup tin, why can't you, there are hundreds of empty ones lying about, and plastic spoons too."

She was just enough tickled by the novelty of this occupation to relax her watch on me. Seizing the chance, I escaped at top speed, reflecting that if Gareth's upbringing, like Laureen's, had consisted of alternate spoiling and rebuffs, it was not surprising that he had turned out so poorly.

I arrived hot and breathless in Brother Stan's den.

"Good that you are come!" he greeted me comfortably. "Today we have even one more baby, making four!" He looked with pride at his row of orange-boxes, but then added, "Poor little abandoned ones," sighing at the folly and fecklessness of parents who could take such a step.

"Never mind, Brother Stan, they probably get much better care from you than they would at home," I said, fishing one out of its box and disrobing it.

"Aha, already you gain confidence with them. I go, then, to prepare the milk."

He gave me an approving nod and bustled out.

I hadn't really expected to see Lucian again, so when he came slowly into the room it was almost as great a shock as it had been the day before. He looked past me without meeting my eye—how well I remembered that habit—gave a glance full of dislike at the babies, and then moved towards the window where he stood with his shoulders, half turned away.

"Hullo, Lucian," I said quietly, when my heart had stopped thumping. And I went on with my job, trying to be as calm and matter-of-fact about it as possible. When it came to Shrubsole's turn she gave a loud crow, and a positive beam of recognition. I couldn't help hugging her.

"That's the one *you* brought, isn't it?" Lucian said suddenly, startling me so much that Shrubsole nearly slipped out of my grasp. "Is it your baby?" He scowled at Shrubsole, who was absorbedly watching the action of her own toes.

"No, she's not mine," I said curtly. "I wouldn't leave her here if she were."

He went on watching me; I could sense from his silence that he didn't know whether to believe me or not. It had often been like that; he would make some unfounded accusation, often a wild one, and wait for my denials; perhaps he hoped they would convince him of my innocence, but they seldom seemed to.

"Whose is she, then?"

"An Italian girl, a model who's in the films we're making. That's why the baby's so dark-haired. The stepfather is—is hostile, and the mother's afraid of him, that's why she's keeping the baby here."

He made no comment. But when I'd finished Shrubsole and started on another baby he suddenly seemed to relax slightly; he said,

"How's old Balfour?"

I was astonished; old Balfour had been head of Lucian's publishing firm. It seemed somehow startling that Lucian should even remember his existence after seven years.

"He died, a couple of years ago, poor old boy; he fell ill and had to retire early. He wrote me a very nice letter when he retired saying he'd always hoped that you'd come back to take over the firm."

Lucian received this in silence; afraid he'd think it had been intended as a feeler into his state of mind or intentions, I diligently spread lather on a baby's back.

But presently, sounding quite friendly and rational, he said, "Do you like being in advertising, Martha?"

"Yes, it's fun. I meet lots of people and I enjoy that."

"You haven't married again?"

"Not yet." I did my best to sound dispassionate and carefree about it.

He looked down at his hands; giving them a long intent scrutiny as if he'd never seen them before. Lucian had always had beautiful hands, long-fingered and distinguished. They were beautiful still, but callused and rather earthy, the nails ridged and broken from poor diet.

In order to fill the silence I started telling him about the work of the advertising agency, making it as entertaining as I could. He listened intently, sometimes even asked a question or two.

"They are an extremely nice group of people," I ended, "I wish you could meet them," and then felt irritated with myself because I was afraid that my voice had sounded wistful.

Lucian looked up quickly at that; seemed about to speak but checked himself. I heard Brother Stan coming along the passage, singing a snatch of some chant as he often did. Without another word, without looking at me again, Lucian hunched his shoulders and slipped out of the room.

"So!" Brother Stan said, coming in with the bottles. "You have had a nice chat, yes?"

He gave me a blandly inscrutable look, and held out a finger to Shrubsole, who grabbed it with an expression of delighted scientific curiosity.

"Aha, she likes the old Brother, this little one! She is full of intelligence."

"Doesn't take after her mother then," I said. "Maybe her father had a high IQ."

I wondered who he had been.

"Well, it's useful to have brains," Brother Stan said placidly.

The room filled with the sound of contented sucking.

Then he added: "Your husband, he has brains. I think, after seven years, he is wishing to begin using them again."

On the way back to the beach I suddenly found myself smitten with an idea about Bom. Bom, never a good seller even in 1889 when invented, had nevertheless managed to struggle on year after year, slowly losing ground as more palatable drinks were produced, but never quite going bankrupt. Its chief defect was not so much the taste as the repellantly gluey consistency.

This was a difficult point to get across to the makers, since consistency was not something consumers found it easy to be explicit about when completing market research questionnaires. However we had now persuaded 64 per cent of a midland sample to admit that Bom was too thick and 34 per cent that it was too thin—the remaining two per cent thought it was a kind of gravy browning

107

or shoe polish and were eliminated. These results, irrespective of what was said about the taste, did suggest even to Cole and Smiley, the conservatively-minded makers of Bom, that the deliquescence, lubricity, inspissation, or whatever of Bom left something to be desired.

Now it suddenly occurred to me to wonder—would it be possible to make. Bom *foamy*? Could yeast, or white of egg, or CO_2 be introduced, at not too ruinous a cost, so that Bom would rush roaring from the bottle?

Phrases began to fill my mind: "It's the rich, vigorous foam in Bom that does you good—crisp, lively bubbles—so easy to digest— each bubble packed with health-giving calcium and riboflavin— Bom—the only foaming beef drink!" As a selling-point it would be not only unique, but probably unaspired-to by anybody else. No use going too far, of course, till I'd checked the possibilities; but I resolved to send off a memo to Cole and Smiley right away.

My mind was so absorbed in these thoughts—after all, one has to think about work *sometimes*—that I nearly tripped over Cara, who was leaving the beach extremely fast, in the company of Barney Soglow. She gave me a sweet, sad smile.

"Is all *well*?" with meaning emphasis.

"Yes, quite okay. Where are you off to?"

"The camera crews will not work on Saturday afternoon, so Barney is taking me to a horse-show. We must hurry—goodbye!" she called over her shoulder as they ran up the cliff path to the field where the cars had been left.

When I came out on to the beach I saw another reason for Cara's hasty departure: Gareth was pacing about among the dismantled bits of equipment, evidently in search of her. He looked furious, but so repulsively handsome that he might have been expected to climb on to a camera trolley and burst into a pop song with all the lights trained on him. I noticed with surprise that in the short space of time since I had last seen him—less than a fortnight surely?—he seemed to have lost about a stone in weight. Stress and strain over Product X? Over Cara? He was being followed everywhere by little Laureen, who was panting, tearful, and stumbling in her efforts to keep up with him. "Wait for me, Dad! Dad, wait for me!" she kept wailing; for the first time I found her rather pathetic, specially as the only reply she had from Gareth was an occasional "Shut up!"

I had started a tactical retreat when unfortunately Laureen saw me, grabbed hold of my ankle, and croaked,

"Come-see the castle I bin building. You *said* you would."

"It's lovely."

"You haven't *look*ed at it."

While I was hastily admiring it Gareth saw me and pounced.

"Martha! Have you seen C-Cara anywhere?"

"She went off with Mr Soglow," Laureen announced self-importantly. "I coulda told you that—I kept *sayin'*—but you never listen."

"Where did she go?"

"To the horse-show at Camelot."

Gareth's face darkened still more. "The h-hell she did! She knew damn well I wanted to talk to her. I've got to go b-back to town this evening too. *You'll* have to talk to her for me, M-Martha."

"Heavens, Gareth, I can't interfere in your matrimonial disputes."

"Oh, f-freeze that! You'll b-bleeding well have to, if you want to get this j-job finished and P-Product X on the market."

"Cara's doing her parts in the commercials all right," I said. "Very well, in fact—if *you* don't go upsetting her." He gave me a sharp look with his pale eyes, which I ducked by arranging three shells on Laureen's castle.

"*Upset* her? C-ripes," in an injured tone, "what's she d-doing to *me*? Now, l-look, Martha, I'm not joking—either you talk some sense into Cara or this whole operation will be k-kaput—dead—washed up. I'm warning you!"

"You mean you'll persuade your father to take the account elsewhere?" I said hotly. "Oh, that's charming—that's what I call really constructive."

"This campaign means a l-lot to you, doesn't it, Martha?"

"No more than any other!" I snapped. "Naturally I want it to go through."

"Then why the h-hell can't you be a bit more h-helpful? L-look, darling, you've got more sense in your l-little finger than that damn stupid Cara's got in her whole bloody anatomy—let's you and me talk things over and s-see if we can't get something worked out."

He was positively shaking with earnestness; I noticed a film of sweat on his forehead.

"I really fail to see—" I began, but then I thought of old George Salmon with his kind, tired face and his distraught home life; he had been so proud and delighted to get the Gay Gal account, he would be really crushed to lose it. And if soothing Gareth was necessary to keep the account, surely it was my duty to George, who had always been very nice to me? I could hear his voice saying, "For heaven's sake, Martha, a little civility won't kill you. Come down off that high horse."

So, warily and very reluctantly, I said, "Oh, well, all right."

"That's the g-girl! Come for a run in the car."

"Can't we talk here?"

"With half C-Cornwall listening? Not bloody likely! Come on, I've got the c-car up at the top."

I hesitated again, looking for Tom or Mimi to support me. But they, with most of the film unit, seemed to have left already.

"Oh, c-come on, Martha," Gareth said sulkily. "I know you've n-never liked me but there's no need to make it so d-damned obvious. I shan't rape you."

This seemed to make my vague notions of violence or abduction slightly absurd, so I followed him, resolving, however, that if his friends Tigger and Mait were anywhere within sight or seemed likely to join the party, nothing would persuade me to go with them, even if I had to run screaming and conspicuous all the way to the Trelawny Hotel.

"I wanna come too," whined Laureen.

"Well you bloody can't," said her loving father. "Who wants *you*? Go along to grandad—he's over there waving to you."

She began to howl.

"Oh, let her come," I said hastily, feeling that she would be a useful third. Gareth's handsome brow grew black; he led the way up the path to the car field in furious silence.

I was disconcerted to see the Crespina.

"I thought you had an E-type, Gareth?"

"So I have," Gareth said. "It's in town. This is Mait's old heap. He lent it to me while I'm here because I flew down—anyway Mait's got himself disqualified from driving for five years because he knocked down an old biddy on the Hammersmith Flyover." He spoke with respect, as if this were an achievement to be proud of.

"How does he get about then?"

"Oh, Tigger drives," Gareth said hastily. I did not believe him.

"Wanna go in front," droned Laureen.

"Oh, be quiet, you." Gareth thrust her into the back. "Now s-stay there and s-shut up!"

He roared the engine and drove out of the field at a reckless pace, skidding on the mud patches.

"Wanna Chocka-Bloc!" Laureen demanded as we flashed through the village.

"Pipe down!"

"Let me get her one."

"Oh, all right, get her one; get her two if it'll keep her quiet."

I got her two, and a bag of potato crisps, and she retired into a sticky rustling absorption. It was horrific to think what a state the back of Mait's beautiful car would be in, but I hadn't any sympathy for him.

Gareth was a vile driver—showy, bad-tempered, inconsiderate. While I gritted my teeth and hung on to the glove-shelf he rushed us with maniac speed, ignoring speed limits and major roads, through a network of tiny lanes only intended for cart-traffic, and finally emerged on to an open stretch of moor.

Here he stopped and sat in silence for some time, apparently thinking hard, an exercise which he seemed to undertake only with reluctance. I watched him in silent hostility, thinking that with his thick light hair and heavy jaw he looked like the Ace of Diamonds; all ready for a crooked deal too.

I too had been thinking, wondering if it would be politic to tell Gareth that I knew about the unscrupulous attempt to snatch Shrubsole. On the whole I felt I'd be in a stronger position if I didn't reveal my knowledge, because of the danger of giving away the baby's whereabouts.

"Well," Gareth said, turning to give me a long, intimate look, evidently having decided on his story, "the point is this. Cara's fed up with me, for v-various reasons—she says I misled her about the size of D-Dad's firm and the sort of l-life she'd have in England. She's fed up with the flat over the works—seems she was expecting something like a p-penthouse in Park Lane. If you ask me, she only m-married me so as to get to England. So on account of all this she's throwing her weight around, fetched that k-kid over from Italy without a by-your-leave, makes dates with all and sundry, c-carries on as if I didn't exist!"

"Well, if you're both disappointed with each other, why don't you separate? Maybe it was a mistake to get married."

"Oh, I wouldn't want to do that," he said, sounding startled. "No, C-Cara's all right really. She's just got a t-touch of swelled head. If you could k-kind of persuade her to see my point of view ... Well, it's like this actually. You see—" He stalled for a moment, looked at me sideways, and finally said, "You see there's something that happened in Italy—"

Now we come to the crux, I thought.

"Well, it's n-nothing *wrong*, only my father mightn't like it, being a bit old-fashioned in his ideas, and Cara knew about it, you see, and has threatened to tell him—"

"Smuggling?"

"Eh? Well, no—not exactly. It was about P-Product X. There was this young fellow in Savona, you see, a chemist, a chap called Dino Soldati—it was through him I got to know Cara, matter of fact. He'd been her boyfriend but she'd given him the chuck. He worked for the same firm she did and he used to do research on his own t-too. Well, we got t-talking, one time, and he t-told me about this perfume he was working on—"

"Oh, cripes," I said with a horrible premonition. "Not Product X?"

"N-n-no, n-n-not *exactly*," Gareth said uneasily. He was sweating again. "But a bit s-similar to Product X. He gave me a s-sample of it. Well then, you s-see, he died last autumn—"

"Had he patented it? Was the idea really his, or did it belong to his firm?" My mind shuffled through the various unpleasant possibilities that Gareth's scrappy story suggested.

"Oh, it was S-Soldati's own idea. He'd been working on it in his s-spare time. But as he died without registering the p-patent, it really belonged to n-nobody, don't you see? His firm didn't know about it. And as he'd given me a s-sample, there didn't seem any reason why we shouldn't have it analysed and p-produce it ourselves."

"Hm," I said. "A bit shady, but not downright illegal, perhaps."

All the same I didn't like it, and I was sure George would like it even less. In fact he'd be horrified at the possibility that the title to Product X might not really belong to Dunskirks at all, but to this defunct Soldati, or even, conceivably, to the firm he had worked for. Some firms, by contract, had a lien on anything their employees invented. I had little doubt that Soldati's perfume was Product X; that squared with my estimate of Gareth's character. He knew a good thing when he met it, but hadn't the creative capacity to invent something new himself. It also, obviously, accounted for Dunskirks' extraordinary difficulty in matching the first sample.

"Wasn't there a formula?" I said, thinking aloud.

"Not a c-complete one. And, you s-see, Dad doesn't know all this—"

"But Cara does." A lot more things became plain.

"Well, yes. If you c-could tell Cara that I'm prepared to d-double her allowance and help her g-get a good modelling job, which is what she wants—"

"All this to stop her telling your father? Isn't it bound to come out sooner or later?"

Privately I resolved that it should come out right away. The sooner George Salmon heard about this shaky title, and our firm's research section got to work on checking the legal position, the happier I would be. In fact, I decided, I'd ring George about it that very evening.

Gareth turned and gave me one of his burning looks. He had become extraordinarily pale.

"L-listen, Martha! P-Product X means a hell of a lot to me. F-first, it'll really put Dad's t-tinpot little firm on the map—"

"I know, you said that before," I said crossly. "Is it worth going to such shady lengths? If you despise your father's firm so much, why work for it?"

"B-because if I don't, Dad will b-bloody well will it away from me wh-when he dies, to my cousin G-Gavin, who's dead keen to get hold of the business."

That added up. Knowing Gareth, I could see that he was not anxious to let an easy living slip out of his grasp.

"So in the meantime you're trying to notch up the image of Gay Gal and make it something you won't be ashamed to let your friends know you make a living from?"

"Oh, s-stop being so s-sarcastic, Martha! You put things in such a b-bloody roundabout way! If you really want to know, D-Dad was beginning to complain that I d-didn't take enough interest in the firm—th-things were getting a b-bit dicey—so g-getting hold of Product X was a stroke of luck in the n-nick of time—"

"And your father never guessed it wasn't all your own work?"

"You didn't, d-did you? Why should he?"

Why indeed? Doting on Gareth as he did, old Dunskirk plainly believed the lad could do anything, if he would only try. Shrewd

113

though he was in all other ways, he had this one blind spot; I suppose most parents do.

"Daddy," said Laureen.

"Oh, be quiet, you! Eat your damn crisps and shut up, or I'll never take you d-driving again."

She subsided, sulkily.

"Had that chemist—what was his name, Soldati—any family?" I asked suddenly.

Gareth shrugged. "Christ alone knows—he never mentioned any to me."

"I was wondering who'd inherit the property."

A very odd expression crossed Gareth's face—startled, hostile, wary.

"N-now, look, Martha, I asked you to *help*, not to start a lot of b-bloody red-herrings. You just get to work on Cara, there's a darling, will you? It would be your f-firm's loss, you know, as well as ours, if anything went wrong now—"

Suddenly little Laureen, who had been fidgeting more and more restlessly in the back of the car for the past five minutes, announced in her carrying croak that she was going to be sick.

"Here, come along then," I said. "Out of the car, quick!"

"Oh, f-freeze it, now you see what you've l-let us in for," growled Gareth.

But I was quite glad to escape and tend Laureen through her spasms and howls—something in Gareth's cold, suspicious stare had fairly unnerved me.

"Well, Gareth—" I said at last when Laureen, pale and subdued, was once more in the car and we were driving back to Trevann, "I'll do my best with Cara, I'll tell her your offer, but of course I can't guarantee results."

"Yeah, you do that," he said. "I wish to god D-Dad hadn't taken such a fancy to her and roped her in for these c-commercials. If he hadn't she'd never—" He broke off, then said, "You m-make her see that she'll be much better off if she'll play along with me. B-but if she won't—"

"I'm not going to pass on any threats," I snapped.

He suddenly twisted round, grabbed my hand, and looked me intensely in the eye. He was still dead pale and his hair was quite darkened with sweat.

"You're a g-great girl, M-Martha, you know that? I've always been n-nuts on blondes," he added naïvely, "that's why C-Cara took a d-dislike to you. You and I could really d-*do* something together—"

"For pete's sake, Gareth, keep your eyes on the road!" I cried in lively anxiety as we swung half across a bend.

He took me back to the field where I'd left the Admiral; he was going on to the Trelawny to pick up Tigger and Mait. Hearing they were staying there, I was gladder than ever that I'd moved to the farm.

"They're keeping a tag on Cara for you, I gather?"

Gareth shrugged self-consciously. "So what? I do favours for them. If they like to do a few odd jobs for me—"

But it struck me that Gareth was not the stuff of which leaders are made and I wondered if his disciples, like the sorceror's apprentice, had not got out of control.

One way and another, I was glad when that ride was over.

CHAPTER VII

Of course, when I tried to ring George that night, and on Sunday, I got no answer at his flat; he had probably gone to the cottage at Maidenhead which wasn't on the phone. I'd have to wait and catch him at the office on Monday. I thought of consulting one of my colleagues in the meantime, but Mimi had departed to spend Saturday night and Sunday with friends at St Ives, Jimmy had flown back to his ever-loving wife in South Ken, and Tom was nowhere to be found; probably escorting Cara somewhere.

I passed a solitary Sunday; the best part was visiting the monastery, where Shrubsole greeted me with rapture and Brother Stanislas like an old friend. True, the ferocious Brother Lawrence suddenly appeared in the nursery while I was trying to weigh the babies on a corn-scale and snarled so formidably that I nearly dropped one.

"Too many infants, Brother Stanislas! *Far* too many! And what's *she* doing here?"

Mercifully he didn't seem to recognise me as the fallen woman that he had turned out of his kitchen garden.

"She is a voluntary worker," Brother Stan explained placidly. "Very useful, as we have such a large intake."

"You are spending too much time on them. Some other arrangement will have to be made."

"The District Council have found homes for two from next Saturday."

"The Council are an inefficient, slow set of bunglers," growled Brother Lawrence. "Make them take the lot!"

"Oh, not Shrubsole!" I said, aghast, when he had swished out of the room.

"Have no fear, my child. Brother Lawrence is feeling his gout today, that is all. (Also Brother Thomas unfortunately fell asleep during his discourse this morning, which upset him.) Do not trouble yourself; I would not part with my little Shrubsole, no, no!" Brother Stan gave her a loving poke in the midriff.

Presently Lucian wandered in, looked at me sidelong and, as before, opened a hesitant conversation, asking questions about people we had known, my present life—where did I live now? could I afford the rent?—inquiring about current affairs, books, films, music. It was curiously painful and touching to see his absorption in the smallest details—he was like a convalescent savouring the naive pleasures of food, fresh air, and sunshine.

My feeling of strain began to abate and presently I even found myself enjoying our talk—I'd almost forgotten Lucian's extraordinary intelligence, how quick-witted he was at returning the conversational ball; any exchange with him, however simple, kept one's faculties at full stretch and exhilarated like a fast game of tennis.

Brother Stan tactfully pottered in and out, leaving me with a large tub of washing and a slab of yellow soap; I scrubbed as I talked, reflecting that the monastery could do with a washing-machine—not a Midinette, either, but something tough and capacious. I resolved to send them one, then remembered Brother Lawrence's antipathy to electrical devices and decided to send a van-load of soap powder instead. There was something pleasant, however, a kind of virtue in rubbing away at the babies' well-worn vests and pants and little petticoats while I answered Lucian's hesitant questions about the world outside.

Brother Stan presently took his charges out for an airing, and Lucian was noticeably relieved; I'd observed that he seemed to have a nervous dislike of the babies, particularly Shrubsole, whom he could not bring himself even to look at; he held his breath distastefully as she was carried past him.

That was a queer, quiet day; happy really; looking back, I think that it was one of the happiest days of my life.

In the afternoon I went along again and worked through a huge pile of mending for Brother Stan. Lucian reappeared and we talked some more; this time I asked him questions about the monastery; he explained that it was really a self-governing community and that each member held his own beliefs.

"Who makes administrative decisions?"

"We take a vote."

"And cases of real discipline?"

"Well—of course they are very rare. I suppose Brother Lawrence would enforce discipline if it were necessary; he is the Elder."

"Elder Brother is watching you," I murmured. Lucian gave a reluctant, rusty smile, and explained that the usual penalty for behaviour contrary to the spirit of the community was "exposure" i.e. being made to do one's thinking aloud for an hour or two. I could well imagine that to these reclusive natures such a penance would be excruciating.

"Must be tiresome for all the others too," I said. "Does it often happen?"

"Oh, hardly ever; we are all here because it suits us, so we wish to conform. If a member stopped wishing to conform, he would leave."

There was a hesitant sort of silence then, broken only by the hen-like noises of the babies, who were rolling about on a blanket on the floor while I tidied up their beds. One of them, a largish hideous boy baby, whom Brother Stan had christened Noah, ogled Lucian, who looked away hastily. I didn't blame him; Noah was really a repulsive object, far too fat, rolls of it like the Michelin man, and large inexpressive pale eyes, and shiny-bald, as if made of soap, utterly different from my dear little Shrubsole with her dark bright eyes and clear-cut intelligent features.

"Lucian," I said at last quietly. "Why did you join the order like that—so suddenly—without ever letting me know or getting in touch with me?"

At once the folded shut-in expression that I had come to know so well, and to dread, came over his face. His mouth tightened and puckered, the corners twitching back into his cheeks; he looked down and away from me.

"Please, Lucian?"

At last his eyes slowly lifted. They had become bloodshot. Their expression was tortured.

"No no, never mind!" I was appalled at what I'd done. "I'm sorry—I shouldn't have asked. It's just that—I was unhappy about you for so long, not knowing—"

"I had to," he muttered. "I just had to get away."

"Okay, my dear. Never mind. Forget it."

At this moment Noah, who spent most of his life in deep sleep from which he could hardly be roused, and had little bodily control in consequence, rolled over on top of Shrubsole and hit her in the eye with his elbow. She started to yell.

"Here," I said hastily, "just hold her for a moment while I finish tucking her bed;" and then, seeing his look of loathing and instinctive withdrawal, "No, all right, you tuck in the sheet, I'll hold her."

He did it quickly, with face averted, and then hurried out of the room; poor wretch, I thought remorsefully, he's gone off to be sick.

I saw no more of Lucian that day.

Monday began all right.

At nine I rang the office and asked for George, only to hear from Susan that he'd gone to Paris in pursuit of Éloise and would be there two days. Poor old George. There wasn't much point in chasing him by phone about Paris if he was going through an emotional *crise*, so I decided that my worry about Product X would have to wait till Wednesday when we'd all be back in town anyway with luck. Meanwhile we might as well get the filming finished, having done so much.

The weather was still fair, but Mr Tregagle shook his head over the glass at breakfast time and was heard to mutter something about a three-day blow.

When I got down to the beach I had my first glimpse of Cara since Saturday. She looked positively radiant; her mournful Rossetti-madonna demeanour had been laid aside for the moment; she was exchanging vivacious quips with Jimmy and the cameramen. Tom I thought looked strained; when I tried to collar him to tell him about Gareth, he made some flimsy excuse and almost rushed away from me. I stared after him, hurt and baffled, but it would have been undignified to chase him all over the beach if

118

he was bent on avoiding me. And I was overdue for a little talk with Cara.

It took ages to extract her from her group in order to tell her about my conversation with Gareth; impatience and boredom shut down over her like a lid at the first mention of his name.

"Gareth?" as if she could hardly remember who he was. "Oh, heavens, what is he grumbling about *now*?"

"You seemed worried enough about him the other day," I snapped, exasperated by her indifference. "He isn't grumbling, he's offering to double your allowance and find you a modelling job."

A wary look came into her eye; she laughed shrilly.

"Double my allowance? Even so, I could make more money scrubbing floors. And as for a job—I can find one for myself, tell him. He will have to do better than *that*, if he wants to buy me."

"Cara, what the *devil* is all this about?" I said, thoroughly irritated by my thankless role of go-between. "This Dino Soldati—Gareth says you knew him—was he the real inventor of Product X?"

For a moment she was completely taken aback. "Gareth told you about *Dino*? How in the world did you get that out of him? Oh, of course," she added spitefully, "I'd forgotten, he likes to confide in you. You are his ideal of English beauty."

"But Cara, is it true? Did Dino invent the perfume? Because if so—"

"Oh, how should I know?" she said evasively. "What do I know about these chemical matters? *I* was not there when they talked."

"But you knew Dino." Something flashed into my mind, Gareth saying, He died last autumn. What had Cara said about Shrubsole's father? Something about a fire.

"How did Soldati die, Cara?"

A look of real terror came into her face then. "Oh, will you leave me alone?" she hissed. "I tell you, I know nothing about it! I was away at the time, visiting my cousin in Bergamo. When I came back it was all over—I knew nothing, nothing!"

"For god's sake, Cara—" Her terror communicated itself to me. "You mean that the baby's father—"

"*Hush!* There, Jimmy is calling for me and you have made me all upset," she whispered venomously, and darted off towards the cameras. I stared after her blankly, feeling as if I'd tried to light the gas and set off a landmine.

My guess that Soldati was Shrubsole's father seemed, from Cara's reactions, to be dead on target. So then—if Soldati was the real inventor of Product X, who would be his heir? I seemed to remember reading in some court case reported in the newspapers that the Italian laws of inheritance favour the blood offspring even if they are not legitimate—was that why Gareth suddenly turned so hostile when I mentioned heirs? Was it possible that the perfume really belonged to Shrubsole?

No doubt the legal position was frightfully complicated, but it certainly seemed as if Gareth feared such a possibility—was that the real reason for the attempted snatch? And what had he intended doing then? Did he, like Richard III, feel it was better to tidy all possible contenders out of the way ahead of time?

I shivered, suddenly aware that the sun had gone behind a cloud and the wind was whipping the grey sea into white tassels. Tom and Harry Kodor, at the far end of the beach, were conferring anxiously, pointing to a great purple bank of cumulus. Mr Tregagle's predictions about the weather seemed to be coming true. But I was less concerned with the likelihood of a storm than the frightening question that kept coming back, no matter how I tried to push it away.

How *had* Soldati died?

"We'll have to pack it in, Martha!" Jimmy yelled. "Light's going—shouldn't wonder if there's a cloudburst presently. We're going to drive in and see rushes at the Camelot Odeon—coming?"

"Okay, I'll follow you in the Admiral."

I could see that it would be quite twenty minutes before they were ready to start—equipment was being frenziedly packed into the vans. There would be time to nip up to the monastery and tell Brother Stan I'd come this evening instead of at lunchtime. And then, I decided, I must somehow, whether he liked it or not, contrive to get a private word with Tom. He was the most senior representative of the firm available, and developments were getting well beyond me.

I made for the jetty and the cliff path at top speed, and saw that old Dunskirk had just stumped down on to the beach and was standing with a disconsolate air watching as tripods and canvas chairs were folded, and cameras hustled under waterproof covers. I couldn't face talking to Gareth's father just then; in fact, unless my fearful suspicion of his son could be dispelled, I didn't see how I could ever face talking to him again.

Brother Stan was in the kitchen-garden, hastily assembling the babies, who had been put out in their orange-boxes to air among Brother Lawrence's neat rows of leeks. Halfcrown-sized drops of rain were beginning to splash down.

"You are come at the right moment to help, my child!" he greeted me.

I grabbed Shrubsole, balancing her on one hip and her box on the other, turned—and came face to face with little Laureen, whose freckles seemed to start out like tattoo-marks under the hood of an orange rain-cape. She must have followed me up the path.

"Whatchew doin'?" she was beginning, when her pale-blue eyes lit on Shrubsole and she croaked, "Why! That's Cara's baby, ennit? What's *she* doin' here?"

"Oh, good lord," I said. "Here—run back to the beach, will you, like a good girl? And hurry—it's going to pour!"

I might have known that would not work; as was her wont, she took no notice, but followed me tenaciously into Brother Stan's nursery. Physical force was the only thing that had any effect on that child. She watched, scowling, while Shrubsole was resettled.

"What's Cara's baby doin' here?" she demanded again.

"Cara wants her baby to stay here where it's quiet for a while. Tired of you bashing her, I daresay"

"Bet you my Dad would like to know she's here! He ast me on Saturday did I know where she'd got to, an he was asting Tigger and Mait, an' he wasn't half wild cos they didn' know. 'It was your effing notion to pinch her,' he said to Tigger, 'so you effing well find her.' But Tigger didn' pinch her, did he? What did Dad mean?"

"Now, look, Laureen," I said. "Where Cara chooses to keep her baby is none of your business. Anyway you don't want her back at home, you don't like her, do you?"

"No," she agreed vindictively, "I 'ates the little perisher."

"So you just hold your tongue about her, there's a good child—Cripes, there's one of the babies still out in the rain." I ran out to grab it, encountering Lucian in the doorway; when I came back he and Laureen were eyeing one another unfavourably, like duellists.

"Why djou wear that funny black thing?" she said. "My dad

doesn't wear clothes like that. My dad's got a car. My grandad's got one too—and a house at Polneath. Why's your shoes tied up with old bits of string?"

"Come on Laureen," I said, dumping the last baby and grabbing her hand. "You can't stay here, your grandfather will be having a fit, wondering where you are. Goodbye, Lucian, tell Brother Stan I'll be back tonight to give him a hand."

"Wanna stay here," Laureen whined. "Don' wanna go in the rain, wanna stay here with Cara's baby."

Forbearing to inquire into her motives I just said, "Well you can't, so come on," and hustled her down the path. She protested and complained all the way, threatening to tell her dad of the baby's whereabouts. Thank goodness Gareth was back in London, I thought, but Cara had better be warned about this development at once, and Shrubsole moved elsewhere.

Of course there was no sign of Cara when we reached the beach; I launched Laureen in the direction of her grandfather and then cravenly fled off to the Admiral, despite howls of "Where you goin'? Wanna come with you!"

I hoped I'd find Cara at the Camelot Odeon, watching the rushes. But she was not there, nor was Tom.

"Tom said he was going to Penrose Head," Mimi told me when I asked her. "He wanted shots of storm clouds for the Funshine Catering Trades series. He's going back to town tonight so this is his last chance."

"Is he? I didn't know. What about Cara?"

"Gone with him, I suppose." Mimi scowled at me, and then scanned the empty rows of red-plush stalls. "She doesn't seem to be here, does she?"

The rushes were good, ominously good; I watched them with a sick, hollow feeling in my stomach; a feeling that Providence was sneering at us. When the viewing was over we had lunch in Camelot, and then Mimi and I drove back to Trewithian; it took us an hour; the rain was still hissing down, sluicing over the roads and the windscreen in gritty torrents. The Cornish landscapes of valleys and wind-hugged ridges wavered through the blowing cloud like a Japanese print.

"Bad luck on the morris dancers if it goes on like this," Mimi yelled cheerfully.

"Morris dancers?"

"Doing their rum-ti-tum capers at Trevann this evening. Tom

wants to film them before he goes, don't ask me why; I daresay he intends to pass them off as Turkinistan peasants dancing the national hokey-dokey. Honestly, mon cher," Mimi added, "you seem to be only *half with us* these days. It's all these trips to the monastery, I suppose. But I wish you'd keep more of an eye on Tom."

I'd told Mimi about Lucian. Mimi never makes judgments on her friends, but I could see that she deeply disapproved of this attempt to wade back into the past.

"How are things going among the holy orders?" she asked in a noncommittal voice.

"Oh, Mimi, I've no idea. Sometimes I could sit down and howl."

"Well, if you ask me—no, I'll wait till we get back to town. It's all this loathesome rusticity that's depressing you really, I daresay." She looked with disgust at the streaming, ferny banks as they flashed by. "Thank god, two days and we'll be back in civilisation. People in the country always behave like Chekhov characters and it's catching; when you're at home you'll have a better perspective on it all."

"I hope so," I said desolately. I didn't feel optimistic. Return to London seemed to present more problems than solutions. I'd have liked to tell Mimi about Shrubsole, but it wasn't my secret.

"Let's sleep all afternoon," Mimi said, "And then go back to Camelot and have the best dinner money can buy."

"I ought to work. That piece about Faireweather frozen scrambled egg. 'You add one egg, we add three, And it's fluffy Frambled egg for tea!'"

"Shucks."

"And what about the morris dancers?"

"Let the natives watch their antics."

I parked as near the farm door as I could and we darted through the downpour like herrings. Mrs Tregagle greeted us commiseratingly and said there was a fire in the parlour; I thought again how lucky we were to have found this pleasant place; the management of the Trelawny Hotel would have gone to the stake sooner than lit a fire in April.

"There's a package for you, Miss Whatname," said Mrs Tregagle, who could never master the uncouth foreign syllables of Dourakin. "Postman was proper sorry it got so soaked, but 'tis a long pull up from the village and turble weather. No van on this round, see, now in't that a shameful thing? And slugs do eat letters if so be as you do put'm in the box at hill-foot, app'n if you want to send a letter 'tis best to give it to postman—"

"Never mind," said Mimi cheerfully examining her sodden package, "this is only jewellery; a wetting won't hurt it. Abdullah said he was going to send me a brooch as a souvenir of our gay evening on Friday, Martha." She peered at the postmark. "Hm—Camelot. I've a lowering feeling that it will be a Cornish pisky, I don't altogether trust his Excellency's taste when he gets away from his oriental setting. I'd really rather he'd waited and sent some trifling bauble from the palace treasury. However, here goes." She cut the string and began pulling off layers of soaked outer wrappings while Mrs Tregagle hurried away murmuring about kettles and tea.

"'Tisn't a jeweller's box," I said, "it seems to have held Snolump Sugar. Maybe he got his aide to parcel up some oddment from the bits and pieces of personal jewellery that he carries round with him; that ruby he fixes his turban with, for instance."

Mimi opened the box and disclosed a nest of wood shavings.

"Unpromising," she said, poking about. "There doesn't seem to be anything here. I thought it felt uncommonly light. D'you think the equerry forgot to—blast, what was that?"

Something smallish and black had darted out of the shavings as she turned them over, and run up inside her loose silk sleeve. With a cry of disgust she shook her arm violently. "Ugh! Get it off me! What was it, Martha? Did you see?"

"Looked like a spider," I said. "Hold still, I'll see. Hold *still*!" But she had clapped her other hand to her elbow with a yelp.

"Damn it, it's bitten me, Martha! What is it?"

She shook her arm again; this time the creature fell out of her sleeve and I swatted it with a newspaper. It was a black spider, about as big as a pea, plump and shiny.

"What a foul thing," said Mimi, rather pale, rubbing her arm as the spider kicked in its death-throes. "Do you suppose that's Ibn Abdullah's idea of a joke; because if so it isn't mine?"

Using a knitting-needle I probed through the shavings, but there was nothing else in the box. No card, no letter.

"Surely his Excellency wouldn't have sent it," I said. "Do you think it's some crazy mistake?"

"I'm sure that's not an English type of spider." Mimi tried to suck two small red spots which had appeared on her forearm.

"I've certainly never seen one like it. There's a red mark on its front like a figure eight."

"Never mind its bloody stomach." Mimi furiously rubbed her arm. "Where do you think it came from? It's given me the dickens of a bite—feels as if someone had stuck in a red-hot needle. Whose writing on the wrapper?"

"Hard to say—it's printed, and the ink's all blotched with wet anyway. Hey, though—good lord, Mimi, I don't believe this was meant for you at all! No, if you look close, it's addressed to Mrs Dunskirk, not Miss Dourakin. It was intended for Cara!"

"Are you sure?"

Mimi snatched the brown paper from me and stared at it. Then she said bitterly,

"Oh that's charming! That's just fine! One of Cara's brushed-off lovers, I suppose, sent it as a memento, and *I* have to undo it! Isn't that just like life? Cripes, won't I give Cara a piece of my mind when I see her. Pleasant friends she must have! Or do you think it's a husbandly attention from Gareth?"

"Mimi, I don't like this a bit," I said, looking at the bites on her arm. They were swelling up and getting redder every minute. "I think we'd better get you to a hospital and ask them to pump some anti-spider serum into you."

"If they've got anything of the kind down here in the outback," said Mimi gloomily. "All right, let's go."

However Mrs Tregagle came in just then with the tea-tray. She was horrified to hear of Mimi's mishap; I tried to be reassuring and suggest that it was just someone's notion of a light-hearted practical joke and that I was only taking Mimi to hospital in case she happened to have an allergy.

"Well, I niver did tell! Drastic goings-on!"

We stayed for a cup of tea; I had a vague notion it might be good for shock. The delay was a mistake, as it turned out; halfway back to Camelot, Mimi nearly collapsed. Frightful waves of pain rushed up and down her back and legs, her jaw clenched, she came out in a cold sweat, all her muscles bunched and quivered as if she were being given electrotherapy. Most of the time she was speechless with pain, fighting it grimly, but between spasma she gasped out vituperations against Cara in a mixture of English, French, and Russian that filled me with admiration; I never knew Mimi had such a wide command of gutter-language. Luckily I found some aspirins in my handbag and she crunched them down

125

while I drove flat out. To distract her, and because I felt she was owed some explanation, I gave her a brief history of Cara's relations with Gareth and what had been going on in the last few days. Her eyes snapped ominously, but by the end of the journey she was in too much pain to comment.

Camelot Hospital was at the top of the town, between the prison and the lunatic asylum, approached by a hairpin bend on a one-in-three gradient. We went up it as if it were Brands Hatch; I pulled up the old Admiral on its haunches and half carried Mimi through the first door we came to, into a highly polished passage that smelt of Jeyes' Fluid.

A fierce old girl in dark blue, with a starched muslin bonbon-dish atop, shot out of a door labelled MATRON and snapped,

"No visitors till seven-thirty!"

"We want the casualty department," I said.

"Not open till six." The old girl's badge said MATRON too.

"But this is urgent. My friend's been bitten by a spider."

"I'm going to vomit," said Mimi, and did, all over the polished granite. She looked terrible, white and gasping.

"A *spider*? Never heard such nonsense. Intoxicated, more likely."

Outraged by our behaviour the matron coldly indicated a little casualty room and then retired. Mimi collapsed on to a canvas-covered trolley. Looking round rather desperately I found some red blankets, which I put over her, and a bell, which I jammed my thumb on. The sound shrilled emptily through the hospital's afternoon hush, but after a long time it brought an elderly doctor.

"Och now, what's all this stramash?" he inquired in a strong Glasgow accent. "Ye're taking me away from the ante-natal clinic, I'll have ye know."

When I started to explain he checked me with an uplifted hand, saying, "Bide now, till I see for masel'," and proceeded to examine Mimi, who was having one of her speechless spells, jaw clenched and eyes almost starting from their sockets.

"Withoot a shadow of doot yon's a perforated ulcer," he said at last, cheerfully prodding Mimi's abdomen, which was as rigid as lignum vitae.

"It's no such thing!" I snapped. "She's been bitten by a spider. Do you have any spider serum here?"

"Lass, are ye oot of yer wits? She has every symptom of a perforated ulcer."

"Except the ulcer!"

"I'll have ye know I've been in medicine forrty years," he was beginning when I said, "Look—those are the bite marks on her arm, and here's the spider!"

Thank god I had brought it in its box; I could see old McSporran practically reaching for his claymore to carve Mimi open. But at sight of the spider his eyes lit up.

"Lassie, ye're richt! Yon's a bonny Black Widow Spider, I do declare! Now isn't that an unco' thing to find in Cornwall? In all the years since I retired frae the Caledonia Star Line I dinna recall ever coming across sich a thing in these pairrts!"

He turned the dead spider over lovingly.

"Have you any serum?" Mimi brought out between her teeth.

"Och, dinna fash yersel, lass—deaths frae Black Widow bite are verra rare, verra rare indeed—" he sounded regretful about it. "Forbye ye should chance tae have a weak hairrt, o' course."

Finding this did little to encourage his patient he relented and admitted that though there was no spider serum actually in the hospital he could have some flown over quite fast, either from Plymouth or Bristol, where bird-eating spiders in fruit boats were among the expected hazards. He gave Mimi a massive shot of sedative and went off to telephone.

"Hey, Martha—" Mimi muttered, just before she conked out under the drug.

"Yes, what?"

"Maybe you should go back and discuss this little contretemps with Cara? Warn her or something?"

"Maybe I should," I said doubtfully. "I was thinking that. But what about you?"

"I'll be all right." She made a stoic grimace; then her eyelids flickered.

"Okay, I'll be back at visiting time."

Her muscles clenched as another shock of pain hit her, and she muttered, "B-b-ring some b-b-brandy and my b-best night-dress...."

On the long drive back to Trewithian I considered the situation. Either Gareth had come to the conclusion that mere financial inducement wouldn't be enough to stop Cara telling old Dunskirk about the shady antecedents of Product X or else—which seemed more probable—Tigger and Mait, ashamed of their first failure and tired of what they considered Gareth's shilly-shallying, had decided to go ahead under their own steam again. The print on the wrappings of the parcel, blotched and indecipherable though it was, had a look of the note in the pram. And the affair had all the hallmarks of Tigger's fourth-form brand of humour. But where, I wondered, would Tigger or Mait get hold of a Black Widow Spider? At a sick-joke shop? Then I remembered Mait's freelance overseas trading connections—very likely he did a roaring business importing tarantulas, rattlesnakes, and Russell's Vipers; such an occupation would fit him to a tittle.

When I got back to the farm the rain had diminished; a wild ragged sunset was painting the moors red. All the branches of the windblown trees glittered and dripped.

Mrs Tregagle was waiting anxiously to hear how Mimi did. I explained that she was staying in hospital for observation and her eyes popped.

"Well, fancy, all for a liddle bite! Int that a mazing thing now! Oh, miss, while I think, a gentleman asked to spake to you on telephone while you was gone, so I said as how you'm taking Miss Whatname upalong to hospital."

"Did he give his name?" I asked. "Did he leave a message?" I hoped it would be Tom. But Mrs Tregagle shook her head.

"Nay, he niver did that."

Disappointed, I collected a case of needments for Mimi, and then went over to Cara's room in the cottage and knocked.

For a wonder, she was there. She opened the door and said, "Oh, it's you," in a flat voice, as if she had expected someone else.

"Cara, do you know this writing?" I'd brought along the parcel wrappings and showed them to her.

"N-no," she said slowly. "Why?"

"This parcel was addressed to you, Mimi opened it by mistake—the writing was wet and smudged, you see, it looked like her name. There was a poisonous spider inside and it bit her."

Cara went yellowish-white and her eyes vibrated.

"Gareth!" she whispered.

"Tigger or Mait, I think actually. Gareth's back in London, isn't he? This was postmarked Camelot."

"Well, Gareth told them to do it, of course."

"Cara, it's time you went to the police with the whole story."

She looked at her watch distractedly.

"Yes—later—perhaps. I must think!" She was evasive—shaken

128

still, but recovering, beginning to think of ways and means, to be angry.

"Come, Cara, you can't let Gareth treat you like this, kidnapping, threats, sending you spiders—it's criminal. He mustn't be allowed to get away with it."

"Indeed he must not!" she agreed vindictively. "And I shall not let him have the formula whatever he does."

Then she clapped a hand to her mouth and stared at me over it in alarm.

"Formula?" For a moment I couldn't believe my ears; I just gawped at her. "Cara, do you mean to say that *you have the formula for Product X?*"

She tried to retract, furious that she had let it slip out, but in the end I made her confess.

"Yes, of course Dino was my lover! He gave it to me—well, all right, if you like, when I heard he had died I took the paper, I knew where he kept it, in the Bible, and naturally I had a key to his room. Has not his child the right to it?"

"You've had it all along? Has Gareth ever seen it?"

"No, Dino would never show him. Dino was so proud of that perfume! He let Gareth smell it once, and then of *course* Gareth wanted to buy the formula. But Dino would not part with it, he only gave Gareth a sample."

"Cara, how did Dino die?"

She looked frightened again.

"His lab caught fire and he was burned to death. I was not there, I was in Bergamo. No one can say I had anything to do with it! But the carabiniere said it was an accident; this lab was only an old shed really."

"Was Gareth there at the time?"

"Oh, how should I know? He says he was not even in Italy then, but on the yacht with Mait. And so then, much later, he comes to Savona again and asks me to marry him. I am unhappy about Dino's death, I am glad to marry Gareth and come to England—specially when he tells me how rich his father is, what a big firm Gay Gal—eccolo, I believe him!" She clutched my arm, to force belief into me.

"You didn't know then that Gareth was trying to make Product X himself?"

"Of course not! Never! How should I, I never go into the factory? Not until that party at your office did I know—you were wearing the perfume, you remember? And I smell it then, and then I know!"

Cara had fainted at the party, I remembered; was this because she suspected for the first time that Gareth might have had something to do with Dino Soldati's death?"

"So you think the formula really belongs to Shrub—to your baby?"

"But of course!" Opening her eyes wide. "She is Dino's child! There is a law called patria podesta which says that an illegitimate child belongs to its father—besides, we were to have been married."

Gareth told a different story, I remembered; he said Cara had already left Soldati—thinking Gareth a better match?—however that probably would not affect the legal position.

"Well for heaven's sake go to the police. And get yourself a lawyer. Tom will find you one, I'm sure; if your case is as good as that you have nothing to lose."

"Yes," she said, but she sounded unconvinced.

"Where's the formula now?"

"Oh, not here," quickly.

"Is it somewhere safe?"

"How do I know you will not tell Gareth if I tell you? There is something else with it that he would much like to have—" She bit her words off suddenly and said again, "How do I know you will not tell him?"

"Oh, come now, Cara, is it likely? Haven't I worked like a beaver to hide the baby's whereabouts from him?"

That reminded me of my second purpose. "Cara, Laureen followed me to the monastery this morning. I'm afraid she knows the baby's there."

"*Dio mio*, then she must be moved, at once! Why did you not tell me? There is not a moment to waste, that little diavolessa tells Gareth everything to gain his goodwill."

"If Tom's driving back to town tonight," I said, "you could go with him and take the baby too. Mr Tregagle says we're in for a three-day blow, so filming's probably out tomorrow."

Cara was evidently thinking hard.

"Who could she go to in London, though? I know no one, I have no friends—"

"Tom," I said. "Tom's sister Rosemary has a lot of children, I daresay she wouldn't mind—"

"Martha, you are a genius!" For the first time Cara sounded genuinely friendly. "She will not object, this Rosemary? No, Tom will persuade her, he will do anything for me, I know. And you will go with him, Martha, to take the baby?"

"*I?* But don't you want to go?" I was thunderstruck.

All Cara's airy falseness returned, she opened her eyes innocently and said,

"But the filming? Suppose it should clear up? And tomorrow is the last day, I should be there in case, no? Oh, I think it would be far better if you went with the baby, Martha. And you are so fond of her you will do this thing for me? Please! I entreat of you!"

There were points to the plan, certainly. I knew that, if the weather should by any chance improve, they could certainly manage without me on the last day's filming, which would be given over to odds and ends; Jimmy could cope. It was all Avalon; Picnic Soup was finished. But what passed my understanding was why Cara should want to stay in Cornwall when Tom was going back to London.

"Make haste!" she urged. "Tom plans to leave straight after this morris dancing—you have little time to lose. Dear Martha, you are so *kind* to do this for me! And listen—I tell you a thing! I tell you where to find the formula. It is best *you* should have it—for the baby! You are so clever, you know about the laws and what should be done."

"Where is it, then?" I said doubtfully, not too keen to be told. Knowing where it was seemed a hazardous responsibility.

"In a Dottore Spock baby book in our apartment over the factory. Here, I give you the keys—for outside, for inside, you see?"

"Oh, very well," I said. "But if I escort the baby up to London, you will have to take Mimi's things over to Camelot hospital. They said she'd have to stay there at least two nights. You can take the Hillman and go to the police at Camelot at the same time."

"Yes, yes, I do this—only hurry!"

She almost pushed me out of the door; I noticed that she kept looking past me as if she were expecting somebody.

By the time I'd explained my plans to Mrs Tregagle and gone to the monastery it was dusk outside and dark inside. Brother Stan greeted me with his usual affability, but seemed greatly upset when I told him that I must take Shrubsole away at once.

"What is this, my child?"

I explained the danger contingent upon her stepfather's finding her, and his kind old face crumpled in distress.

"But this is ill-advised! This must not be! The little Shrubsole tonight has a grippe—a cold from the rain this morning—she sneezes twice, it will be a folly of the most calamitous to take her into the cold night air! This I cannot with my conscience easy permit. Surely it is not necessary? The monastery is big, we can hide here here. She would be safe—surely she would be far safer than carried helter-pelter about the country?"

"No, truly, Brother Stan, I must take her—her mother is really scared, she has asked me to. You can wrap her very warmly, absolutely cocoon her—and Mr Toole's car has a heater. She'll be all right, I promise."

I didn't entirely believe that her state was as serious as he made out—she had looked thriving and healthy enough earlier in the day; it was probable, I thought, that Brother Stan's strong partiality for Shrubsole was weighing with him and he didn't want to part from her; I sympathised, because I knew I'd feel the same myself.

"I will take good care of her," I said as he hesitated. "And I'll be coming back tomorrow or the next day, so I can tell you how she stood the journey. Please, Brother Stan!"

He still seemed unconvinced, but said, sighing,

"Wait here, then, till I fetch her. They are all asleep." Placing his finger to his lips, he tiptoed away up the dark passage and reappeared, after a fairly long interval in which I had time to grow anxiously impatient, with a cocoon-like bundle, wrapped in a large piece of blanket.

"Fast asleep!" he whispered. "Take care not to awaken! And whatever you do, make sure the head remains covered. Night air may be injurious. Here is also a basket with spare clothes and a bottle of milk."

"I'll take care, I promise. And bless you, Brother Stan—I don't know how to thank you for all your kindness. But I'll be in touch very soon." I hesitated, and then, on an impulse, said, "Is Brother Lucian about?"

"I regret he has gone out, my child. He went with the donkey, to fetch paraffin from the village."

"Will you say goodbye to him for me please?"

"Of course, my child." Brother Stan seemed strangely troubled—he did not linger, but, hastily muttering his usual blessing, shut the door on me. I felt sorry for him—evidently he minded the parting from Shrubsole very keenly.

It seemed like old times to be carrying her across country again, I thought, as I hurried along the field-path which was a shortcut to the village. She had put on weight in the monastery.

By the time I reached Trevann it was full dark but I was in no doubt as to the whereabouts of the morris dancers; from several fields away their cheerful piping could be heard and as I drew near I could see the dark, clustered group that had assembled to watch, forming a ring on the road outside the pub. Tom's car was parked on the verge, I saw with relief; I worked my way along the outskirts of the crowd, looking for him, and had gone about half-way round when a voice greeted me.

"Aha! Do I not see before me the lovely but elusive Mees Gilroy?"

I nearly jumped out of my skin.

"Good heavens, Excellency, what are you doing here?"

"I am driving past when I see the dancing, so I stop to study your strange English customs," the Emir said happily. "This is a fertility rite, yes?"

"Oh, almost certainly," I answered at random, peering about for Tom.

"And connected in some way with the production of your excellent Morris cars, no doubt? I think I have heard that the morris dancing is very prevalent in Oxfordshire, where your good Lord Nuffield has his manufactury?"

"Just a coincidence, Excellency, I think; I've an idea the name really means Moorish."

"Ah, so, indeed: Not a local custom of Cornwall, then?"

I was obliged to admit that this particular brand of morrisers had their origin in St Johns Wood. Nobody could deny their enthusiasm, though; dressed in the traditional white, with bells, ribbons, and straw hats, they capered, waved kerchiefs, and cudgelled one another with uninhibited vigour. An accordion and a flute poured out jiggety bouncy music, and a man disguised as a hobby horse pranced about, snapping at the crowd when they pressed in too close, exchanging repartee with the girls and making them squeak, accepting coins in the horse's pelican-like jaw.

"Brought along the bubba to see the fun, then, missis?" the horse inquired, stopping by me. "Or is that your weekly wash? Spare a penny for the poor morrisers?"

"Allow me, please!" The Emir gallantly slipped a fistful of half-crowns—he probably never carried any smaller denomination—into the snapping pouch.

"Blimey? Who have we here, the old Aga Khan?" the hobby-horse yelped, starting back in exaggerated astonishment. Heads turned our way.

'Forgive me, Excellency," I muttered. "I have to go and speak to Mr Toole over there."

I'd just caught sight of Tom on the far side of the ring. Sidling away among the spectators I made for him, pulling the blanket well forward over Shrubsole's head. Luckily she seemed to be in a profound slumber; even the rousing shouts of "How do you *do*, sir!" failed to disturb her, as the dancers cuffed at one another's heads amid approving laughter from the crowd.

The scene was intermittently lit by car headlights and the flash-bulbs of the local paper's reporter; Tom had his movie camera and was filming the hobby-horse which had crossed the ring and was gambolling obligingly in front of him. Avoiding the lights as much as possible I sneaked up behind him and twitched his sleeve.

"Tom. Tom! Here a minute. I want to speak to you."

His face, as he turned and saw me holding the baby, went blank with astonishment.

"Martha! What on earth are you doing here with—"

"Hush!" I hissed. "Listen—when do you start for London?"

"Right away. In fact I might as well leave now—I've nearly run out of film."

"Well, will you take me, please—and *this*? I'll explain on the way. It's rather urgent."

"Yes—all right. I'll just collect my other camera—go and get in, the car's not locked." Blessed, reliable Tom! He was as matter-of-fact as if I'd asked for a lift to the post office.

I started back round the ring. At that moment the crowd broke away, with squeals of mock fright, as the hobby-horse did another of his rushes. A flash-bulb popped right beside me; in its tinselly white glare I found myself face to face with Tigger and Mait. Their startled faces swung towards me as the light died. For a moment I was stunned by this unexpected piece of ill-luck, my feet seemed fused to the ground—why hadn't I ever considered that they might be watching the morrisers?—then sense came back to me and I bolted into the shadows.

"Hey!" That was Mait's voice. "Hey! You! Come back here!"

"Stop her!" That was Tigger.

Without looking round, I made for Tom's car at top speed. This seemed no time for dispute—my sole aim was to get Shrubsole into safety. Mercifully Tom had reached the car first, and was leaning out of the driver's window to say goodbye to the hobby-horse and thank it for its co-operation.

"Quick!" I muttered. "Let's go! I'm being chased."

"Stone the crows!" said the hobby-horse. "Are the Cornish wolves that bad, then?"

Tom opened the rear door nearest to me; I whipped in, avoiding a largish crate on the floor. As he started the engine, Tigger and Mait came pounding up; with a magnificent gesture the hobby-horse lurched round and swept them both into a grotesque embrace; the whole group fell over sideways, giving us time to accelerate and get clear of the crowd. As we roared up out of the dip and over the ridge of the headland, all the noise and light fell away behind us like a dying rocket; in two minutes we were out on dark moor, with nothing but white road streaming ahead and blackness at our back.

"Please hurry," I said. 'They may have the Crespina."

Tom obligingly accelerated; the needle crept up towards ninety. But he said, "What *is* all this, Martha? Is that Cara's baby you've got there?"

"Oh, Tom, such a lot has been going on."

"Begin at the beginning," he said. "If we're presently going to be followed and held up by Gareth's undesirable friends, I might as well know exactly where we stand."

So I told him about Laureen's following me to the monastery, and the Black Widow Spider, and that Soldati, the baby's father, seemed to have been the real inventor of the perfume. This was news to him, apparently; I hadn't been sure if it would be.

"Why don't we go to the police?" he said.

"I hope Cara's doing just that. She said she would. I'd rather concentrate on getting the baby to a safe place."

"Where are we taking her?"

"Cara wondered if your sister Rosemary would have her for a little while?"

"Indeed?" Tom's voice was dry.

"I suggested the idea," honesty compelled me to add. "Do you think Rosemary would mind?"

"Oh, I daresay one more among six won't make much odds. You really think this is necessary?"

"Heavens, Tom, I'd rather be safe than sorry! A baby's so—so vulnerable. After all, babies die every day just of natural causes—what do you think this one's chances are worth if Gareth decides to use her as a pawn—or those two sorcerors' apprentices?"

"Gareth wouldn't really do anything, surely?"

"I'd as soon not take the chance," I repeated.

"No.... It was crazy of Cara to bring the child to England," Tom said, half to himself, as he smoothly guided our headlong course down an extended curving slope and up the other side. Pale creatures, sheep or deer, fled away from the long lances of the headlights, jumping the uneven, tufted banks. A smell of wet gorse, sweet, like peaches, drifted in through the air vents.

"I don't think Cara intended to bring the baby to England. It was because her cousin got tired of looking after it." Then I bit my lip, in case he thought my remark sounded derogatory. It was not easy to talk to Tom about Cara. But he didn't seem to have noticed, he was brooding over the legal position.

"I should have thought Cara's title to the formula is quite a good one, while the child is a minor—but she ought to see a lawyer, of course. I wonder why she didn't raise it earlier?"

"Didn't realise it was valuable till she found out that Dunskirks were making it, I suppose."

"Yes.... I shouldn't imagine old Dunskirk would wish to go to court about it; he'd probably agree to settle and lease it from her, as it's rather discreditable to Gareth. Of course the crux of Dunskirks' claim would be how Gareth came by his sample, and whether he could prove that Soldati intended him to have either the formula or a regular supply of the perfume."

"I'm pretty sure he didn't, from what Cara said—" I stopped abruptly and looked over my shoulder. "Tom." My voice sounded thin and queer. "There's another car coming behind us at an awful lick. Do you think it's Tigger and Mait?"

"What if it is?" Tom said. "You really think they mean trouble?"

"Cara was scared enough. And think of the spider...."

"Yes," he said reflectively.

He applied himself to his driving. We were climbing a great rampart of moor in a series of tremendous zig-zags; the road seemed to push at us over the car's bonnet, first on one side, then on the other. I was glad we were in Tom's Rover and not the poor old Admiral. At last we slipped over the head of the hill and temporarily lost sight of our pursuers—if they were pursuers—who were still a couple of miles back.

We went on in silence. I was scared, and felt a constraint with Tom; not knowing how deeply he was involved with Cara made it difficult to discuss the situation. Tom, too, seemed reluctant to talk. The baby, thank god, was still fast asleep. I had huddled into a corner with my feet curled up to avoid the crate—dud Picnic Soups, I now remembered—and laid her out along the back seat as comfortably as I could.

"I can see the headlights again now; they're drawing up a bit," I ventured presently.

"Yes." Tom sounded detached, almost absent. "There's a right fork about a mile farther on, to Excombe; I'll turn down it and see if they follow."

In a couple of minutes the signpost flashed up to us and Tom swung right; craning round I presently saw the pursuing lights do likewise. We were leaving the moor now and the road, through a deep valley, was too winding for us to be able to do without head-lights.

"They're still behind us," I said presently, after we'd passed a number of turnings.

I was really frightened; I wished I had something, anything, in the way of a weapon. I was embarrassed at the idea of suggesting this to Tom, who would probably think I was being hysterical. In the end, for lack of better, I sneaked out one of the Picnic Soup cans and put it in my pocket where it felt comfortably heavy. At least it would be something to throw....

"Hm," Tom muttered. "There's another very empty stretch of moor beyond Excombe; going at this rate they'll probably overhaul us there. Not too good. I'd better drop you at Ex-combe."

"Drop me? You mean, *leave* me?"

"There's a station," Tom said calmly. "And the ten o'clock train from Doynen Road stops there; I know, because I travelled up on it last time and I remember looking out. It's—" he lowered his watch-wrist into the dash light—"five past ten now, the train ought to get there in fifteen minutes or so, you'll catch it nicely. Got any money?"

He was perfectly matter-of-fact, but the thought of being abandoned appalled me. It had been so restful leaving the decisions to Tom.

"Suppose they follow me?"

"Don't you see, they'll follow the car. If I'm on my own I can lead them a tremendous chase, without you two to worry about." Tom sounded as if he relished the prospect. "If they ever do catch up with me and discover you're not on board, you'll be well away."

"But Tom—"

"Don't fuss, darling. Be ready to nip out fast, now. Excombe's a small place, you shouldn't have any trouble finding the station. Here we go...."

The 30-mile restriction sign loomed up, and Tom slowed, correctly.

"Mercy, Tom, they'll be on our heels before I can get away if you slow down to this pace."

"It's all right," he said equably. "Look what's ahead."

The village of Excombe had a pleasantly wide street of timbered, thatched cottages, made postcard-pretty now by the watery moon. The inhabitants were all snug indoors. But in front of us a long file of heavy transport lorries rumbled slowly through, taking advantage of clear night roads.

"We'll get in among them," Tom said. "Lucky we overtook them here where the road's wide. It narrows farther on. In among them it'll be easy to shed you inconspicuously."

He swept alongside the lorries and slipped into a gap ahead of the last three. Then, rounding a curve in the main street, we passed a road repair sign and saw ahead the red blink of traffic lights.

"It's that temporary kind," I groaned. "They always take for ever to change."

"Then you'd better get ready to jump while we wait," Tom said calmly.

But luck was always on Tom's side—another reason that made me feel bereft at the thought of leaving him. The lights changed just as the front lorry reached them, and we passed through almost without having to slow. Two of the lorries behind us got through, and then the lights changed again.

"Right, my dear, now's your chance, while our friends are stuck behind the lights. The station must be over to the right somewhere and you've got ten minutes to find it. Have a good trip, you and your kidnapped baby."

He sounded as if he were smiling; for the first time some of the familiar warmth came into his voice.

"But Tom—where shall I see you?"

"At Rosemary's, of course. Or—this is a slow train as far as Reading—I might even get to London before you. If so, I'll meet you at Paddington. You get there about half-past seven in the morning. Run, now—"

He slowed the car to a crawl and opened the rear door without even turning his head.

I gathered up the warm bundle of baby and slipped out as we passed a road entrance on the right-hand side. Its shadows received me—but not before I'd had time to read the sign *Station Avenue* on a garden fence; Tom's luck was still in charge.

CHAPTER VIII

Excombe station was tiny, and dead as a doornail at this time of night. I found the booking-office door locked, but a wicket-gate led through to the line. An up train was signalled. Wandering along the unlit, chilly platform I heard a lugubrious whistling and tracked it to a small duty room at the end of the station. Here, in the dim light of an oil lamp, a lad of nineteen or so was sitting with his feet on a table, reading. He was pale and spotty. The title of his book was *The Mastery of Sex*. He seemed very surprised to see me.

I asked for a ticket to Paddington.

"Oh, you don't want no ticket," he said. "No sense in going along and unlocking the office just for that. You can get one on the train if you want." He yawned, looking at his watch. "She'll be along in a coupla minutes."

"Any chance of getting a sleeping compartment, do you suppose?"

"Shouldn't think so," he said unhelpfully, and returned to his book.

Presently the long lighted snake of train appeared with dramatic suddenness round a bend in the valley, grew larger, and came hissingly to a halt. Spotty Muldoon slouched out and threw a sack of mail on board. I found a couple of coaches of sleepers but the attendant told me politely that all his berths were occupied.

"There's plenty of empty compartments up the train, though, miss. You can lay out along the seat and have a nap; nothing to stop you."

He was right: the train seemed to be only a quarter full. I found an empty non-smoker and tied my blue scarf over the light to dim it. Shrubsole, still carefully muffled, slept peacefully. I began to wonder if Brother Stan could have given her an aspirin or one of his herbal concoctions—would he do such a thing? She slept on, relaxed as a roll of putty, when I laid her on the seat, turned towards the back with a fold of blanket, burnous-like, over her head. I was uneasy, though, that a sudden jolt of the train might roll her off, so I didn't lie down myself but cat-napped in a corner opposite her, or tried to; sleep was a long time coming.

Bom, tiddly om-Bom, the train said. Bom for Mom. Bom for Tom. Herbert Lom drinks masses of Bom. Nourishing Bom, so rich and green, nastiest drink you've ever seen.

Why had Cara given the impression that she was expecting somebody? She kept looking nervously out of the window; was it just general apprehension?

Perhaps she was afraid that Tigger or Mait might turn up, to see the results of their practical joke with the spider. Could it have been one of them who rang Mrs Tregagle? Who was it that took and died, With a spider inside her inside? If at first you don't succeed, try, try again. Bruce and the spider. Was it wise to have left Cara in Cornwall? But she *wanted* to stay. Surely she'd be safe enough there, if Tigger and Mait were chasing after us? Supposing they caught up with Tom.... Bom-tiddly-om. Yo, ho, ho, and a bottle of Bom. Nom d'un nom, buvez Bom. Gareth was in London, that was one comfort. London was a big place, no need to run into him. So long as I didn't follow Cara's suggestion....

That certainly was a vile train. It never maintained a constant speed for more than five minutes at a time; it would stop, jerk, hiss, clank, drag itself whiningly up some tiny incline, rush with manic enthusiasm down an equally tiny gradient on the other side, and then come to another of its grinding halts before it ventured on the long, slow, cautious, rumbling progress across a viaduct. The west country has innumerable steep wooded hills and valleys which the railway creeps and leaps through as best it can; after a couple of hours I felt the contours must be recorded in my brain like an electroencephalogram. And the train stopped. How it stopped! It stopped at junctions, crossings, tunnels, stations large and small, signal-boxes, and wayside halts. At each legitimate stop milk-churns were rolled and rattled on and off; at the illegitimate ones, driver and guard shouted unintelligible tidings to one another along the coaches. When Tom told me it was a slow train he made the understatement of his life. From time to time I looked out and noted with small joy that we had reached Taunton, Bristol, Bath or Swindon, where we spent a couple of lifetimes and I longed to nip out and get a cup of tea, but didn't like to leave the baby or risk disturbing her slumbers. After Swindon a dismal, rainy twilight trickled in; the Thames valley looked dank and suburban, an outer valance of London. Thank God, I remembered, Tom had said the train became fast from Reading on; crawling at this pace through the Ealings would be enough to squeeze one to the verge of suicide.

At Reading there was another interminable stop while mail was hurled about; then the train, starting suddenly, worked up into a brisk, purposeful rhythm; no more dawdling through milk-stops, we were bent on getting to London in time for breakfast. We rattled along, lurching; people hurried up the corridor, looking for empty carriages, being thrown from side to side. The baby stirred and stretched a sleepy arm.

And it was at this moment, glancing up, that I saw a man pause by the door of my compartment, look through the glass, and start to slide the door back. He was joined by a second. Tigger. Tigger and Mait.

"Well, well," Tigger said facetiously, as Mait moved in behind him and shut the door again. "I'll never believe them again when they say it's quicker by rail. Ask me, we could have driven to Monte Carlo, time this poor old train was dragging its weary way from Excombe." He nodded at Mait and said, "That was a nice hunch of yours, Maitie."

I felt sick; my mouth was as dry as a dustcart and my heart did horrible banging thumps which I felt must be visible to the naked eye.

"You don't seem very pleased to see us, darling," Tigger said. "Aren't you flattered that we chased your train all the way here just for the pleasure of getting in with you?"

"It's a public train," I said. "There's nothing to stop your getting on it."

"Hey, listen to her!" Tigger was thoroughly enjoying himself. "I know what it is, she's worried about the boy-friend. No need to fret, darling, there's nothing more the matter with him than a smashed wing; he'll live to fly again."

"Cut out the witty stuff, Tigger," Mait said shortly. His country-club tones jarred on my nerves even worse than Tigger's thin facetiousness. "She's not amused by it and it bores me."

"Thank you," I said.

"Oh, all right, very well." Tigger was affronted. "In that case we'll just relieve you of the kid and be on our way, take our unsavoury selves out of your high-class proximity." He leaned down to pick up the baby.

"Don't you dare!" I snapped. "Touch that baby and I'll have the communication cord half way across the carriage."

"Ah, now, darling, take it easy." Tigger eyed me warily. "We don't want to have to get unpleasant, do we, Maitie? But we will if we've got to, make no mistake. Now or later."

"You must be mad!" Anger began to overcome my fright. "How can you possibly hope to get away with this? Clear out of my carriage."

"We've just as much right to be here as you, dear. As you said, it's a public train."

"You've no right to touch that baby."

"Ah, now, that's a matter of opinion," Tigger said. "She ain't yours, is she?"

"Her mother asked me to look after her."

"Can you prove it? Got anything in writing?"

Heavy official steps came along the corridor. Doors had been opening and shutting. Over Tigger's shoulder I saw a brass-buttoned dark-blue-clad figure reach our door and slide it back.

"Tickets ready, please!"

"Oh, thank goodness you came along," I said to the guard with inexpressible relief. "These men are annoying me. Will you tell them to leave me alone, please?"

"Here what's all this?" the guard said disapprovingly. "What are you doing to the young lady?"

Mait leapt smoothly into the breach. "The young lady's giving you something of a false impression, I'm afraid," he said in his plummy bonhomous voice. "For reasons best known to herself she chose to abscond with the baby of a friend of ours and we've just caught up with her."

"That's a lie!" I said indignantly.

"Abscond—? Here, this'll be a police matter, this will," said the guard. "I'll have to report this when we get to Paddington, nothing to do with me. *In* the meantime, I'd better have your names and addresses. And your tickets, please."

Tigger and Mait produced tickets from Reading. I said,

"I haven't one, I'm afraid. I got on at Excombe."

I could see this made a very bad impression. The guard looked at me suspiciously.

"Will you tell me how much it is, please?" I dug out some pound notes. But he ignored them.

"You *say* you got on at Excombe?" I nodded. "How do I know that's the truth? How do I know you haven't come all the way from Penzance? You did ought to buy a ticket before you board the train; that's the regulation. I'll have to report this; travelling without paying the fare is a prosecutable offence, you know."

"For heaven's sake! I would have bought a ticket, but the clerk at Excombe said it wasn't worth opening the booking office."

That didn't go down well either.

"I'll have to get my book and make a full report of this occurrence," the guard said. "Don't any of you ladies or gents leave the compartment till I return, please."

He stomped off, leaving me thoroughly uneasy. Outer London was all around us now; we couldn't be more than ten minutes from Paddington. I could foresee sessions at police stations, and Gareth, as the baby's blameless stepfather, being summoned to give evidence. Tigger and Mait were were evidently of the same opinion, for they arranged themselves smugly on the seat facing me; Tigger set up a frightful tuneless whistling.

The baby began to cry.

"Oh, do shut up!" I snapped at Tigger. "Your whistling's enough to make anyone yell."

He didn't look at me. His face suddenly fixed in a curious grimace; he was staring at the baby, which at that moment kicked off the blanket and would have rolled to the floor if I hadn't made a quick grab.

"Now see what you've done, coming in and kicking up all this disturbance."

I up-ended the baby to put her to rights, and received the shock of my life.

It wasn't Shrubsole.

For a moment my mind did a dotty cartwheel through improbabilities—had I put her down somewhere, picked up someone else's baby, left Shrubsole on the bench at Excombe station? Then, frantically scanning the infant I held, I recognised the shiny, unprepossessing features of Noah, who, wakened from a healthy night's sleep, was lustily yelling for his breakfast.

Somehow or other, whether by mistake or on purpose, Brother Stan had contrived to give me the wrong baby.

I have never seen such a glazed look as appeared on Tigger's face.

"Hey!" he said, nudging Mait. "*That's* not the kid we're after. Cara's kid had lots of black hair, and black Eyetie eyes. It was smaller, too; nothing like the size of that one."

"Are you sure?" Mait eyed Noah doubtfully.

"Poz. Hers was a real little Wog. This one ain't nothing like."

"Furthermore," I said, seizing my chance with both hands, "if, as I now gather, it's Cara's child you want, I can assure you that you're on a fool's errand. Her baby is a girl; this one's a boy. Do you want proof?"

"No—no," Tigger said, getting up hastily. "Never mind, sorry you've been troubled and all that. Come on, Mait, let's beat it before old Whiskers comes back raring for a session with the law. In present circumstances it would be pointless."

"Now we've got to go all the way back to bleeding Reading to pick up the car," I heard Mait say sourly as they left the carriage.

"Well, whose bright idea was this? Ask me, she's done you proper."

Tigger looked back at me and grinned.

"Dunno how you fixed it, darling, but I take off my hat to you, I do really. You couldn't have worked it neater if you'd been bred up in the con business."

When the guard came back he looked about in a puzzled way.

"Where's the two as wanted to lay a complaint?"

"They discovered they'd made a mistake," I said coldly.

My relief at getting rid of Tigger and Mait was so great that I was able to take a much firmer line with the guard than I had before. By the time I'd scolded him for the behaviour of the

Excombe booking-clerk and for the way defenceless females had to suffer from assaults and unpleasantnesses while travelling on his train he had become quite humble and was glad to give me a receipt for the single fare from Excombe to Paddington, in return for which I kindly promised not to report the clerk for dereliction of duty.

At Paddington I was pleased to see Tigger and Mait running like mad for a Reading train. I hoped they'd get caught travelling without tickets. There was no sign of Tom, though I waited for ages, praying that he would turn up. The thought of him was like a jarring ache under all my other worries.

At last I went into a callbox and rang Rosemary. It wasn't easy; Noah, dismayed at all this change from monastic routine, had started to yell and thrash like a possessed thing. But I was gaining confidence now in handling babies; I tucked him grimly under my arm and held the receiver as far from his bellows as possible.

"Hullo?" I heard Rosemary's voice, rather puzzled. "Hullo—I say, what's going on?"

"Rosemary? This is Martha, Martha Gilroy. I say, has Tom rung you?"

"Why Martha," she said, sounding pleased. "No, he hasn't, should he? I thought you were all skylarking down in Cornwall."

Tactfully she didn't inquire why I was ringing her at eight ack emma and six-inch range from a persecuted baby.

"I hoped he might have got back by now," I said. "If he does ring, can you tell him I'm all right?"

"Of course," she said, sounding more puzzled than ever.

"And, Rosemary—"

"Yes?"

"Can I possibly come and see you? I've got—I've got a baby with me—"

"I thought perhaps you might have."

"It's not mine. I'm looking after it for someone, but I haven't much in the way of baby facilities at my flat—"

"Do come," she said cordially. "Come to breakfast. Are you at your flat now?"

"No, I'm at Paddington. You're a lamb; I'll be along as soon as I can."

Rosemary had a big house on Wimbledon common; I'd been there once with Tom. I took the underground to Waterloo which completed poor Noah's demoralisation; the escalators and tube-trains gave him the screaming hab-dabs. However he was slightly pacified by Brother Stan's bottle of milk, cool, but still acceptable. On the suburban train down to Wimbledon he took another of his coma-like naps; it was clear, now, why I'd had such a peaceful night.

Rosemary greeted me placidly, gave me coffee, and dealt with Noah in a way that put both Brother Stan's and my amateurish efforts to shame. I wasn't very well acquainted with her, but liked her—she was plump and rather untidy, with short dark curling hair; not at all like Tom in appearance but sharing his reposeful attitude to life. Her large old house was littered, comfortable, full of bright, unusual colours. She had started in to be a painter, but decided to put her career aside until the youngest of her children reached the age of five, and meanwhile diverted her creative energies into decorating her house and making clothes for her large brood. When I first arrived, children seemed to be everywhere, hopping, scrambling, and crawling, but presently two boys, aged five and seven, disappeared to school, two maternally-minded twin girls of four took charge of Noah "the lovely new baby" with cries of joy, while the youngest pair, aged two and six months, were put into cots and slept peacefully.

"May I use your telephone?" I asked Rosemary, while this operation was going forward.

"Of course, help yourself."

I felt I must warn Cara straight away that Shrubsole, because of Brother Stan's extraordinary mistake—how *could* he have done such a thing? could it have been on purpose?—was still at the monastery. After some delay I got through to Trewithian Farm; Mrs Tregagle's daughter-in-law Lily answered the phone.

"Could I speak to Mrs Dunskirk if she's not out filming? It's Martha Gilroy here."

"No, she's not out filming, Miss Gilroy—" Lily sounded thoroughly bothered. "Raining cats and dogs it is, anyway. But Mrs Dunskirk isn't here! Nor I don't know where she *can* be! She never told me she was going to stop out, but when I went to call her this morning, her things was all there but her bed hadn't been slept in and there wasn't a sign of her! We didn't know what to think!"

"Oh my goodness!" All sorts of sinister possibilities suggested themselves. "Did anybody come to call for her, do you know?"

"I couldn't rightly say. You've all been coming and going up to

146

the farm such a lot these last few days—Nobody came this morning, that I do know. But about last night I couldn't say."

"Has she taken my car?"

"The Hillman? No, that's right here in the yard."

Worse and worse. What could have happened to Cara? I didn't like it at all.

"I think you ought to tell the police."

"Did we?" Lily sounded doubtful. "You don't think she might have gone off with a friend, like, and stopped the night?"

"Well, she might, perhaps—" Barney Soglow? "But you'd think she'd have rung up to say. She might have been in an accident. I'll tell you what, ring her father-in-law at Polneath—" I gave her the number—"and then, if he thinks it would be sensible, ring the police. I'm so sorry you're having all this trouble."

"That's all right, miss. I'm glad you rang up. We didn't know what to do for the best."

I rang off and sat biting the telephone pencil and worrying. One of my anxieties was that, if Tigger and Mait were now heading back to Cornwall, they might have the wit to realise that Shrubsole was still there. But did they know where? How far would Laureen have spread the news by now? Did her sphere impinge on that of Tigger and Mait? How could I warn Brother Stan, I wondered, and blasted Brother Lawrence for his reactionary attitude to the telephone.

In the end I sent Brother Stan a telegram: Wrong package received from you yesterday, please keep right one carefully, and hoped it would put him on the alert without arousing too much attention.

"Now," Rosemary said, coming in and sitting down with her elbows on the kitchen table among the wreckage of breakfast for eight. "My curiosity will hold out no longer. Do tell me what this is about. Have some more coffee."

So I gave her the gist, and she listened wide-eyed.

"Honestly!" she said. "It's like something out of James Bond! What are you going to do now?"

"I suppose I'll have to take Noah back and swap him for Shrubsole as quickly as possible, if you're sure you won't mind having her for a bit?"

"Not a bit, my dear, the girls will be thrilled, won't you, honeys?" she said to the twins, who bustled in just then to find a different variety of rattle to tempt Noah with.

"I wish Tom would ring up," I said miserably. "I'm worried to death about him too. And there's poor Mimi stuck in hospital. Really I'd better get the first flight back to Cornwall and find out what's happened."

"Oh, don't you bother your head about old Tom. He always falls on his feet," Rosemary gave me a shrewd look. "You know, you're just about dead; your face is the colour of Camembert. Why don't you get a couple of hours' sleep and take an afternoon plane back? I promise to wake you if any crisis occurs. The spare room's up at the top of the house where the children don't go, so you can have a real rest."

She was right, I knew. I could hardly keep my eyes open. I let myself be shepherded upstairs to a cool room with a pleasant view of London gardens; Rosemary had hardly drawn the curtains and left, shutting the door behind her, before I fell on the bed and sank into a trough of sleep.

When I woke, evening sun was slanting between the curtains; I shot off the bed in a fright, thinking I must have overslept horribly, but at that moment Rosemary came in with a cup of tea.

"Oh, you're awake," she said. "I let you sleep on because Tom rang at ten—"

"Oh, thank goodness! What happened to him? Is he all right?"

"Yes, he's all right, relax! Drink your tea. I told him what had happened to you and he said to give you his apologies; it wasn't his fault that he got caught. Apparently not long after he dropped you some young ass on a motorbike shot out of a side road without stopping and crashed into his wing. While Tom was phoning the police and an ambulance from a nearby house, the men who were after you came along, evidently got from the girl in the sidecar the fact that you hadn't been in the car, and guessed that you'd caught a train somewhere; Tom said they went blazing off before he could get out. And since then—well, you know what ages it takes making statements to the police, and he had to get his buckled wing pulled clear of the wheel and make sure the Rover was safe to drive, and inquire about the boy."

"Is he all right otherwise?"

"Only concussed, the silly young fool. It was all his fault."

"No, I meant Tom."

"Bump on the shoulder and cut by flying glass, otherwise unimpaired." Rosemary chuckled. "And he's got a superb shiner— the girls were most impressed."

"He's *here*?"

"Got here about one, so I put him straight into Phil's bed; he's going to sleep till half past seven and then he says he's prepared to drive you back to Cornwall. He did say it was rather careless of you to have collected the wrong baby, but perhaps all for the best as things turned out."

"Do you think he ought to drive me back?"

"Don't see why not," Rosemary said placidly. "You can take spells with the driving, can't you? He seemed quite anxious to return as a matter of fact."

"You told him Cara was missing."

"Yes."

"I wonder if I could have a shower?" I said.

"Of course, my dear. First on the right."

While I was showering my mind worked feverishly on the problem of Cara's disappearance. Could Gareth have had anything to do with it? One obvious step was to discover his whereabouts; as soon as I thought of this I grabbed Rosemary's terry robe, ran downstairs, and rang the Gay Gal factory. I got Miss Edwardes, old Dunskirk's secretary, just on the point of going home, and asked to speak to Gareth.

"I'm sorry, Miss Gilroy," she said. "He isn't here. I found a note from him this morning—he'd had an urgent call from his father and flew down to Cornwall on the last plane yesterday evening."

Oh. "Would you happen to know if it was anything about the Avalon filming?"

"I don't think it was," she said. "Something personal, I think."

So Gareth was in Cornwall, and probably Tigger and Mait too, by this time. We couldn't hope to get there before them. And if Gareth should happen to pay any attention to little Laureen....

Suddenly it struck me that there was one way in which this wholesale absence from London could be turned to account. I began putting on my clothes again at lightning speed, with hands that shook slightly. I was sick with fright, so the only thing was to make all possible haste and get the job over as soon as possible. Besides, I wanted to get away before Tom woke because he would be certain to disapprove; Tom was a very law-abiding citizen.

But after all, Cara *had* given me the keys.

And we badly needed a bargaining factor.

I ran down to the kitchen and told Rosemary that I was going to fetch something from my office, collect a change of clothes from the flat, and would be back by seven.

"Take Tom's car, why don't you? You'll never get a taxi round here at this hour."

"That's a stroke of genius."

The Rover was outside with a badly dented wing. Rosemary sneaked the keys out of Tom's pocket and came out to see me off.

"Poor Tom," I said, "he'll think twice before he comes to my rescue again."

"Nonsense, it's good for him," Rosemary said calmly. She started to add something, checked herself, and finished, "Besides, he enjoys it. Don't be late now. I'll have a meal ready for you at seven."

Driving across south London was easy enough at that time of the evening; the main flow of traffic was north-south. It took only fifteen minutes to get to the office, where I left some Frambled egg copy and picked up a batch of Midinette proofs that needed correcting. Then I called at my flat for a torch and change of clothes; then I drove back to Wimbledon.

Here I paused. I didn't want to involve Tom in any way in the felonious enterprise I was planning, so I left his car up at the top of the hill, on the Ridgeway. I couldn't park near the High Street; roadworks were going on, there was a trench, with trestles and red lanterns. At last I found a gap. It would be easy to find the spot when I came back because there were a couple of those huge wooden drums like giant cottonreels that they use for electric cable. By now it was nearly dark, and spitting with rain, which suited me; the less visibility the better, I felt.

I locked the car. I'd stopped near the top of a little alley, Ridgeway Passage, which ran down towards the railway; judging it ought to bring me out near the Gay Gal factory I set off down it, using my torch because it was dark and too narrow to qualify for more than one street lamp, half way down.

My guess proved correct: I crossed Worple Road, found a continuation of the alley on the other side, and came out opposite the factory gates. They were shut, but one of my keys unlocked a wicket-gate. If there was a night-watchman he wasn't about.

I went up the fire escape and through old Dunskirk's flat. Even with Cara's permission (for what that was worth) I still felt hideously guilty. Using my torch, because I wasn't anxious to attract attention to my presence, I tiptoed upstairs to the younger Dunskirks' apartment.

I'd never been there before; it was revolting, as I would have expected, ankle-deep white carpets, and lots of wrought-iron-work, and tables with thick bumpy glass tops, and Botticelli reproductions with icing-sugar frames; my torchbeam picked out these and other features as I prowled about looking for a bookcase among a wealth of stereos and cocktail cabinets.

There wasn't a proper bookcase, only a tiny revolving affair with a few chemical textbooks and *No Orchids* and the AA handbook for 1958. But I presently unearthed Dr Spock's manual on baby and child care from a pile of women's illustrated magazines on the bedside table in Cara's glass-and-satin-and-sheepskin bedroom. I whirled hastily through its pages, found a sheet of paper with some scrawls on it, and tucked it into my pocket.

Then I tiptoed down two flights of stairs to the lab.

The place still seemed quite deserted. I paused at every step and listened; because if someone found me in Cara's apartment I did at least have my excuse ready, and the keys; but there was no excuse for what I was going to do now.

Not a sound anywhere, except a car pulling up several blocks away; I crept on.

It had struck me, that, while I was in the factory, it would be stupid not to try and get hold of another sample of the original Product X, if any were left, as we had long ago finished our small bottleful. We could take it to an independant perfume analyst and get an objective report on it, which would be necessary in any legal inquiry. My only doubt was, could I remember where the stuff had been stored? I vaguely recalled old Dunskirk pointing it out to me in a big black glass carboy that must have held about five gallons; presumably this was Soldati's entire supply which Gareth had pinched after his death and somehow ferried back to England by legal or illegal means. I imagined Gareth would be quite capable of faking up bills of sale and lading if put to it.

The familiar cloying violet scent of the perfume department enveloped me cosily as I slipped through the double doors from the main lab. One thing: no sleuth could detect a woman's presence here by her perfume, I thought, feeling my cautious way round the walls to the windowless closet where essences and large containers were housed.

As I passed the fire-exit I was inspired to unlock it and pocket the key in case of emergency. The whole building seemed empty, dark, and silent, but I had little stomach for this enterprise; I felt horribly uneasy.

Once I was in the store-room with the door closed it seemed safe to switch on the light and conduct a hasty search among the forest of different containers that were lodged in there, higgledy-piggledy. I saw forty-gallon steel drums, and great oriental-looking glazed earthenware urns, leather barrels, all sorts of kegs, firkins, and flagons; at first the task seemed hopeless since many of these bore no more identification than some inscrutable hiero-glyphic. Then in a corner I found a dusty glass carboy in a wicker basket, labelled simply X, and above it, on a shelf, ranks of little green and brown sample bottles marked X_1, X_2, X_3, X_4, X_5—witness to Gareth's fruitless attempts to reproduce the original. Two or three of them had the mark X without a numeral, so I grabbed one of those and put it in my bag, feeling more burglarious than Bill Sykes ever did. Triumph! Then in a hurry back to the door, where I switched off the light and waited a moment. No sound. Opening the door inch by inch I crept out; I moved perhaps three or four steps towards the fire-exit and then froze—I'd felt a puff of cool air from my left, I heard a faint sigh as the double glass doors leading to the main lab swung open and shut.

Somebody else had come into the room. Somebody was stand-ing there in the dark, just inside the door maybe, motionless, listening—somebody who, like myself, had no wish to switch on the light.

Who? Surely not the nightwatchman?

Along to my right the glass-paned fire-door was visible as a faint blur of slightly lighter darkness. It was too far to make a bolt—there were things in the way, I knew, but couldn't remember exactly what: stools, crates, a heavy balance-scale; there would be too much danger of falling headlong.

I began to glide stealthily sideways.

A whisper from near the door stopped me. It said, "Cara? Is that you? Cara?"

For a moment I was more startled than afraid. Why should anybody expect Cara to be there?

"It's no use playing hide-and-seek, darling, I can hear you breathing," the voice went on gently. "Anyway the old guy on the gate said he'd seen a young lady go up the fire-escape and let herself in, he reckoned it was Mrs Dunskirk."

I was wearing a headscarf, and the light was bad; even so, he must be remarkably short-sighted.

I cut my breathing down to a minimum and crept on, inch by inch. From somewhere across the room there was a faint sound of movement; the speaker was coming slowly towards me.

"Are you listening?" he said. "You might just as well answer—I know it's you. You got scared, didn't you, when we sent you the spider? Too bad it bit the wrong gal, but plenty more where that came from. Mait's got a pal who breeds them. Versatile, isn't he? You were going to run off with your gentleman-friend, weren't you, but you couldn't bear to leave without helping yourself to a sample. By a funny coincidence I had the same idea.

"That was a neat trick of yours, getting the girl to lead us astray with the dummy kid, but if I've got you I don't need the kid, do I? Here we are all cosy and no one within earshot. The deaf old boy downstairs is swigging char in his little hut; anyway he knows me. And it would take more noise than an H-bomb to fetch him.

"You know what I want, don't you? I want that formula you're hiding. Oh, I know women; I know you've got it on you, tucked in your corsets most likely. If I'd been Gareth I'd have had it off you long ago. Old Gareth's too soft. He's finished, you know that? Too much has come out now that should never have happened in the first place. Christ, he didn't have to *kill* Soldati; the young fellow would have parted for a good enough offer and a bit of moral pressure; we could easy have made it hot for him over the drugs he sold on the black market. But you can't trust old Gareth; bull-at-a-gate, that's him, soft when he ought to be tough and runs amuck just when he ought to be diplomatic. He's gone blinding down to Cornwall again to talk round his old dad, but he's missed the bus, hasn't he? Because little Tigger guessed you'd be calling in here before you left. Gareth doesn't really know how to handle women, they make him nervous, but I'm not like that. Just hand over that formula, darling, and then you can go your way and I'll go mine."

All this time he had been slowly advancing and I had been slowly shifting sideways, inch by inch, feeling my way, until I was only eight feet or so from the fire-exit. But now, unfortunately, my groping right hand slightly displaced an enamel tray balanced on top of a stool. Tigger heard the sound and took a couple of quiet steps in my direction.

"Don't try to take off that way, darling," he said in a mild,

153

reasonable tone of voice. "Because I've got a little bottle of sulphuric acid here, la vitriola, you know, parla inglese?—it would make a nasty mess of your pretty complexion. No more modelling jobs, and the gentleman friend mightn't like you so well if you'd only half a face."

My scalp tingled. Could he possibly be speaking the truth? The rational part of me doubted it. But he might have picked up a bottle in the main lab. Though it might equally well be menthol or ethyl cinnamate, the trouble was I wouldn't know till it was too late.

Acids terrify me—the sour smell of them, and that white choking vapour they give off, horridly potent—*evil* looking—the thought of acid on one's face, in one's eyes, turns the spine to water....

"Hey, Tigger," I whispered. "What are you going to do with the perfume? You can't use the formula once it's known to be stolen?"

I kept my voice down, with a vague feeling that as long as he thought I was Cara, I had a sort of tactical advantage over him.

"Do?" he said. "There's plenty I can do. There's plenty of parts of the world where they haven't heard of Dino Soldati. Or of Dunskirks. And before that I'm going to use it to lever a little cash out of old Dunskirk; reckon he'd pay up quite handsomely to keep his precious son's name out of the courts. Quit stalling now, darling, just hand over that bit of paper."

Martha, you're an abysmal fool to have come here. You might have known something like this would happen, and what *do* you think Tom will say when he hears?

The thought of Tom's fury somehow heartened me. My fingers felt protectively for the paper in my jacket pocket, and on the way encountered something else—a tennis-ball-sized cylinder, the can of Picnic Soup. Good heavens, I'd had it on me all the time and never thought of using it. I turned it over in my fingers, feeling for the little triangular foil flap.

"Tigger," I murmured, "You're making a mistake, you know."

"Oh no I'm not," he said. "I know you're planning a walk-out on Gareth. I know who with, too. I've had my eyes open down there in Cornwall. So, all right—good luck to you. I'm not standing in your way, providing you hand over. What use is a formula to *you*? You can't make scent. So why be obstinate?"

The can of soup in my pocket had been growing hotter and

hotter ever since I'd peeled back the flap, until it was almost too hot to touch; I judged the ultimate point of safety had come. Easing it out of my pocket I slung it like a hand-grenade in the direction of Tigger's voice; there was a splendid splashy crumping bang, and a strong smell of hot lobster bisque. Tigger made a muffled noise and hurled something at random but I'd snatched up the enamel tray off the stool and, using it as a shield for my face, I darted for the door. He didn't try to stop me; I supposed he was wiping hot soup out of his eyes. Serve him right, I thought vengefully, locking the door behind me.

The rain was coming down quite hard now, and the iron treads of the fire-escape were slippery as glass, but I hardly noticed; I shot down like a lamplighter and round the corner of the building. I'd got halfway across the asphalt forecourt when I saw the Crespina parked by the gate. Mait was standing on the off-side, chatting to the nightwatchman. Thanking providence for rubber-soled shoes, I slid quietly up on the near side. I was just passing them when there came a yell from a first-floor window:

"Mait! Stop Cara!"

"Cara? Where is she?" Mait called back, bewildered. I heard Tigger shout something else as I ran out through the main gate, which had been opened for the Crespina. A door slammed and I heard the engine start, but that didn't worry me; I nipped straight across the road and into the alleyway. He could never drive up there, it was far too narrow.

In a moment, though, I heard footsteps coming after me; I wasn't clear yet.

The only thing that consoled me, as I hared up that dark little passage, was that for once I hadn't the handicap of carrying a baby. I would have given a lot for a couple more tins of lobster bisque, though; with the hysterical part of my mind that functions all the faster when things are going wrong, I thought up a testimonial campaign:

Mrs Jones of Llandivwlli always keeps a can of Picnic Soup under the counter of her sub-post office in case of bandits. "Just the soup for the job," she says, "and on the days when no bandits come it makes a tasty supper dish for my hubby and me." Voice over: Bang-on Picnic Soup! A can a day keeps the bandits at bay. Have a go with Picnic Soup!

Meanwhile my faithful legs were toiling up the hill and my lungs were opening and shutting like Harrods' doors at sale-time;

155

I began to worry obsessively about getting into Tom's car. Where had I put the key? In my purse or my wallet? And was the lock in the handle of the door or under it? And did the same key fit both door and ignition? My mind had gone blank, I couldn't remember, and I very much doubted if there was going to be time to find out before my pursuer caught up with me; I could hear those heavy purposeful footsteps gaining on me, only twenty yards back. It would be Mait, I thought with a sinking heart; the skinny Tigger, when not armed with sulphuric acid, I thought I could have dealt with.

Bursting out into the Ridgeway I ran slap against one of the big wooden cable-drums. It had about half its cable on and rocked alarmingly, top-heavily; I grabbed both rims to steady it—the thing was taller than me, about seven feet in diameter. Inspiration hit me then like the apple hitting Newton, and I screwed the drum round by its huge bolts, rocked it even farther, once—twice—and sent it bowling down the alley into the darkness below. There was a crash and a yell—I didn't wait to hear what happened, but flew to the car, found the key, opened the door, started up, and was away without even noticing the process. I never did discover where I'd had the key.

Just to be on the safe side I drove off towards the Kingston Bypass, circled round half a dozen blocks till I was sure no one was after me, turned back into Wimbledon High Street, and, ten minutes later, pulled decorously to a halt in front of Rosemary's house. After all, there was no possible reason why they should think of coming here.

It was exactly ten minutes to seven.

Rosemary let me in and said, "Tom's in the sitting-room. Make him give you a drink. I'm just dishing up a sort of high tea—shan't be a minute. Phil's away, so I'll eat with you."

Philip, Rosemary's husband, was an economist who seemed to spend most of his time on fact-finding missions to places like Tristan da Cunha and Tierra del Fuego, possibly because his home was so overrun with small fry.

I went into the sitting-room, which looked untidy and peaceful, with wooden bricks and dinky toys strewn about the carpet. Tom was standing in front of the fire with a glass in his hand and a thoughtful expression. He had a noble black eye.

"I borrowed your car. I do hope you don't mind," I said, and held out the keys.

He extended a hand—and then stopped, sniffing.

"What's that on you?"

Looking down at my left lapel I saw a long dark smear of oily fluid.

"Oh, heavens! Sulphuric acid." Then I sniffed it and said, "No, oil of peppermint."

"You keep a vat of peppermint at your flat?" Tom eyed me suspiciously, squinting between his puffed eyelids.

"What's that you're drinking? Whisky? May I have some please? No," I explained, as he moved to the drinks tray, "I went down to the Gay Gal factory. Cara gave me the keys and told me where she'd hidden the formula—"

"*What?*" Tom spilt the best part of a glass of Scotch over a battered pink orlon bear. "You mean to say that *Cara had the formula?*"

"Yes, didn't you know?" I was interested to see that Tom was quite as surprised as I had been at this bit of news.

"Of course I didn't! So that's why Gareth's been harrying her! Nothing to do with jealousy of the baby."

"Fetching over the baby merely added fuel to the fire."

"Why did she tell you where she'd hidden it?"

I'd rather wondered that myself; I hadn't expected it.

"Perhaps it was a sort of insurance," I said reluctantly. "Whatever happened, she didn't want it to get into Gareth's hands, and she knew I'd look after Shrubsole—the baby's interests."

"How do you mean, whatever happened?"

"Tom, I'm worried to death about Cara! You know she's missing—never came back to the farm last night? Gareth's down in Cornwall too—he went down last night, Miss Edwardes told me. If Cara went on taunting him and holding out against him—last time I saw Gareth he seemed frightfully nervy and unbalanced—"

"Aren't these rather lurid fears?" Tom said. His tone was sceptical, but I could see him thinking about what I had said and not liking it either.

"I don't know, Tom. I honestly think Gareth's capable of flying right off the handle if he can't have what he wants. He's been Daddy's cherished boy for so long—and now he risks losing the whole thing."

"We'd better get back to Cornwall fast, then, and make it plain to him and old Dunskirk that it's all up with marketing Avalon until its origins and ownership have been properly established."

157

"That ought to be sobering," I agreed. "Do you think that's what George will say?"

"I know. I rang him up at his flat twenty minutes ago; he's back from Paris with Eloise in tow."

"Oh, thank goodness!" I said with heartfelt relief. "*Dear* George, I'm so glad. You told him the whole thing?"

"More or less. So if you've got the formula—how *did* you come into contact with all that peppermint, by the way?"

"Oh, just a minor mishap," I said airily, but grinning to myself at the thought that for once Tigger had received more than his just deserts. "It's of no consequence."

"Well, where is this bloodsoaked formula?"

I pulled out the paper.

And it said: Total 30 ounces. 6 ounces in 5 bottles or 7½ ounces in 4 bottles. 15 ounces evap. milk, 15 ounces water, 3 tablesp. gran. sugar or 6 tablesp. Dextrin and Maltose prep. 5 drops crystalline Vit. D. 50 milligrams Vit. C.

"What in heaven's name is that?" Tom said.

Rosemary came in at this moment and read the paper over my shoulder.

"Goodness, what a *pother*," she said. "Breastfeeding for me, every time."

I began to laugh helplessly, thinking of my epic terrors and triumphs in the lab. And all for this.

"It's a formula, all right," I said. "The one for Giovanetta Soldati's feeds. Cara has outsmarted me, I fear."

CHAPTER IX

The journey back to Cornwall was uneventful. We took it in turns to drive and sleep. Noah slept all the way; that infant really had a talent for the arms of Morpheus. If he hadn't been such a dormouse, I reflected, I'd have discovered the substitution much sooner and we'd never have got to London in the first place, which would have saved a lot of trouble. On the other hand, then we wouldn't have acquired the sample of Product X which we had left with George, who was going to take it to an analyst right away.

"What do you want to do first?" Tom said, when we had passed Launceston and the moor stretched ahead of us, purple-black in the light of the wild and gory dawn under high-piled rainclouds. Mr Tregagle had been right about his three-day blow. "Shall we go to the police and inquire about Cara?"

At bottom, I was feeling pretty sore against Cara. Naturally I hoped she hadn't come to any harm; granted it wasn't her fault that we'd had the wild-goose-chase with the wrong baby. But she needn't have gone out of her way to tell that gratuitous fib about the formula and make a fool of me. Why had she done it? To ensure I took the baby up to London? So as to draw the pursuit off her?

I wasn't looking forward to meeting old Dunskirk either, and having to face him with the knowledge that his cherished son was a thief and possibly a murderer, that his super new product was stolen goods and instead of raising the image of Gay Gal was more likely to drag it through the mire, that our beautiful campaign was blown sky-high, and that his exquisite daughter-in-law, even if she hadn't known about the theft all along, had certainly connived at it by keeping silent when she did realise what had happened, probably because she feared she was an accessory.

"Tell you what," said Tom, who possibly read my thoughts. "You'll want to go and see how Mimi's getting on."

"I certainly shall. Poor Mimi—she'll think we've all died or something."

"And I expect you're anxious to get back to the monastery."

The cool, dry note was back in his voice again; he kept his eyes expressionlessly on the road ahead. So I merely said, "Yes."

"While you're doing those things I'll have a talk with Dunskirk and try to discover if he or the police have any clue to Cara's whereabouts, and tell the film unit to pack up. It's lucky the Picnic filming's all finished. Then I'll ring you at the farm about one, or shall we meet at the pub for lunch?"

"You're a saint," I said gratefully. It was nice of Tom to be so thoughtful when he must be worried to death about Cara. "Ring me at the farm, just in case either of us gets held up."

When Tom dropped me at Trewithian I found the case of Mimi's things outside Cara's bedroom door, just where I had put it down. Tom stayed only long enough to hear from the Tregagles that no news of Cara had been received, and then went on towards Mr Dunskirk's house at Polneath.

159

Lily Tregagle was longing to gossip about Cara's disappearance.

"The police did come up, asking questions," she said, big-eyed, "but Sergeant Pearce he told me confidential, that there wasn't much they could reckon to do. If a young lady runs off, well, ten to one it's not a police matter, is it? By rights, he said, they couldn't be called in unless a breach of the peace was likely to take place. And that doesn't seem likely, does it, though of course foreigners are more excitable."

To me, nothing seemed more likely than a breach of the peace when Gareth caught up with Cara, but I didn't go into this, only asked Mrs Tregagle if she would be so kind as to keep an eye on Noah while I paid a hasty visit to poor Mimi in hospital. She agreed cordially, sent her regards and a bunch of daffodils to Miss Whatname, and said allergies was funny things, wasn't they?

I fully expected, when I reached the hospital, that the matron would boot me out because no visitors were allowed before seven-thirty p.m., but it turned out that in Mimi, even in a Mimi writhing under the effects of spider-venom, Matron for once had met her match.

Since there were no private rooms available, Mimi, who would rather die in a ditch than recover in a public ward, had managed to get herself accommodated in a spare sluice, where there was just room to park a narrow bed. I was allowed to go and see her and found her almost rigid with fury because she had been obliged to wear a boy's blue-and-white striped flannel pyjama suit several sizes too large.

"That's right—laugh!" she snarled, as I put the case on her bed and some grapes, anemones, and the daffodils into a large kidney-dish. "A fine friend *you* are! Who promised to come back in a couple of hours with brandy?"

"Oh, Mimi, I'm truly sorry. You'll forgive me when you hear what a time I've had."

"No I shan't," she said vindictively. "Not unless you've been bitten by a spider too. Look at the guy they've made of me!"

"I think you look marvellous," I said. "I only wish Tom were here to take pictures."

She did look extraordinarily funny, quivering erect with rage in the blue and white stripes, with her Roman nose, and black hair standing on end, and eyes blazing with fever.

"I hope you got some brandy out of the matron," I said, helping her into a more acceptable garment.

"Well, I did, as a matter of fact," Mimi confided. "We've struck up quite a bosom friendship. But tell me what's been happening to you? Did you find that miserable Cara—?"

Suddenly a spasm of cramp hit her, she went stiff all over and her muscles quivered like banjo-strings.

"Pass me the dish," she gasped. "Quick, I'm going to vomit again."

Much concerned I dumped the flowers on the floor and held her head till the seizure was past and she lay back weak and sweating.

"Mimi! Has this been going on ever since Monday?"

"Every blasted hour," she said between her teeth. "If I'd realised when that creature called in on Monday night—"

"When who called in, Mimi?"

"Tigger, or Mait, I never know one from t'other. He turned up at visiting time that night. I was pretty well doped. When they said I had a gentleman visitor I made sure you must have sent Tom or Jimmy with my stuff. He was obviously rocked back on his heels when he saw me—he mumbled something about all a mistake and he'd thought it was Cara who'd been taken to hospital. So I said she'd gone back to London; thought that would be the best way of getting rid of him. Loathsome little tick—coming to see the effects of his prank, I suppose. If I hadn't been so slowed-up at the time I'd have given him a piece of my mind before he beat it."

"Never mind; I threw a can of red-hot soup at him and rolled an exceedingly heavy cable-drum downhill on to Mait, so you are fairly well avenged."

"I'm delighted to hear it." Mimi's knuckles whitened as another paroxysm hit her.

A sister who came in just then confirmed that she wouldn't be allowed to leave the hospital for at least another day; they were obviously proud of this unusual case and wanted to make the most of it. I left fairly soon, promising to come back at visiting-time.

"I'll believe *that* when you turn up," Mimi said darkly.

I'd hardly got back to the farm and begun telling the Tregagles about Mimi when the phone rang. "It's for you," Lily said, so I went into the comfortable, cluttered farm kitchen with its milk records, and stacks of egg trays, and pot of potato peelings always boiling for the hens.

"Hullo? Oh, Tom. Where are you ringing from?"

"I'm at Polneath." He sounded very subdued.

"What's the matter? You sound upset."

"It's poor old Dunskirk." He lowered his voice still more. "He's had a stroke."

"Oh, no!"

"I'm afraid so, yes. Apparently—can you hear?"

"Yes."

"The housekeeper told me that two notes were delivered by hand on Monday night, one for Mr Dunskirk, one for Gareth. Mr Dunskirk read his and it made him frantic, he rang Gareth in London and told him to come down at once and explain himself. Gareth flew down, read his note, and he and his father had a blazing row, she heard them shouting at each other but didn't know what about; then Gareth went storming off into the night. Old Dunskirk rang his lawyer in London, said he wanted to change his will, and told him to come down first thing next day—yesterday. But in the night he had the stroke and they found him paralysed all down his right side. Could only mumble."

"Oh god. Poor old boy. Has a doctor—"

"Yes, the doctor's been, and the lawyer. Lawyer couldn't do anything because the old boy couldn't communicate; he talked to the doctor and went back to town again."

"What about Gareth, where—"

"That's what I was coming to. Apparently he was absent for the whole of yesterday, but turned up again unexpectedly this morning, unshaven, bloodshot, and wild, stayed only a moment or two, snatched off little thingummy—"

"Laureen?" I said, with a sick foreboding.

"Yes; the housekeeper saw him through the window dragging her into the car, but came downstairs too late to ask what was going on. She's all of a tizzy anyway, poor woman. They're getting a nurse, and an ambulance to move old Dunskirk back to London, and I said I'd stay here and shut up the house after it's gone; shouldn't be long now."

"The notes—who sent them?"

"Haven't a clue—Cara, perhaps?"

"No news of her there?"

"None. But Martha—"

"Yes?"

"Please be careful, will you? I didn't like the sound of Gareth at all. I think you were right about him. Let's hope he's gone back to town, but if he's somewhere in the neighbourhood still—"

"Who's being lurid now? No, all right—" as he made a protesting noise. "I'll be on the lookout. Still, why should he bother me?"

"Well, you watch out."

"When shall I see you?"

"I'll come over as soon as the ambulance has left and I've left the keys at the house-agent. I rang Jimmy and the film unit's on its way back to town."

"Just as well," I said. "The weather's hopeless."

Dawn's brief red promise had long ago been swamped by frantic grey clouds following one another across the sky in hurrying droves like lemmings. Mrs Tregagle's fuchsias tapped and scraped restlessly at the window and the daffodils in the orchard were being whipped against the ground.

I told Tom about Mimi and suggested that, as she wouldn't be well enough to travel till the weekend, I should go back to town with him in his Rover next day, taking Shrubsole, and then return to collect Mimi and the Admiral on Saturday.

"Good," he said. "We'll make final arrangements when I see you. Take care, then, lovey—"

"Okay, okay."

"God bless," and he rang off.

I put the receiver back on its rest and found Mrs Tregagle standing at my elbow.

"Sorry Mrs Tregagle, didn't see you." Why did I feel so light-hearted suddenly? Heaven knew, all our affairs were in a sorry tangle. Poor old Dunskirk—

"It's a message, miss; a gentleman left it for you."

Gareth's handwriting on the back of an envelope: a smeared, uneven scrawl.

I have something you want, you have something I want. Better inquire at the monastery.

Shrubsole!

Quick, take Noah, put on raincoat, hurry—

No, first phone Tom again, see what he says.

"When was this note left, Mrs Tregagle?"

"About two hours ago, midearr, about twelve."

Exasperatingly, it took ages to get the Dunskirks' number again: engaged, engaged, engaged. Doctor, perhaps, ambulance, arrangements for journey. At last I got a woman's voice, anxious, tearful. The housekeeper, what was her name?

"Oh, Mrs Oldcastle?' This is Martha Gilroy, of Salmon and Bucknell. I'm very sorry to trouble you, but might I speak to Mr Toole, I believe he's there?"

"Mr Toole just went in to the chemist's at Camelot to get a prescription made up. Can I take a message?"

I thought feverishly. No sense in worrying this poor woman with news of Gareth; she sounded as if she already had more than she could take.

"Could you ask him to join me at the monastery as soon as he possibly can? Say I've had an urgent summons there."

"Yes, miss, I'll tell him." But would she remember? She sounded distraught.

"Oh dear," Mrs Tregagle said, watching me wrap up Noah. "Turble weather to take out a baby, idn' it?"

"Never mind, I'll go quick, in the Hillman."

Vicious little gusts of rain slammed against the side windows as the old car swayed down the lane; wind whistled in the telegraph wires. After I'd done the short stretch along the main road, and turned up the monastery track, I was astonished, looking out, to see one of the Brothers at work in the big russocky meadow on the left-hand side. Oblivious, apparently, of the rising storm, he strode about whacking at thistles with a hoe; he looked the epitome of dejection. His cowl flapped up and down rhythmically like the crest of some rusty old black bird, and he seemed to be talking to himelf.

When I drew closer I saw that it was Brother Stanislas. I was shocked at his miserable expression.

"Brother Stan! What's the matter?"

"Oh, my child! Need you ask?" His anguish would have been comic if it hadn't been so piteous. "*You* are the one whose pardon I must seek above all."

"Because you gave me the wrong baby? Well, it was a bit of a nuisance, but in the end it turned out for the best. Anyway, I'm sure it was only a mistake."

"No, I made no mistake," he lamented. "It was because I thought she had a cold and should not go out. I knew you were returning to Cornwall soon; by then, I thought, she would be better. And I was sure she would be safer here than anywhere else.—No, those were not the real reasons. It was wicked, wicked selfishness, because I could not bear to part with the little Shrub-sole. I loved her so. It was a thoroughly stupid thing to do. And I have caused you great trouble and Brother Lawrence is very angry with me—rightly so."

"Oh dear," I said sympathetically. "Have you been put to hoe thistles as a penance? Do stop now—it's absolutely pouring down. And I'm sure you have done enough."

"No, my child, I have not done nearly enough. I committed a wickedness and must be purged." He thumped his chest punitively and set to work on the thistles again as if each one represented a Deadly Sin, mumbling something to himself that sounded like Latin principle parts.

"But, Brother Stan, who's looking after the babies while you do this?"

"Brother Lucian is," he said dolefully. "Which is as much of a penance to him as thistling is to me. Sinful, sinful Stanislas, to bring all this trouble."

It was Lucian, he disclosed, who had discovered about the sub-stitution of the babies and had angrily reported the matter to Brother Lawrence; because Lucian seemed to show unsuitably acrimonious feelings about it, Brother Lawrence immediately turned round and punished him by putting him in charge of the nursery.

"Oh heavens," I said, "poor Lucian, I'd better get up there fast and give him a hand. Do let me take you along too, Brother Stan, I'm certain that you're as sorry as you can be."

But he would not come; hunching his shoulders against the downpour he stomped off to the other side of the field, so fast that he was out of earshot and did not hear me when I called after him, asking if Gareth had been to the monastery.

I went on to the nursery in anxious expectation of chaos. Lucian, I felt sure, would be hopeless at infant-care, particularly if the job were dealt out as a punishment. My heart misgave me for the poor babies left in his charge, particularly Shrubsole.

Without bothering to ring the bell I walked straight along the concrete passage and was taken aback to find not Lucian but Brother Lawrence, dourly presiding.

"Why didn't you ring?" he snapped. "Well? Speak up? What do you want?"

"I came to fetch Shrub—" my voice faded away. Only two orange-boxes were occupied. Shrubsole was not there. "Where is she?" I said hoarsely. "And where's Lucian?"

"Brother Lucian is doing penance," shortly.

"What for?" I asked, but received a quelling look.

"If *you* hadn't pushed your way in here, young woman, meddling where you'd no business, we should have avoided a lot of trouble. Now; perhaps you'd be so good as to go back where you belong, and leave us in peace." He dumped Noah in a box.

Tired and worried as I was, I longed to slap him, but it wouldn't have helped.

"I'll go, and gladly, if you'll tell me where the baby is that I've come to fetch—the little black-haired one?"

"Her father came for her."

"Oh *no*—you mean her stepfather? A blond man, rather handsome?"

"I did not myself see him. Brother Lucian admitted him, and handed over the child."

"Oh my god. Was this long ago? Did he say where he was taking her? Can I see Brother Lucian?"

"I have told you, young woman," Brother Lawrence said, frowning repressively. "He is doing penance."

"Yes, but, honestly, Brother Lawrence, this is urgent! The man who's taken her is irresponsible—he may even be a murderer."

Brother Lawrence seemed to hesitate. At last he said reluctantly,

"I must admit that I was angry when I found what Brother Lucian had done. He should not have handed over the child without consulting me. That is why I relieved him of his duties in the nursery."

He picked up a stick and gave a distasteful stir to a bucket of small garments soaking in soapsuds.

"Please let me see him, Brother Lawrence."

"Oh, very well. You will find him cleaning the pigsties. Kindly go the outside way, *not* through the community precincts, and stay no longer than is strictly necessary."

He turned his back on me and began, at arm's length, a fastidious investigation of one of the babies which had started to whimper. It was plain that he held me wholly responsible for the misdemeanours of his two brothers and, sadly, I supposed that he was right.

Leaving the east door I turned left, towards the sea. The lane led on, beside the high wall surrounding the kitchen garden, and ended at a gate into a rough narrow field which ran out to the very tip of the headland. By now it was raining so hard that all distant objects were veiled in sheets of greyness. After bumping the Hillman down the track as far as it would go, I left it by the gate and hurried through the downpour to the collection of breeze-block dwellings inside the field which housed the community's herd of pigs. The smell and the squeals were unmistakeable.

I could see Lucian forking straw; he wore gumboots and a sort of black boiler-suit with a hood, which he had thrown back; with his dark hair hanging in streaks and his thin preoccupied face he looked like a Dürer engraving. He had turned the disgruntled pigs out into the field and was tossing their bedding after them with furious energy; from the violent start he gave when I leaned over the pigsty wall and called him it was clear he had not heard my approach.

Without looking at me he said hastily, "I'm busy, I can't stop now."

"Lucian I've got to talk to you. Brother Lawrence sent me down here."

At that he half turned, still keeping his face averted. I could see the nervous twitching of his cheek.

"Please, Lucian—the man who took Cara's baby—was he tall and fair? Did he say where he was going? Was there anybody else with him?"

For an interminable time he didn't answer; just stood, staring down at the tines of his fork, half buried in smoking straw.

"Look, Lucian, this really is important! For all I know he may be going to kill that child. Why won't you tell me? Don't you know? Didn't he say *anything*?"

Silence. Twitch, twitch. His knuckles were white on the rough wooden handle. My patience felt like the safety-valve on a boiler in which steam was accumulating at thousands of cubic feet a second. But I waited, and at last said as gently as I could,

"You really must tell me, Lucian. This is important for you too."

"Why?" he said tonelessly, without turning.

"Because of the baby. You hated her, didn't you?"

He turned then, and gave me a long, strange look out of his bloodshot eyes.

"You were angry with me, I suppose, because she was my favourite, and angry with Brother Stan because he played a trick so as to keep her. So you were glad to get rid of her when this man turned up, was that it?"

"What affair is it of yours, anyway?" he muttered, frowning. "*You're* not her mother."

"No," I said slowly. "No, I haven't any children."

Illumination came to me then so fully and clearly that I couldn't think why it hadn't all been plain years before; phrases even recurred from some unimportant-seeming, long-forgotten conversation. An idle remark of mine: "How many children shall we have, Lucian? Is four a good number, do you think?" Lucian apparently absorbed in sorting manuscripts, apparently not hearing; presently coming out with some irrelevant reply, leading the talk elsewhere. How long after that was it that he began to turn away from me, in on himself? Quite soon? The very next day?

Following this trail, heedless of consequences, I said,

"The baby that died with your mother when you were ten—was it a boy or a girl?"

"Oh, spare me the half-baked psychology, please!" he said furiously. "What does it matter?" And then sullenly, after a moment or two, "It was a girl."

Poor Lucian. With that gap, that rival in his past.

I had not spoken aloud but he glared at me as if I had and said,

"*Don't pity me!* Yes, all right—I know I was jealous, I acknowledge it! I acknowledge the whole damn shoot! I hate children! But I've had it all already once from Brother Lawrence, I'm not taking it again from you."

"You don't have to," I said, though filled with astonishment. Brother Lawrence! Well, well, well! "But I promised the baby's mother that I'd look after her and get her to a safe place in London. Being taken by her stepfather is the very worst thing that could happen to her. I must know what's happened. Please tell me, Lucian."

"I don't know."

At that moment I felt real despair. I knew that he was lying—everything about him proclaimed it, his face, his voice, the whole set of his body. There had always been a fanatical, terrifying obstinacy about Lucian; if he didn't want to do a thing, no force could make him. And meanwhile time was passing; although by rights it should be hours till darkness, the heavy clouds were now so low that we stood in a sort of dusk. I could feel the relentless rain beginning to penetrate the shoulders of my coat. What could I do? Appeal to Brother Lawrence?

"Lucian," I was beginning reasonably, when something plucked at my hand. Thoroughly startled, I turned to see little Laureen standing beside me. She was a deplorable sight—soaking, her dirty face smeared with rain and tears, her draggled hair hanging in rats' tails. One knee was cut, both were grazed, and her untied shoes were covered with mud.

"Laureen! What ever are you doing here?"

She was crying so miserably that it was almost impossible to make out her answer.

"He s-s-said to stay in the car but I didn' want to, I was c-c-cold! S-s-so I went arter him b-but he wasn't there, oh, oh, oh, oh. An' it was steep an' I fell, l-l-look!"

Gulping and hiccuping she held out two muddy, bleeding hands.

I knelt and put an arm round the wretched little object.

"Poor Laureen—that *was* a bad fall. Where did it happen?"

"On the cliff." She jerked her head towards the point.

"Is your father there?"

"I d-dunno where he is."

"Where's your car?"

She pointed vaguely down the field.

"He left the car in the field and went down the cliff? Did he have Cara's baby with him?"

"Ye-yes, he *did*," she gulped, "b-but he wouldn' take me. He tole me to stay in the car."

How long ago? I wondered.

"Lucian," I said, "please take Laureen up to Brother Lawrence, will you? Ask him to clean her up and give her a hot drink. You can take the Hillman, it'll be quicker. And then ask someone to come down to the beach—can you get a message to the police? There's no time to lose. I'm going to see what's happening. Please hurry!"

I tried to speak briskly and calmly, as if there were no possibility of his not helping me. It worked. He scowled at Laureen as if he disliked his task, but turned and made his way gingerly towards the Hillman. Laureen nearly wrecked everything by howling and clinging to me.

"Don' wanna go with the black man, don' wanna!"

"Oh, look, Laureen, there's a kind man in the babies' nursery who'll wash those nasty cuts and make them better. And he'll probably give you bread and honey and lovely hot milk. Fetch Brother Stan if you can, for god's sake," I muttered to Lucian as I disengaged Laureen's clinging hands and tried to urge her, sodden, jibbing, and mutinous, into the car.

He nodded, without looking at me, intently examining the controls.

Laureen kicked furiously at the car door.

"Oh, come on!" Lucian snapped suddenly and showing, to my astonished relief, a natural, healthy exasperation, he reached out an arm and hauled poor Laureen smartly on to the seat beside him. She was so aghast that she stopped crying for a moment and he said, "Right! Now don't make any more noise or we'll probably hit the wall. I haven't driven for seven years."

I slammed the door on Laureen and found that Lucian with averted face was reaching past her to hand me a piece of paper through the window; before I'd had time to see what it was he had roared the engine, spin the front wheels, and shot the old car jerkily but fast up the narrow track to the monastery.

It was almost too dark to read the sodden, inky blur:

Cara says she gave it to you so I know you've got it. Better come to the island if you want the baby.

Oh, the stupid, mischief-making fool! I thought furiously, as I ran at a headlong pace up the rough, stony field to the gorse hedge that marked its boundary at the edge of the cliff. Why did she have to tell Gareth a lie like that? Didn't she *want* to save her child?

I came within sight of Gareth's E-type, which was parked in a dip at the end of the field, empty.

Then it occurred to me that of course Cara must have assumed Shrubsole to be safe in London by now. Brother Stan's unfortunate lapse certainly had landed us in trouble.

I reached the boundary hedge and looked down.

From here I could see the whole of the little bay. The tide was coming in, and white-fringed breakers were rolling angrily far up the beach where the Picnic Soup pastoral had been filmed. The rainswept shingle lay in a clean curve, now, unmarked, as if no human had ever set foot on it. In the middle the island was hardly visible; just a grey blur.

I looked about for Gareth but there was no sign of him; from where I stood, though, I couldn't see the jetty down near the point, where the monastery boats were kept. I started down the cliff path at a run, slipping and scrambling. It was plain that this was the way Laureen had come; her footprints were visible in the clay, and, here, the long slide mark where she had fallen and finally turned back, discouraged. One of her hair-ribbons lay in the mud at the side of the track.

The path plunged through a tangle of sloe and gorse and fuchsia to emerge abruptly on the huge concrete landing-barge, jammed in at an angle against rocks, which served the monks for a pier. I remembered how Mimi and I had sunbathed on it, baking in the hot spring weather, while the film unit were shooting the broncho sequence; now grey, hurrying waves were washing over the lower end, hurling pebbles raspingly along the rough concrete; that idle, sunny morning seemed a lifetime away.

Gareth was not here either.

But one of the monastery boats was missing, and I could see the deep groove where it had been dragged down the beach to the sea's edge. I stared across at the island, straining my eyes to peer through the blowing rain and spume. Had I imagined it, or was there a flicker of something white, moving on the rocks?

I knew that I would have to go and see.

The monastery boats were heavy, lumbering craft, used for mackerel fishing and setting lobster-pots; it took all my strength to pull the remaining one down to the water. On a normal occasion I probably shouldn't have been able to do it. But I was in a rage by now, a thoroughly reckless, satisfactory rage, against Cara for getting me into this situation with her lies and machinations, against Gareth for his crazy, obstinate blackmailing tactics; what could he hope to gain by such an act? He must know, by now, that he had done for himself.

My mind turned aside from the obvious deduction: that Gareth did know he was done for, that ordinary selfishness and obstinacy had now tipped right over into paranoia.

By now I was so wet that my raincoat was only a hindrance. Impatiently I flung it off and left it on the beach, with my handbag. The trousers and shirt I had on were soaked too, and clung to me uncomfortably; the thought of a small baby being exposed to this weather was horrifying.

Starting the cranky old engine was a long struggle. As soon as I had gone a few yards, I found that the wind caught the boat and drove it across the bay; I had to keep it headed to the right of the island, and made very slow progress, two yards sideways for every yard forward. It seemed to take about twenty minutes—I daresay it was no more than ten really—to make the short crossing. Out in the middle the waves were big and choppy, but once I reached the lee of the island the water was calmer; although I was scared of crashing the boat against the other landing-barge pier I managed to run her alongside and tie up in shallow water by the tiny scrap of beach without doing much damage. The other boat was beached there too.

Gareth was on the island then.

The light was a little better now; overhead the clouds were still inky, but to the east a belt of yellow sky above the sea cast a pale theatrical glow over the little hummock of ground. I couldn't see Gareth, but there was plenty of cover: jagged rocks down by the water, the castle wall, higher up, and the Victorian gazebo inside it, on the topmost point. He might be anywhere. I searched for him, calling, "Gareth!" but the wind blew my voice back towards the shore.

The cold biting rain and unnatural light completely changed the island's aspect. I'd hardly have recognised it for the halcyon place where I'd sat on a rock and written Midinette copy and wondered about ringing up the monastery, where Jimmy had complained about gulls spoiling his shots. The rocks were slippery with rain and spray; I climbed cautiously up them on to the landing-barge, wondering again who had had the notion of bringing the unwieldy thing here, how they had ever manhandled it into position. It was about seventy yards long and over ten feet high; up on top of it I was exposed to the full blast of the wind and found it hard to keep my feet. The rising waves slapped its hollow length resoundingly and the lower end was under water, but it was plain from the tidemark that it would never be completely covered. At the shore end the monks had built a sort of rock grotto for meditation and prayer, facing out to sea. Although this seemed an unlikely hiding-place I made my way along to it gingerly, skirting an open manhole in the barge's concrete deck, and rapped on the door, shouting, "Gareth, are you in there?"

No answer came, so I opened the door and looked in. He was not there, only, I was annoyed to see, some props left behind by the film company, a camera tripod, bows and arrows, one of the crowns Cara had worn, and a shaggy sweater of hers. Inefficient clearing up; somebody hadn't thought it worth making another trip to the island for these odds and ends in the rising gale. Salmon and Bucknell would foot the bill, no doubt. I came out again, slamming the door, and scrambled up the skiddy little track to the gap on the castle wall.

By now I was becoming thoroughly uneasy; if Gareth had been on the island he must—surely?—have seen me coming, have heard me calling. Could he have decided to make away with himself, and the baby too, having waited, perhaps, until he had begun to be certain I wasn't coming? If the baby had been on the island, wouldn't I have heard her cry by now, even in this wind?

The circle of short turf inside the castle wall was bare, and so was the little arched summerhouse in the middle; rainswept through it and the black-and-red paved floor shone with wet. Something white lay by one of the supporting columns; with a dreadfully sinking heart I picked it up. A baby's sock, already sodden and dripping. Had it been left there on purpose as a final mockery of my vain pursuit?

With less and less hope, I searched the rest of the island, making a circuit of the castle wall, investigating behind every rock and gorse-clump. Not another sign of occupancy did I find; I might have been Crusoe.

Even when I had been everywhere I could not convince myself that the island was really uninhabited; I retraced my steps, miserably plodding back to all the places that I had already searched, because I could not bear to face the thought of what must have happened.

At last, unutterably low-spirited, I made my way back to the little bit of beach in the lee of the pier where the two boats had been left.

Mine was gone.

But it had not gone far. I could see it, about thirty feet away, drifting fairly fast across the bay to the opposite point where waves were exploding in clouds of spray. Its chances of survival were negligible. The monks would have to manage with one boat until I could buy them a replacement. But how could it have drifted free? I had made it fast, with a perfectly adequate knot, to an iron staple in the landing-bar. The staple was still there, secure enough to hold the Queen Mary.

It was while I was examining it that I was grabbed from the rear. My hands were violently clamped together behind my back and a rope was jerked tight over them with agonising force. I

173

yelled, and twisted round, struggling to pull away, but I might as well have tried to drag my hands out of a power wringer.

It was Gareth, of course. The frightening thing was that, despite his wetness and dishevelment—soaked jeans, velveteen jacket black with rain—he still looked so *normal*, calmly tying knot after knot in the rope that bound my hands.

"Gareth! What the *hell* do you think you're playing at? Will you please let me go?"

"There," he said, ignoring my rage, studiously testing his handiwork and deciding, apparently, that it would do. "I d-don't think that will s-stop the circulation. But we'll s-see, won't we? Now, where's the formula?"

"I haven't got it," I said, trying to keep calm, to treat him rationally. "Do, please, let me go."

He frowned.

"Don't lie, that's s-stupid. I know you h-have it. Cara said so."

"Gareth!" I burst out uncontrollably. "Where *is* Cara? What have you done with her?"

A look of quite extraordinary malice came over his face. He said,

"You'll never see h-her again. Aren't you glad? She'd pinched your boy-friend, hadn't she?"

"What did you do to her?"

"W-wouldn't you like to know?" There was something blood-chilling about his complacency as he stood smiling at me; with the water running off his thick blond hair and light eyebrows he could have posed for one of those tough, red-blooded ads of chaps who enjoy a real he-man's smoke; all was right except for the look in the eyes.

I didn't dare ask outright if he had murdered Cara. Or about the baby. Instead I said,

"I can see there's a lot to discuss, but please undo me first."

"There isn't anyth-thing at all to d-discuss," he said. "I want that f-formula. Is it in your bag? Was that wh-why you left it on the other s-side? I was watching you through th-these."

He pulled up a pair of binoculars on a strap; Jimmy's, I thought. Had they been left in the grotto with the arrows and Cara's sweater?

"It's not in my bag. I haven't got the formula at all."

"I d-don't believe you. Cara s-said she'd p-posted it to you."

With a chill of misgiving I wondered what Cara had hoped to

achieve by her lie. Postponement of a showdown? *Had* she achieved it?

In my mind I juggled between the alternatives of humouring Gareth to gain time, thereby risking his added rage later, or continuing truthfully to deny all knowledge of the formula. But these considerations fled abruptly when from somewhere above me, on top of a barge, I heard a faint cry.

"The baby! Where is she?"

"Waked up, has she?" said Gareth irritably. "I g-got so fed up with both of them b-bawling that I put her under with a c-couple of aspirins. Left bloody L-Laureen on the other side when she'd shown me where you'd got th-this one hidden; never thought the whining little b-brat would come in so useful."

He swung himself up on to the concrete barge—I was uncomfortably struck by his easy display of muscular strength, confirming the impression I'd already received of his hands' grip—and jumped lightly down again with a bundle which was beginning to stir and stretch and wail. I recognised Shrubsole's tussock of black hair emerging from a bit of tarpaulin.

"T-taken to her, haven't you?" he said, watching me with a sour, unfriendly grin. "C-Cara said you were dead k-keen to look after her. Well, you're welcome to her s-soon's you hand over that bit of paper."

Now I was really terrified. I had thought that I'd plumbed the depths already but you can never tell how much more is coming. The sight of Gareth standing there with Shrubsole tucked carelessly under his arm waked up a whole new series of atavistic impulses in me.

I said: "I can't stop you looking in my bag if you want to. But the formula's useless to you now, you realise that?"

His eyes lit up. He said, "Th-then it *is* in your bag," with a triumphant inflection, ignoring the latter half of my remark.

"I didn't say so."

"We'll soon see."

He started untying the boat.

"Let me loose and I'll help," I said. Hopefully I reckoned that by the time the boat had made the crossing—wider now, for the tide continued to rise—Lucian or Tom or the police or *someone* would have appeared on the beach. I moved casually towards the dinghy.

"Ah, n-no—not *you*," Gareth said. He gave me a violent shove,

175

so that I staggered backwards up the beach and fell over a rock. Painfully winded and with my hands tied behind me, I was at a hopeless disadvantage; by the time I'd struggled upright, Gareth had dumped Shrubsole in the boat, pushed off, and jumped nimbly aboard.

"I'll c-come back to undo you if it's th-there," he called. "If it's not there I'll come back even f-faster."

There was nothing to do but huddle shivering on the rock and watch the boat creep slowly through the choppy waves.

Visibility was decreasing again. But I could see well enough when Gareth finally reached the opposite shore, eagerly seized my handbag, and rummaged through the contents. His final gesture was unmistakable as he hurled it from him, scattering bits of paper and small articles all over the sand. He got back into the boat and, with despair, I saw it begin to grow larger again, coming towards me. I had thrown away the last chance because now even if—which I was not absolutely certain—somebody had come down to the beach from the monastery, how would they get across?

When Gareth came into the calmer water in the shelter of the pier he did not beach the boat, but waited, idling the engine, when he was about twelve feet out where it was still deep.

"You th-thought you'd fool me, I suppose?" he said. Again, there was something deeply disquieting about his unnatural calm. He should have stormed and raved because I'd tried to trick him. Instead he behaved with a sort of brisk composure, quite different from his usual manner, as if my ruse was something he'd reckoned on.

I strained my eyes, looking past him. The figure I'd thought I'd seen on the opposite shore had vanished; I must have imagined it. In any case, help could not now possibly arrive in time. But still one must do something.

"Gareth," I said, "please think. What can you do with the formula now? You can't make Avalon, or market it, you must see that? Everybody knows it's not your invention."

"What have you done with that paper?" he said. "Have you got it on you?"

His restless light eyes scrutinised me, hunting for possible hiding places. Neither my shirt nor my trousers contained pockets; if they had, any piece of paper in them would long ago have been reduced to pulp, but plainly he was far beyond thinking of that.

The flesh shrank on my bones, anticipating his next move. He started the engine again.

Then Shrubsole, who had been whimpering faintly in the bottom of the boat, began to cry in good earnest. One part of me was relieved; I'd been terrified that the dose of aspirin he had given her was a dangerous one. But her wails sounded healthy enough.

"Blast you, shut up," Gareth snapped at her. But she continued to howl. He stopped the boat, now only a few feet from the beach, and stood up, holding her.

"M-Martha," he said, still with that queer crazy serenity. "I've had enough of being m-mucked about. And I've had enough of k-kids yelling. I'm going to chuck her into the water unl-less you tell me where you've hidden that formula."

"No!" I shouted frantically. I ran down to the water's edge with clumsy haste and began wading out, in some vague hope of stopping him.

"This is your l-last chance," he said. "Are you going to t-tell me or not? No? Here goes, then, one—t-two—three—"

"*Don't!*"

He wasn't really listening to me. He was past listening. "*Go!*" he shouted gleefully, and tossed the baby from him. Her wail, crescendo, described a long curve, and a corolla of water shot up where she landed.

But it wasn't all water; I saw hands upraised to receive her; incredibly, *Lucian* was there, treading water beyond the boat, looking, in his black, cowled boiler suit, like some extraordinary Saint Christopher rising from the water. There should have been a halo.

Gareth's vindictive swing had unbalanced him. He fell headlong in about five feet of water, and disappeared; the boat rocked and shot seaward towards Lucian, who did the obvious thing; he put Shrubsole on the bottom boards and swam to the pier, pulling the boat after him. There it was easy enough for him to climb in. He started the engine.

"Lucian!" I shouted. "Take the boat back to the other side. Get the baby dry or she'll catch pneumonia. Go quickly—is she all right?"

He glanced down, nodded, and turned the boat's head away from the island, Gareth by now had scrambled to his feet, dripping and cursing—but Gareth was no swimmer, evidently; he hesitated, baffled. A wave slapped against him and that seemed to settle it; he started wading to shore.

Lucian idled his engine a moment while he called to me doubtfully, "What about you?"

"I'll be all right, if you can send someone soon. Only hurry!"

I had no doubt that if the two men came to grips Lucian, thin, undernourished, and exhausted from a fairly long and rough swim, would not stand a chance against the ruthless, well-set-up Gareth. The chance to save Shrubsole was not to be lost.

"And thank you, Lucian," I shouted belatedly. He didn't turn his head; I was not sure if he had heard.

"D-darling Martha you th-think you're such a c-clever girl, don't you?" Gareth said to me menacingly as he staggered dripping up the beach. He didn't stop by me as I had expected, but swung himself up on to the pier and disappeared inside the monks' hut. Next moment he emerged with one of the bows and a fistful of arrows. Running down to the end of the pier he notched an arrow into the bow and took aim at the retreating boat.

"Gareth! Stop it! Don't be a fool!" I yelled, wrestling ineffectually with the rope that tied my hands. I might as well have spoken to the wind. I could only hope that the wind itself, and Gareth's probable ignorance of archery, would prevent his doing any harm. The bow was a powerful one and it seemed horridly probable that the slowly progressing boat was still well within range.

An arrow whistled off into the dusk and struck the water with a fin-shaped flick of white, beyond the boat. Taking more careful aim, Gareth shot another. The wind deflected this one and carried it to the offside of the boat. A third fell short. By now the boat and the black shape, all that was visible of Lucian, were almost merged in the general greyness, but Gareth seemed to have fantastically good eyes; his fourth arrow fell just this side of the boat and after the fifth he gave a shout of triumph. I saw Lucian move sideways, violently, but no sound came back. Had he been hit? It was impossible to decide, or, if he had, how badly; the boat continued to move and soon became really invisible. Gareth shot off a couple more arrows but plainly they were nowhere near target, and with an exclamation of disgust he tossed the bow from him off the end of the pier.

In the same instant I realised that I had better make myself scarce; deprived of one prey, he would probably wreak his frustration on another. It was not easy to run fast up the steep slippery little path from the beach with my hands tied behind me, but I achieved a turn of speed that would have done credit to Dorothy Hyman.

I might have known it would be hopeless.

But still I managed to elude him for ten minutes or so. The trouble was that the little island wasn't built for this odious game of cat-and-mouse; there just wasn't room to manoeuvre. In the end, gaining all the time, he chased me down on to the pier; I had despairing thoughts of diving off and trying to float to land, though with tied hands I doubted if I could make it.

Gareth caught up with me halfway along the pier and dragged me, kicking and struggling, back towards the monks' grotto. Then he took me utterly unawares by knocking my knees from under me and twisting me into the open manhole.

I went down through it with a gasp of pure terror; to fall ten feet is no treat to me at any time, but to fall ten feet in the pitch dark into water of an unknown depth—ugh! I still have nightmares about that moment. Water closed over my head; I heaved and thrashed, managed to stand up, and found with relief that it was only up to my chest. But what else was in here? My imagination peopled the huge, hollow barge with giant squids, moray eels, and man-eating crabs.

"M-Martha?" Gareth's voice boomed resonantly in the concrete shell. I looked up. His head was framed in the manhole, five feet above me.

"Gareth! Look, I *swear* I haven't got your blasted formula. Please don't leave me in here."

Waves struck thunderously against the lower end of the barge, and it quivered; I felt with horror as if the whole thing were so precariously perched on its ledge of rock that it might roll over at any time into the harbour, taking me with it.

"N-now listen," Gareth said. "You know there's a big hole down at the bottom of the barge, s-so it fills right up when the tide comes in? I was h-hiding in there when you c-came to the island, that's how I f-found out."

"How did you get out again?" I asked cunningly.

"Th-there's a ladder. I've put it in the h-hut. I'll let it down when you tell me what you've done with the f-formula."

"Why should you think I've got it?"

"C-Cara told me," he said patiently. "She s-said she'd posted it to you on M-Monday."

"To my London flat?"

"No, to the f-farm. You *m-must* have it by now," obstinately.

"I haven't, though. When did Cara say this?"

"Yesterday."

Where had Gareth been yesterday? I had no idea. Something glimmered, phosphorescent, down at the dark lower end of the barge. There was a detestable smell in there—morbid, oozy, fishy —had he given Cara this treatment too? Where was she now?

It was deathly cold. The rising water slopped against my ribs—it seemed scummy, oily—not clean sea-water. Near panic I called the first thing that came into my head,

"Perhaps Tigger and Mait have the formula, Gareth?"

"N-no, they haven't," he said. "They've ratted. Cara wrote one of her little notes to them too, as well as t-to me and Dad. They told me yesterday they were quitting. I d-don't care, I'll be b-better off on my own."

"What did Cara say in her notes?"

"Oh," indifferently, "about Dino Soldati's death."

"So you did kill him, Gareth?"

"It was an accident," he said in an irritable tone. "I wouldn't have if he'd been c-c-co-operative. S-so then I took the perfume, what there was, and s-set fire to the lab. I couldn't find the formula."

"It wasn't there. You didn't know Cara took it?"

"N-not till she t-told me that day at the f-farm. The b-bitch," he said coldly. "I might have known she'd d-diddle me somehow. I'm glad I caught up with her and g-gave her a piece of my m-mind."

"Do you know your father has had a stroke?"

"What d-difference does it m-make to me if he dies? He s-said he was going to change his will."

"He hasn't changed it yet. The lawyer came too late."

"I d-don't believe you. Anyway, wh-what do I care?" with sudden passion. "I'm f-fed up with the whole p-piddling cosmetics business."

"Then why do you want the Avalon formula?"

"I shall s-sell it," he said dreamily. "It'll realise a big sum, you know that? It's a great, a c-classic perfume. I knew that at once. Even S-Soldati didn't know what he had there."

"And what will you do then, Gareth?"

The water was up to my chin, by now. Every now and then, unable to balance because of my tied hands, I was washed off my feet, and had to struggle, kicking desperately, to catch a toehold on the gritty floor.

"Then I sh-shall take the money and go to Italy and h-have my voice trained."

"Your *voice*?" I was thoroughly startled.

"I always wanted to b-be an opera singer but D-Dad wouldn't let me. He said s-singing was only fit for S-Sundays and the M-Messiah at Christmas, not a p-proper career for a man. S-stupid old fool! I hope he's dead. L-learning to sing would have cured my stammer."

"That's true," I said thoughtfully. "So it would...."

He peered down at me again.

"You're a n-nice girl, Martha. I wish I'd met you s-sooner, instead of that stupid Italian bit. You're much more my t-type. If you'd only give me the formula you could come with me, if you l-like. We'd have f-fun in Italy," he said coaxingly.

Poor Gareth; I could have wept. My heart was wrung for his hopeless, adolescent dream.

"I'm so sorry, Gareth. I'm afraid I really haven't got it. I think Cara must have been fooling you. Please let me out of here now; the water's up to my mouth."

An oily wave broke over me, and I wasted energy kicking, trying to keep my head above water, and missed the first half of what he said next.

"...have to leave you there, then." The tone was regretful. "I'm s-sorry, Martha. You know too much, you see. About Soldati and all..." He stood up and began moving away.

"Gareth!"

But it was hopeless trying to shout; another wave filled my mouth and I went under again, struggling to remember some instructions we'd received at a school camp one summer about keeping afloat with the minimum of effort. Let your head drop forward, hang suspended like a sea-horse. Reduce your breathing to the slowest possible tempo. By this means, you can float for up to four hours even with your hands tied behind your back....

Ideal conditions here, I thought. Just so long as I keep my health and strength and don't stupidly lose consciousness.

The only trouble was that it was so cold and dark, and I was so cold, so cold, and so deadly tired.

I must try to think about something intelligent, to fend off weakness. Bom, perhaps. It's the lively active bubbles in Bom that keep you on your toes. Easily digested Bom, packed with haemo-globin, glyceryl mono-oleate, and mineral salts, is *so* nourishing, *so* full of pure goodness, that the energy from it passes *straight* into your bloodstream. Bom is full of digestive enzymes, too—not only easy to digest itself, but actually *helps* you to digest other food!

Oh, I'm on a winning streak there, I thought. I must remember that one. Do you suffer from tired stomach? Find the lightest meal is too much for you? Why not start with an aperitif of piping-hot Bom? Soothes, *helps* your stomach. Or, in summer, cold, jellied Bom...

Ugh. The phosphorescent object seemed to have moved; seemed to be drifting in my direction. It was large; it rolled, sluggishly. Perhaps a submerged log? The best thing would be to turn my back on it. By working my shoulders I managed to move round. I didn't like feeling that it was behind me, but anything was better than *looking* at it.

My head grazed the roof. There wouldn't be much air left, soon. Where was the manhole? Insensibly, I had moved away from it; now I tried to propel myself back with a sort of flapping move-ment of my arms. At least I'd have fresh air there. And if Gareth had gone, perhaps there would be a chance of getting my head out, somehow working my way up with elbows and shoulders? The sudden hope made my heart thump and my breath come too fast; I gulped and nearly foundered.

But Gareth had been expecting me. He was there, squatting by the manhole; I could see the shape of his head against the sky.

"Is that you, Martha?" he said in a conversational tone. "I'm afraid you can't come out. If you try I shall have to hit you with this rock."

He had something in his hand. He raised it up.

There was a shout then, and running footsteps thundered along the deck of the barge. Gareth was swung aside. The rock flew out of his hand into the dark.

"*Martha!*" Tom's voice. "What *are* you doing in there?"

"My goodness, Tom! Is that really you?" And I added in-adequately, "I'm awfully glad you came."

He wasn't alone. I could hear other voices. Someone shouted "Get him!" and there was a scuffle, even the sound of a shot. Overhead I heard a formidable stuttering roar which I vaguely associated with Picnic Soup. At the time I didn't pay much attention.

"You'll have to pull me out, I'm afraid," I said to Tom. "My hands are tied behind my back."

"For Christ's sake." He knelt down, took a grip under my arms, and levered. Someone else—I had a glimpse of dark-blue uniform—helped him, grabbing my elbows from behind. We all lurched over in an undignified heap. I felt Tom's cheek against mine, bristly, and for some reason remembered that we'd driven down from London last night and he'd never had a chance to shave.

Stupidly, I began to cry.

"Tom—Tom! I'm horribly afraid that Cara's body is floating about inside the barge."

CHAPTER X

"Have another drop of brandy." Mimi passed the bottle hospitably.

They had squeezed another bed for me into the sluice, and packed me about with hot-water-bottles until I felt like a Sunday joint surrounded by potatoes. In uncritical gratitude I sank back on the lovely hard, narrow mattress. Somewhere a baby was crying...

"Shrubsole?" I said with hope.

"Tough as an old boot, that baby. They only brought her in as an extra precaution. I suppose she'll grow up to be a sort of female Commando."

"And Lucian?"

"Remarkably well, I gather, considering he had an arrow through his arm. One of the other old boys came and fetched him home in your car when he'd been bandaged up in Casualty. Dr MacGregor says yon hocus-pocus film business is an unco' ploy for dacent, honest folk; we've filled his hospital wi' more morrtal eenjuries than they usually reckon to see in a twel'month."

"Hut now," said Dr MacGregor coming in, prompt on his cue. "Less o' the converseetion, Mistress Dourakin. The young lady's fair worn out, and I'm aboot tae put her under for a kittle nap tae see her through till the morn's nicht. Bide ye still a meenit—"

The blessed needle came down on my arm and let me out of my aching body into a welcome void of sleep.

When I next woke, level evening sunbeams were illuminating all the mysterious aluminium and copper fitments in the little room; I could hear a cheerful clink of teacups from the main ward, and the strains of Schubert's *Marche Militaire* on the BBC Light Programme. Tum tiddle tum tiddle tum tum tum. What a marvellous theme tune that would make for Bom, I must remember to suggest it sometime.

Then I focused properly, and discovered Tom sitting by my bedside. I had never seen anything more beautiful than his kind, ugly face.

"What happened to Gareth?" I asked at once.

"He jumped off the pier. A policeman went after him but couldn't get to him in time. He was drowned. Just as well, really, for his father's sake. And it'll save you having to give evidence."

"His father's getting better, then?"

"They aren't sure yet."

"Cara?"

"No trace, up to now. They're still searching."

"Then what was that thing in the barge?"

Tom said apologetically, "It was a dead seal."

"I must say," remarked Mimi with a strong shudder, "I'd hardly admit that *anybody* could suffer a nastier fate than mine, but to be boxed up in a barge with a dead seal—ugh! I really do feel for you, Martha."

"How did you get to the island?" I asked Tom, thinking back a few more notches. "Mrs Oldcastle passed on my message, did she?"

"Did you leave a message with her? It never reached me—I suppose she forgot in her worry about the old boy. No, I went along to the farm after his ambulance had gone, and Mrs Tregagle said you'd had a note asking you to go to the monastery, and had started at once. So I followed you. I'd just got there when—your husband—" Tom hesitated, oddly at a loss.

"Lucian?"

"Lucian came in, soaking wet and bleeding, with the baby. Then that formidable whiskery old Brother—"

"Brother Lawrence—"

"Arrived with some police in a coastguard helicopter which he'd rustled up. So I went across with them."

"I was pleased to see you."

"You were a charley to go off on your own, weren't you?" But he didn't sound too cross.

"It was the baby. I didn't dare wait."

"I know." He stood up. "Are you all right now?"

"Fine. I want to get up." For the first time I noticed that I was wearing boys' blue-and-white striped flannel pyjamas. Mimi gave me a fiendish grin.'

"I don't expect they'll let you up yet."

"Where are you going, Tom?"

"Back to town. Someone has to hold poor George's hand."

He held mine a moment first, though, waved goodbye to Mimi, and was gone.

A cold chill seemed to pass over the evening. I said, "I do wish they could find out about Cara. It's horrible, not knowing."

"Actually I have a theory," said Mimi. "But let's wait and see."

They let us both get up next day. I had to make statements to the police. Then, while Mimi packed and kept a severe eye on little Laureen at the farm, I went to say my goodbyes at the monastery. I took Shrubsole with me; she seemed miraculously unaffected by her adventures, as sweet and cheerful as ever. All the time I was talking to Brother Stan he held her on his knee, watching her intently as if he were trying to learn her by heart.

"Oh, what a wicked, foolish sinner I was," he sighed. "You see how far astray we can go when the desires of the self are not kept in check! Poor little Shrubsole, who will have her now?"

Shrubsole, looking up at him, smiled her radiant, conspiratorial smile.

"That's what I really came to tell you. I thought you'd be pleased." For some reason I had to clear my throat. "The police here have been in touch with the Italian authorities about her father's death, and they've discovered that Soldati had parents living in Piedmont. They were thrilled to hear they have a grand-child and have asked for her."

His face lit up.

"Ah, that is good, that is the best! And she will replace for them the son they lost."

"Yes," I said rather sadly.

Brother Stan gave me his kind, shrewd look and said, "You have all life before you yet, my child. Now, I go away to do more penance. Oh, the penances I shall have to do before I am purged of my sinful covetousness! Here is Brother Lucian to say good-bye." He gave Shrubsole a last yearning look, and then bustled out as Lucian came in, pale, with his arm in a sling, but clear-eyed and carrying himself straighter than I remembered. We gazed at one another rather shyly. Then I said,

"Thank you for saving us, Lucian."

"I nearly didn't."

"But in the end you did."

"Yes," he said, still seeming slightly surprised. "And in the end it wasn't so bad as I'd expected."

"That awful swim?"

"No," he said seriously. "I wasn't thinking of that. I meant the children."

While I was still wondering how to answer he said,

"Martha?"

"Yes, Lucian?"

"I'm sorry about the way I left you."

"You couldn't help it. And it doesn't matter any more. What will you do now, do you think?"

"I'll stay here a bit longer," he said slowly. "In a year or so I may be ready to leave. Then perhaps I'll go back into publishing. And you?"

"Oh, back to my job."

"Will you get married, do you suppose?" His speech was simple and direct, like that of a child.

"I—I don't really know...."

"That man who helped rescue you—"

"Tom Toole?" Just saying his name gave me a feeling of warmth.

"I talked to him a bit. He seemed very nice."

"Yes," I said. I picked Shrubsole out of the orange-box where Brother Stan had put her and moved towards the door.

Lucian said, "I'm sure Brother Lawrence doesn't agree, but I'm glad you came here, Martha. Goodbye, and good luck." Much to my surprise, he gave me a quick, gentle kiss, and Shrubsole a funny, reluctant pat. I kissed him back warmly and made my way out, rather blind-eyed, to the Admiral.

Back at the farm I found Mimi bursting with news.

"Look what the Emir's sent me!" She flourished a great black cabochon ruby with a red gleam in its heart that must have been worth god knows what. "Just buzzed through the post like a bar of soap."

"Good god! I'm surprised you had the courage to open it."

"I didn't! I got Mr Tregagle to, with the tongs. And you've got a fat letter with Turkinistani stamps; hurry up and open it. I'm dying to know what old Ibn Abdullah's been up to."

It was in violet ink, heavily scented with ethyl phenylacetate, and all covered with royal seals and flourishes.

"My dear Martha,

You perhaps will be surprised to have heard from me but Abdullah says I must write and explain why he would not let me keep the formula. He says it would be wrong and he could not allow me to if I am to be one of his wives...."

My voice died away in total astonishment. I turned the letter over and looked for the signature. Cara.

"Well, go on!" said Mimi.

"... If I am to be one of his wives. So, when he took me away on Monday, he made me stop at the bottom of the lane and post it to you in an envelope, together with the note Gareth writes to Soldati, making appointment for the night of his death.

"Abdullah says the formula should be given to Dino's child. He says you will do this because you are upright and honourable. He says I am not upright but he loves me. We will have Giovenetta in Turkinistan unless you wish to adopt her.

"I left a note for Mr Dunskirk telling him of Gareth's wickedness, and one for Gareth that he should meet me at the airport, and there, with Abdullah, I tell him I will have nothing more to do with him as he is dishonest and not even successful. And anyway I am afraid the police will say I am his accomplice which is not at all true."

Poor Gareth! I thought, remembering that wishful *I gave her a piece of my mind*. How different the reality must have been—Cara's scathing indictment, given in the presence of the Emir. And then Tigger and Mait had told him they were quitting; no wonder he had driven raging back to Cornwall, grabbed Laureen, and gone off to try and extract the formula from me by kidnapping Shrubsole. No wonder he hadn't wanted me to know what had become of Cara. Cara would be in clover for the rest of her life, so long as she behaved herself. It was too galling.

"Gareth can divorce if he wishes," the letter went on. "Abdullah says I shall be his number one wife, or anyway number two. This is better than work on television, as he is very rich. He says to give his love to you and Miss Dourakin. And I send mine to dear Tom. I am so happy. Your friend,

Cara."

"*Friend*," said Mimi. "The last irony. Whether she meant to or not, she nearly got you killed off by her parting gift. But if she posted you the formula, why have you never got it?"

"I have an idea Mrs Tregagle told us the letterbox at the foot of the lane isn't used for some reason. Do you remember? We'd better ask the post office to open it up and have a look."

Mrs Tregagle was horrified when I told her.

"'Tis slugs," she said. "They do be always getting in and eating letters—'tis desprit inconvenient. When would it have been posted now—Monday? Five mortal days? Eh, deary me..."

An official from Camelot came out post haste and opened up the letterbox for us. But Mrs Tregagle's gloomy prognosis had been all too accurate. Nothing was left of the incriminating note, or Dino Soldati's precious formula, but a limp, damp, shredded mat, like a lace doiley, liberally coated with slime and utterly illegible.

"Ah, they Cornish slugs be doddy voracious eaters," the postman said, shaking his head. "Would that be anyways important, now? Mebbe you did oughter claim for compensation?"

"I don't think the owner will be very worried," I said, turning to look at Shrubsole, who lay on the back seat of the Admiral, gazing admiringly at her own pink feet.

I took the children straight to Rosemary's. Tom, who met me there, said old Dunskirk was recovering and asking for Laureen.

"So that he can bring her up as badly as Gareth, poor old boy. Does he know, yet?"

"Just that Gareth was killed in an accident. But I gather Cara spilt most of the beans in her note; that, and the row, was what brought on the stroke. Do you remember George was going to take your sample of Product X to an analyst? The man said someone from Gay Gal had brought him the very same perfume several months ago, but he'd been quite unable to track down all the ingredients."

"Gareth, I suppose, getting desperate. Isn't it amazing news about Cara?"

"Funniest thing I've heard for months," said Tom, who seemed very cheerful about it.

"You don't mind?" I said cautiously.

"Mind? Why should I?"

"You seemed to be seeing quite a bit of her in Cornwall."

"Well, good heavens," said Tom, "I had to pass the time somehow. You were always so—were always visiting the monastery, and poor Cara seemed rather odd-man-out. I must confess though, a faint anxiety did cross my mind, about the time when she lost the baby, that she had got me cast as Number Two; it was a great relief when old Abdullah turned up and she transferred her attentions to him; anyone could see from the start how that would go. Even the genius that you so kindly attributed to me couldn't compete with ten thousand a day *and* a throne. I saw her one day gazing into a mirror with one of the Avalon crowns on her head; I thought at the time that she had a very considering look in her eye. She ought to enjoy herself to the top of her bent, queening it around as a sultana."

"And thinking smugly of us back in our dull old office."

"You aren't going to start up again with Lucian, then?" Tom asked in a carefully neutral tone.

"Goodness, no! You were quite right, we'd grown poles apart. But I'm glad I saw him, I understand the whole thing a lot better now." Hurrying away from dangerous ground, I said, "So it looks as if poor little Shrubsole will never have her inheritance."

"Never mind, at least she has a family. That reminds me," Tom pulled out a sheaf of air tickets, "I thought you'd like to come with me to Italy and see her safely delivered. Best to get it over quickly, don't you agree?"

Four days later we were walking, in hot sun, down a dusty mountain path. I carried in my mind a picture of a small white house among cypresses, two radiant, weeping old people—now I knew where Shrubsole had her eyes from—and sisters, aunts, cousins, cats, goats, hens, roses, lemon-trees, and donkeys. A family.

We walked rather fast.

"Don't cry, Martha," said Tom at length.

"I'm not—really. It's only—" I stopped and hunted vainly for a handkerchief.

"Here." Tom tucked one into my hand. "I always seem to be doing this." There was a smile in his voice.

"Thank you." I blew and wiped. We went on our way.

"We can have lots," he suggested after a while. "Six, like Rosemary's, say?"

"That would be nice. I shan't have quite so much time for copywriting then, shall I? Goodness!" I said, stopping suddenly as an idea hit me.

"What's the matter now?"

"I've just thought. All our marvellous campaign that was to have made advertising history is utterly *wasted*. What shall we do? George will be in despair."

"I tell you what," Tom said, tucking his arm through mine and walking even faster. "Why not just alter the wording a little and use the films for Bom instead? I don't suppose the consumers will notice the difference."